KEY GRIP

BLACK STALLION STUDIOS BOOK 2

VICKI THARP

JPC PUBLISHING

KEY GRIP

Key Grip is a work of fiction. Names, characters, places and incidents either are the product of the author's imagination or are used fictitiously, and any resemblance to actual persons, living or dead, business establishments, events, or locals, is entirely coincidental.

Original Cover Design by Designs EE

ISBN 978-1-948798-20-4

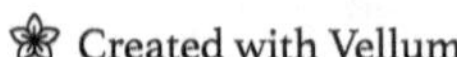 Created with Vellum

1

———————

Again.

Early Monday morning, Sebastian Stavros hid in the makeup room at Black Stallion Studios trying to convince himself he could fix his screwup without his uncle completely losing his shit.

Not that Niko would punch him, or even raise his voice. Instead, Niko would level those dark eyes at Sebastian with the same intense disappointment Sebastian had seen in his father's eyes too many times before.

But unlike his father's opinion, Niko's mattered.

Coming from Niko, that disappointment would cut a swath through Sebastian's self-esteem like a reaper at harvest time.

Rose Galloway, Black Stallion's resident mom to the talent and general grand master of the Black Stallion realm, poked her gray-haired head into the makeup room. "I would tell you that Niko is looking for you, but you sitting here in the dark tells me you already know this."

"I just..." Sebastian's guts churned. Bile climbed up the back of his throat, even though he hadn't been able to eat since the night before when he'd found out that he'd entered the incorrect dates on a talent's contract.

Scratch that, not *a* talent. *The* talent.

Jacoby Winters. If gay porn had a king, it was him.

And by some miracle, he'd agreed to a shoot with Black Stallion.

Until said fuck up.

Which meant Jacoby Winters had signed a contract to do a scene with Black Stallion ten days *after* the date they needed him.

Chances of contracting a guy of his caliber again were remote. A guy like Jacoby had few openings in his shooting schedule.

Rose flicked on the light, and Sebastian squinted at the brightness. She plopped down on the loveseat beside him. "You need a hug?"

Rose's hugs beat all hugs, but even they wouldn't solve Sebastian's problem. "I need to figure out a way to make this better, then I'll go talk to Niko."

"The only way to unscrew this pooch is if you can get Grant Hardy back into Black Stallion's stable."

Sebastian laughed, the dry sound scraped up the back of his constricted throat. "The Cory Center needs him more than he needs us."

"You could ask. Maybe he'd make an exception for you."

The same way you wished Grant would make an exception and jump on your dick even though he's straight?

If only.

Note to self: No more pining after men you can't, and will *never*, have.

"That's not going to happen."

Rose made a face. It was her sympathetic I'm-trying-to-be-positive-when-there's-nothing-to-be-positive-about face.

Man, he was so fucked.

Niko strode past the open door, his shoes squeaking on the concrete floor when he stopped. He backed up and eyed Sebastian through the doorway, that enigmatic, calm façade tacked firmly in place. "In my office. Now."

Niko didn't wait for a reply.

"What am I going to tell him?"

"You'll think of something." Rose patted his hand. The gesture didn't bring him any comfort.

"Wish me luck."

"It'll be fine. He hasn't killed you yet."

Reluctantly, Sebastian stood and trudged after his uncle, catching up with him by the New York skyline set in the studio. He preferred to not have the conversation in Niko's office where he'd feel like the delinquent facing the principal.

"I've got it handled," Sebastian said as Niko walked away.

Niko stopped. Turned. "*How* do you have it handled?"

Even though Sebastian knew that question would be the first thing out of Niko's mouth, he wasn't prepared to answer.

Niko planted his hands on his hips, his eyebrows raised in question, as if waiting for something brilliant to pop into Sebastian's head.

"Hardy agreed to do the scene with Matek Kattan."

"Grant Hardy." The blatant disbelief on Niko's face came just short of calling Sebastian a liar. Which, granted, he was. But Niko didn't know it. Not for sure. "The same Grant Hardy who stood in my office a month ago and told me he was out of the business for good?"

Sebastian swallowed, the muscles in his throat working hard against the constriction. Lies didn't roll off his tongue like greased lightning. He cleared his throat. "The same."

"You got the okay from Matek?"

"Sure." The hesitation hardly showed.

"And where's Hardy's signed contract?"

"Still working on the particulars, but—"

"You've got two days to have it on my desk, capisce?"

"Yeah, I've got it." Sebastian started backing away. He had favors to call in and a capricious amount of groveling in his near future.

———

AFTER SHOOING ALL THE AFTER-SCHOOL KIDS OUT OF THE building, Grant Hardy locked The Cory Center's front door. He leaned against the cool glass and raked his eyes over the mess he needed to clean up before he went home for the night.

Which made an already long, exhausting day even longer.

Not that he wanted it any other way.

Unless the grant from the Forsythe Foundation he'd applied for came in. Then he could afford to do more, including hiring someone to clean up at the end of the day to take some of the pressure off him. Until then, the majority of the Center's responsibility fell on his shoulders.

He went room to room, wiping down the kitchen counters and putting away the basketballs in the gym. By the time he heard the rattle of the locked front door, he'd moved on to the disaster in the art room.

He ignored the rattle.

Whoever stood outside, tried the door again and then rapped on the glass. Hard. Insistent.

"We're closed," Grant hollered out as he plunked the used paintbrushes into a container of water to soak overnight.

The knock came again, only louder. Grant headed for the front before someone shattered the glass.

A patrolman stood at the door, a hand on a teen's shoulder,

in either comfort or to keep the kid from running. From a distance, Grant couldn't tell which.

He unlocked and opened the door. "Officer Brewer, what can I do for you?"

"I told you, it's Connor," the stocky officer said. "And, I need a favor."

Grant backed up as Connor thrust said 'favor' through the door on reluctant legs. Grant held his hand out. "Grant Hardy."

After a scrutinizing beat, the kid shook his hand. "Tavi."

"Tavi, what?" Grant prompted, looking for a last name.

Tavi stared at him, his eyes weary, wary, and wry. "Just Tavi."

Okay, then.

Grant's nose wrinkled as Tavi's days-old, pungent body odor assaulted him in the enclosed lobby.

Connor hooked his thumbs in his duty belt. "I was hoping you could take him."

The kid cut his eyes to Connor. "I'm not a package he can sign for."

Connor did an admirable job keeping his eye roll in check. "I picked him up for hustling in Denton Park. I didn't want to arrest him. A record isn't going to do him any good."

"Plenty of people hustle in that park. T-shirts, DVDs, crappy watches. The cops usually turn a blind eye. When did you guys start arresting people?"

"Since he was selling sex."

"It was a blowjob," Tavi said, his gaze direct on Grant as if waiting for him to be appalled. Considering the things Grant had done in his life, it would take a hell of a lot more than the mention of a blowjob to make him clutch his pearls. If he'd had pearls. "That's not even real sex."

"'Sex' is oral sex's last name," Grant said, "I'm pretty sure that counts."

"I guess you would know," the kid fired back, his cagey eyes defiant and almost... triumphant, as if the kid knew something the two of them didn't.

Grant cocked his head and narrowed his eyes, but let the comment go. To Connor, he said, "I still don't know what this has to do with me. The Center is an after-school program. A safe space for LGBTQ kids to meet others and find the services they need. It's not a shelter. We don't have beds. There's a men's shelter a couple miles down the road and the group home—"

"Fuck the shelter. It's safer for me on the streets."

"And I contacted the group home," Connor said. "They know him. He's not welcome there."

A hard case then. At what?—Grant took Tavi in from head to toe. From the rumpled dirty clothes to the unwashed hair and world-wise eyes—fifteen-years-old, sixteen tops.

"Can you—" Connor's radio cut him off.

The dispatcher rattled off some numbers. Grant had no idea what the codes meant, but Connor responded as he backed toward the door.

"*Connor.*"

"I gotta go, man. Take him, please?"

This was a bad idea. The *worst* idea.

Isn't this why you started the Center, to help these kids?

Fuck.

Even though Grant had zero idea what he'd do with the kid, he said, "Yeah, go. Save the world."

In parting, Connor turned his attention to Tavi. "Do what Grant says, kid. He's one of the good ones. He's got your back."

Connor disappeared with a hollow clank of the bell against the glass door. Grant locked up, and considered his options. He knew the guys running the group home. Maybe he could sweet-talk them into taking Tavi for the night if the kid promised to behave.

Grant turned around and found Tavi's hackles raised. "I don't need a do-gooder to have my back. I can take care of myself."

"Says the kid turning tricks in the park."

Grant had dealt with kids like him before. Coddling and cajoling wouldn't earn Tavi's trust. And pity would only piss him off. Grant brushed past the kid and headed for the lost and found box.

"Says the straight man who shoots gay porn."

Grant stopped and turned. Clearly, Tavi knew him from his work. Grant wasn't ashamed. Not when his work had helped build the Center. He had no idea what the kid had been through or why he was on the streets, but plenty of kids like him ran in and out of the Center. Maybe not as hard or as jaded, but not much different. "I'm not the bad guy here."

"Then what are you?"

"A friend."

"I have all the friends I need. And if you want me to blow you, it's twen—" Tavi looked Grant up and down, taking in his clothes as if gauging what he could get away with charging. "Thirty bucks."

Yeah, well, the only person's mouth Grant wanted around his cock was Sebastian Stavros'. Maybe then he'd stop fanticizing about the man almost every night.

Tavi had propositioned him for shock value, he guessed. Mostly.

The only way to shock these kids was to not allow them to bait you. Grant turned back down the hall. The kid needed a shower and clean clothes before he stunk up the whole place. "You think real highly of yourself if you think you can charge that much. Besides, I'm straight."

"That's what half my clients say, but I've got skills," came the kid's voice as he followed from behind. "Mad skills."

In the supply closet, Grant rummaged through a cardboard

box until he came up with a pair of sweats and a T-shirt that would fit. He handed the clothes to Tavi.

"Take yourself and your mad skills down the hall. There's a bathroom with showers at the end on the right. I have spare toothbrushes under the sink as well as sample sizes of deodorant. If you toss out your clothes, I'll throw them in the washer for you."

In the meantime, Grant would make a discreet call to the group home while Tavi got cleaned up.

The mulish expression cemented into place on Tavi's face. "Fine."

Wow. This kid didn't have any soft spots. All prickles and hard edges. Grant rubbed a hand at the tension knotting his neck muscles. "You hungry?"

The circles under the kid's eyes Grant attributed to the lack of sleep—the street kids were always being roused from wherever they'd bedded down for the night—but the hollowness in Tavi's cheeks, and the way his clothes draped his body made it clear Tavi didn't have regular access to food.

"I could eat," Tavi admitted after the briefest of pauses.

Grant hitched his thumb over his shoulder, indicating the side hall. "Kitchen's that way. Meet me in there when you're done."

Tavi bobbed his head once and disappeared into the bathroom while Grant made a beeline for his office phone and what turned out to be a short-lived conversation with the group home.

Grant grumbled to himself as he scooped up Tavi's dirty clothes outside the shower stall. Not only had the group home said 'no,' they'd said an emphatic 'oh, hell no.' Now, what was he supposed to do with Tavi?

It wasn't like he could take him home. Some of the local conservative religious groups in the area had already opposed him opening the Center. If they ever found out he was gay *and* taking kids home with him? Fuck. His haters would burn him at the stake.

Being in operation for less than a year, he couldn't jeopardize the Center for the sake of one kid.

After starting the washing machine, Grant headed for the kitchen. He kept it stocked with simple food for the kids, many of whom lived on the street or surfed their friends' couches—places where a regular meal wasn't something they could always count on.

At least at the Center, they could make themselves a sandwich or eat some fruit.

Grant's stomach grumbled as he slathered peanut butter and jelly onto four thick slices of bread. He then added a sliced apple and a handful of chips to the two plates. He slid one across the table in the middle of the kitchen as Tavi rounded the corner, his damp hair dripping onto the shoulders of his shirt.

Tavi dropped into the chair and tore a large bite out of his sandwich. Grant leaned against the counter and started in on his own.

They ate in silence until Grant finally asked, "What did you do at the group home to earn your spot on the blacklist?"

Tavi shoved the last corner of his sandwich into his mouth and mumbled something Grant couldn't make out.

He poured Tavi a glass of water, and when the kid had washed the bite down, Grant said, "Come again."

"What's it to you?"

"Look, kid, if you don't want my help, I can't keep you here against your will. I've got a couch in my office you can have for tonight. I just wanna make sure you're not gonna burn the place to the ground overnight."

"Fire has never been my thing."

Fair enough. "What about work. Is work your thing?"

"When I can get it. I tried Black Stallion Studios, but they wouldn't hire me."

"That's because they don't do kiddy porn."

Tavi's eyes narrowed. "I'm not a kid. I'm almost sixteen."

Grant raised a brow and crossed his arms over his chest. Now that Tavi had scrubbed off the dirt and grime, he looked even younger. "Define 'almost.'"

"I'm sixteen in April."

Grant barked out a laugh, and Tavi slumped in his. "It's June. That's ten months from now." Which meant Tavi was spitting distance from fourteen.

Tavi shrugged. "A month on the street is worth a year anywhere else."

"I get it."

"Do you?" It came out more like an accusation than a question.

"More than you know," Grant allowed, but he wasn't getting into it with the kid.

Tavi contemplated Grant's non-answer and polished off the rest of his food. "About that couch…"

"It ain't free."

Kids like Tavi rarely got something for nothing. Besides, Grant didn't believe in a free ride, no matter who you were.

Tavi's gaze flicked from Grant's face to his crotch and back again.

"Jesus Christ, kid. That's not what I meant."

"What *did* you mean?"

"Mop the floors and finish straightening the art room, and the couch is yours for the night."

There wasn't much of anything of value Tavi could steal, besides food, and he could have as much of that as he wanted, so Grant wasn't too concerned about leaving him alone for the night.

"If you do a decent job, you're still here in the morning, and the building is still standing, I've got other work you can do if you want it."

"You're gonna lock me in here by myself?"

"Is there a reason why I shouldn't?"

"What if there's a fire?"

"The back is locked from the inside. You can get out, but the alarm will go off, and the police will come, and we'll be right back where we started."

"Why do you care?" Again, that defensive accusation permeated Tavi's words, a quick-to-blame and slow-to-trust mentality that the streets had beat into him.

"Right now, all that matters is that I do."

2

Darkness had settled by the time Sebastian watched Grant pull into the parking space. He'd waited on the steps to Grant's second-floor apartment, his gut twisting into knots so tight he could barely swallow any of the water he'd brought with him.

Sebastian stood as Grant climbed out of his Civic, looking rumpled, worn, and hot as hell. "Hey."

Sebastian's smile faltered when the lines between Grant's brows only grew deeper.

Grant trudged up the steps and brushed past him. "What are you doing here?"

Sebastian turned and followed. "I have a favor I need to ask."

"The answer's no."

Grant didn't slam the door in Sebastian's face, so Sebastian nudged the door open that had been left ajar. Sebastian walked into the space he'd dreamed of being in for much longer than he wanted to admit.

Of course, in his dreams, it wasn't the living room with a cushy leather couch and big screen TV that had caught Sebastian's imagination, but the bed in the room beyond.

With Grant in it, of course.

Naked.

And inside him.

"Hey."

Sebastian tore his attention from his thoughts and concentrated on Grant. "Yeah?"

"I asked if you wanted a beer."

At least Grant wasn't kicking him out before he had a chance to ask the teeny, tiny, itsy, bitsy favor, in spite of Grant's previous automatic 'no.'

Man, you are so fucked.

And not in the way you want.

"Why not?" Sebastian squeezed into the tight, galley kitchen. It was California, after all, and an apartment, even on the outskirts of the San Fernando Valley, didn't come cheap.

Grant twisted off the top on a bottle of Dos Equis and handed it over before opening one for himself. Sebastian watched the play of Grant's throat as he guzzled half the bottle.

"Tough day?" Sebastian asked.

"Yeah, there's this kid..."

Sebastian leaned against the opposite counter and sipped at his beer while Grant told him about the street kid the cop had dropped at his doorstep. "You left some kid at the Center? Alone?"

"What?" Grant started on his second beer, this time drinking it more slowly. "It's not like his mommy comes and tucks him in on a park bench every night."

"I guess."

"Trust me. It's much safer for him to spend the night alone at the Center than out there on the streets."

Sometimes what's right is the least-worst option. So that's what Grant had done.

"You're doing a good thing."

"I don't know." Grant glanced down at his beer bottle,

running his thumb through the condensation gathered there. "Like that kid. Am I making a difference?"

"For tonight, you did. And you can hook him up with services that help him get his GED and get him off the streets."

"Maybe. But it's been my experience that kids like Tavi don't stick around to take advantage of what little help is available."

"Maybe he'll surprise you."

Grant made a non-committal noise. Some middle ground between derision and hope. Then Grant set his bottle on the counter and glanced up at Sebastian, his blue-gray eyes filled with caution.

"Speaking of surprises... Why are you here?" Grant's eyes flicked to Sebastian's lips, lingering just long enough that Sebastian knew he hadn't imagined it. "What do you want?"

The sexy dip in Grant's voice Sebastian attributed to the beer, even though Grant had barely drunk any of the second bottle. All knotted up, Sebastian's stomach flipped at the favor he needed to ask.

Then their eyes locked, and Sebastian couldn't tell who'd moved first, only that they'd met in the middle, so close he smelled the hops on Grant's breath.

Maybe now that Grant no longer worked for Black Stallion, he would come out of the closet Sebastian had always suspected he'd locked himself inside of.

Maybe if Sebastian gave him a little shove...

Reaching up, Sebastian cupped the back of Grant's neck and pressed his lips to Grant's. The grunt of surprise made the semi Sebastian sported almost painful behind the fly of his slacks.

He'd watched Grant in many scenes, with many men, wondering what it would feel like to have Grant's lips on him.

Heaven.

Okay, maybe heaven was a stretch, especially because there was nothing sweet or airy or light about the kiss.

Grant angled his head, taking the kiss deeper as he stepped Sebastian back and pressed him against the counter, Grant's muscular arms caging him in. Sebastian gave in to Grant's demand, and he dove into a place where it felt deliciously dark and dangerous as if an ominous cloud had blotted out the sun.

Sebastian couldn't get enough.

He reached for Grant's belt, for that magnificent cock pressing against his hip. The words spilled from Sebastian's mouth before he could stop them. "*That's* what I want."

Grant stilled, then gripped Sebastian's wrist before he could take it any further. Grant's breath coming as fast as his. "There are many reasons why you can't have it." Grant pulled away and took himself and his beer into the den.

Time to call Grant on his bullshit. "I suppose one of those reasons is because you're straight."

"Exactly," Grant said, as he leaned against the window frame and pressed the beer bottle to his forehead.

"Yeah." Sebastian slathered the cold heat of sarcasm on thick. "Nothing screams 'straight' like sticking your tongue down another man's throat."

"It means nothing." The way Grant glared at him, Sebastian almost believed him. But that glare couldn't erase the desire still lingering in Grant's gaze or the way Sebastian still felt the pressure of where Grant's cock had pressed against him. "I fuck men for a living, Bass. It's what I do. Fuck. *Did*. I mean, did."

"Is that why you're still in the closet? Because of Black Stallion, because of the Center?"

Grant didn't confirm or deny. *Shocker*. "What I do and why I do it is none of your business. Especially now that I don't work for you anymore."

"For my uncle."

"Same difference."

"About that…" Sebastian gestured toward the couch, asking Grant to sit.

Grant stared at the couch a beat too long, then walked over and plopped down. "What?"

Keeping his distance, Sebastian slung a leg over the armrest on the opposite end of the couch. "I fucked up."

If that came as a surprise, it didn't show on Grant's face. "Have you ever thought about going into another profession? Maybe—"

"No. I'm good at what I do. But… I don't know what happens. I drop a ball—"

"Or two." The flash came back into Grant's eyes, a hint of the man who'd seemed at one point to live to tease Sebastian.

"In this case, it dropped and splatted everywhere. Niko is on my ass and, nepotism or not, this time, I really think my job is on the line."

Grant leaned forward and set his bottle on the distressed wood coffee table. Real distressed wood—like wood that has survived four years of college at a frat house, not Joe Bob down at the factory with chains and a dull chisel. "Jesus Christ, what did you do?"

"I mixed up the date on Jacoby Winters' contract and—"

"Wait. Black Stallion signed Winters?"

"The one and only. Except now, because of the screwup, I have Matek Kattan showing up in two days for some scenes and no one of Winters' caliber to shoot with him…" *Okay. Deep breath. You can't get a yes without asking.* "Besides you."

Sebastian painted on his best pretty-please smile. Grant didn't smile back. He also didn't laugh in Sebastian's face, which had also been a viable option.

"Not gonna happen."

"I'm begging. Just—"

Grant ran a hand down his face, looking more exhausted

than Sebastian had ever seen him. Even more rung out than that week in Cancun when he'd shot scene after scene for Black Stallion.

"I can't risk it. There's an asshole on the city council. If he ever got wind of my association with Black Stallion, he would fight until he'd slammed the doors on the Center. For good. I've worked too hard, and those kids need our services too much for me to let that happen."

The knots in Sebastian's stomach unraveled after Grant's death blow. He was dead. At least Sebastian's career with Black Stallion was. And then who would hire a man whose uncle fired him?

"Yeah. I get it." Sebastian stood and stuffed his hands into the back pockets of his slacks. "Thanks. For the beer, for hearing me out, and..." he glanced over his shoulder at the kitchen where Grant had kissed him and left Sebastian wanting. Wanting more of Grant and more of the connection they shared but that Grant refused to acknowledge. "Anyway... I'll see myself out."

Grant stood but didn't move any closer. "If it makes you feel any better, I would do it if I could."

"No. It doesn't." Sebastian shook his head. *That's not Grant's fault.* It wasn't Grant's job or obligation to fix Sebastian's fuckups.

A WAKE MOST OF THE NIGHT, GRANT HAD EXPECTED A CALL FROM the security company telling him the alarm at the Center had tripped. Which was a piss poor excuse for his insomnia.

The blame for his sleepless night belonged to the hard-on he'd sported for a man he couldn't, shouldn't, *wouldn't* have.

As Grant approached the Center's front door, he swallowed the last of his coffee and tried to rub the grit out of his eyes, half expecting to see a Tavi-sized hole in the glass from the kid escaping back to the streets in the middle of the night.

But the door remained intact.

The Center sat in the middle of a strip center with a tax lawyer on one side and a vape shop on the other. The section the Center occupied had once been a gym with high ceilings, making it the perfect space for his needs.

He unlocked the door and made his way through the building, his shoes squeaking on the freshly mopped floor as he went through the building, flipping on the lights. Damn. The kid knew how to drive a mop.

He poked his head into the art room and found it tidy. Even the paintbrushes Grant had left soaking had been washed and placed on a pad of paper towels to dry.

Heading straight to the kitchen—because no way could he get through the day without a pot or two of coffee—he spotted Tavi on the couch in his office, his back to the open door, the thin blanket over his head, and the overhead light still on.

After brewing a pot, Grant headed to his office.

"Hey." Grant tapped his foot against the base of the couch, a mug of coffee in each hand. "You're still here."

Tavi rolled over with a groan and sat up, taking the mug of coffee Grant held out to him. "You thought I'd be gone." A statement, not a question.

Grant sat in the chair behind his desk. "Pretty much." He reached over and turned his computer on, half expecting it to be chock full of viruses from Tavi spending half the night looking at porn, but when it booted up, everything seemed fine.

"You look surprised. Like you thought I'd mess it up somehow."

Grant wasn't going to lie. That was no way to build trust. "I did."

"I didn't even turn it on. And if I had, you never would have known. I know how to cover my tracks."

"You some kind of computer whiz?"

"I'm homeless, not stupid."

Grant leveled him with a look, shooting for a patient, open expression that would encourage conversation and maybe knock a chunk or two off that thick wall the kid had built to protect himself. That early in the morning, with little sleep and even less caffeine, Grant wasn't sure he pulled it off.

"I had a computer," Tavi said at last. "You know... before."

The *I got kicked out* part of that sentence hung in the air between them, the expression on Tavi's face almost daring Grant to press for more. But Grant knew better. Pushing Tavi now would only drive him away.

"You did a good job on the floors."

Whatever Tavi had expected Grant to say, it wasn't that. Instead of saying thanks, the way most people would, Tavi said, "Yeah, well, when I'm hired to do a job, I do my best. Whether it's floors, paintbrushes, or blow—"

Grant raised his hand to shut Tavi up. "Yeah, yeah. I get it. You hungry, kid?"

"Starved."

Grant opened the Center, and by the time the bell on the front door clattered, they'd both finished scarfing down a couple of pieces of toast with jelly. A voice called out, "Grant, baby, are you in here?"

Tavi sputtered out a laugh, spewing breadcrumbs across the table. "*Baby?*"

"It's my grandmother," Grant said. Then he called out, "In the kitchen."

As the patter of his grandmother's feet echoed down the hall, Grant stood and pointed a finger at Tavi. "Behave."

"There's my baby boy," his grandmother said as she came

into the kitchen. She hugged him, her frail arms surprisingly strong as they wrapped around his waist.

He kissed her cheek and kept his arm around her shoulder. "Nana, I'd like you to meet Tavi."

"Hello." Tavi had yet to tame his bedhead, but he managed to tame his tongue.

His grandmother was pushing eighty, but her eyes shone bright, her mind remained clear, and her wit sharp. "You keeping my boy in line, young man?"

"Tryin'." Tavi didn't crack a smile, but when Grant's grandmother called him 'boy' again, Tavi's eyes lit with laughter.

Grant folded his grandmother's hand into the crook of his arm and ushered her out of the kitchen before Tavi figured out a way to use the term of endearment as blackmail.

He pushed aside the pillow and blanket and sat beside his grandmother on the couch. This time when he looked at her—really looked at her—he noticed the tension around her eyes dulling the brightness usually dancing there.

"What's wrong?" As soon as those words came out of his mouth, he realized it was Tuesday. The day his grandmother usually spent volunteering at the hospital. Those days were sacred. She'd never missed a Tuesday for as long as he could remember.

The saliva dried in his mouth. Whatever had brought her there had to be cataclysmic. Or nearly so.

"Promise you won't get mad, dear."

Her inability to meet his gaze dropped his stomach to the floor. "I can only promise I won't get mad at *you*. Anything and any*one* else is fair game."

His grandmother grimaced at 'anyone.'

"Who is it, and what have they done?"

"Maybe I shouldn't have come. That boy needs you and..."

His grandmother started to rise, but he gently sat her back down.

"Hey." Tavi poked his head into the office. He'd changed into his now clean street clothes, and he put the folded sweats and T-shirt on the low filing cabinet near the door. "I'm outta here."

Fuck. Grant turned to his grandmother. "I'm sorry. Give me one minute."

He walked Tavi down the hall. "Where are you going?" And yeah, that sounded like every parent everywhere right before their teen left the house.

Tavi's eyebrows rose at Grant's tone. "Back where I belong."

"You don't belong out there."

"Yeah? Well, I don't belong here either. And if I'd known you would be all weird about it, I'd have left without letting you know."

"I'm not being weird."

"Parental then."

"Big word."

Tavi tapped a finger to his head. "Not an idiot. Remember?"

Grant blew out a breath but held his frustrations in check. These were the kids the Center wanted to reach.

Grabbing a business card out of his wallet, Grant scribbled his cell phone number on the back. "Be careful. If you need anything, call me. That's why we're here."

"I don't have a phone."

"A wise kid once said, 'I'm homeless, not stupid.' You need me, I'm sure an Einstein like you will figure out how to get in touch."

Tavi took the card and stuffed it in his back pocket. "Later, dude."

To Tavi's retreating back, Grant said, "And stay out of the park."

Turning, Tavi walked backward, his hands raised in a what's-a-kid-to-do kind of way, his smile cocky, but glum around the edges. Grant would call it a win if Tavi made it through the day without being arrested.

Grant waited in the hall until the front door opened and closed, and then waited a good thirty seconds longer, hoping Tavi would change his mind and walk back through the door. But this wasn't an over-scripted, feel-good after-school special.

This was real life.

Cory had taught Grant one valuable lesson: You can't save someone who doesn't want saving.

Grant returned to his office, his grandmother, and hopefully a problem he could solve.

"Sorry about that." Grant reclaimed his seat. His grandmother's eyes were now rimmed with red, and she tore the tissue in her hands into tiny pieces. "Just spit it out, and we'll deal, okay?"

His grandmother took the deepest, shakiest breath that nearly shattered Grant's heart. Through the years, he'd seen all of her emotions, from anger and disappointment to joy and determination, but never... never had he seen her so distraught.

"I mortgaged my house to loan your father money. Yesterday, I got a letter from the mortgage company telling me he defaulted on the payments, and they put the house into foreclosure."

Grant shot off the couch and paced to the opposite end of his office. His father. His *fucking* father. "That bastard."

How the hell had someone so vile spawned from a woman so sweet?

He leaned against the far wall, his knees threatening to buckle. "This is all my fault."

"No. You didn't sign those papers. I did."

"If I hadn't answered his call last year. If I had left well enough alone. If I hadn't thought... I don't know what... that maybe, just maybe, he'd changed? That perhaps he wasn't the same shit-hole, drunk-ass, lying, stealing, piece of shit that I've known him to be my entire life, this never would have happened."

"I thought he'd changed, too. He wanted to start a business and—"

Grant's derisive laugh cut her off. "He's not qualified to run a lemonade stand."

"I know that." Her voice broke, and a piece of Grant's heart cracked and broke away. "I don't know what to do."

Grant went over, helped his grandmother up, and hugged her bony body to his chest. "Don't worry. I'll take care of everything."

3

______

After a morning spent trying to get ahold of his piece-of-shit sperm donor, Grant left the Center in Vondra Mumbee's capable hands. If anyone understood living life on the streets as a teen and survival prostitution, it was her. Maybe she could talk some sense into Tavi if he showed back up.

Or, if nothing else, scare him away from rando dicks in the park.

Grant roared up Black Stallion's circular drive in the San Fernando foothills, a place he swore he wouldn't return to for work. Not because he'd hated his time there, but because, in a way, his association with the studio was part of what kept him closeted.

The demand for straight guys doing gay porn meant the compensation for talent like him remained relatively high. Unlike other studios, Black Stallion had a contractual clause you had to sign stating you were straight.

If word got out that he was gay... bye-bye residuals.

Residuals that allowed him to pay his expenses and pour his time and efforts into the Center where they were needed most.

He threw his Civic into park in front of a Frank Lloyd Wright wannabe, built with a lot of glass and straight lines in two interconnected parts. One part for the studio and accommodations for the talent, the other part for offices and Niko Stavros's private home.

Locking his car, Grant strode through the front door of the office, nearly knocking down Rose Galloway as she passed by the door.

"Grant!" She caught her balance and threw her arms around him. "It's so good to see you."

"It's great to see you, too." He kissed her cheek and held on tight. She was soft and warm against him, and hugging her felt like coming home. Like hugging the mother he'd wished he'd had but never known. "Hey, is Bass around?"

She pulled away. "Please tell me you're white-knighting the Kattan shoot. The tension between Niko and Sebastian is a living breathing behemoth. Everyone's on edge and afraid to take a wrong step."

Grant ran his hand through his hair. For the normally laid-back Rose, the stress in her eyes almost made him feel guilty for turning Sebastian down outright. "He hasn't found someone else?"

"There *is* no one else."

"That's not true. There are plenty of other great guys out there."

"None that are available. And none who'll make the website forums buzz the way it will if you do the project. You're the fan-favorite at Black Stallion. My inbox is stuffed with people writing me wondering where you are."

He didn't want to give Rose false hope, so he told her the truth. "I've come to talk. That's all I can promise."

She got on her tiptoes and kissed him on the cheek, the smile on her face infectious. "You're back. I know you are. We're family, Grant, don't you forget it."

He watched her disappear down the hall and didn't realize until it was too late that he hadn't asked where to find Sebastian. He searched the office wing, peeking in open doors, but the area remained quiet and Sebastian AWOL. Hopefully, Niko didn't have him strung up by his toes somewhere.

Though the thought of Sebastian tied up, brought a smile to Grant's face. If anyone was tying up Sebastian, Grant wanted it to be him.

Good luck with that straight *boy.*

Fuck me.

Or, in his case, not. Unless it was in front of the camera.

Grant wandered over to the other side of the building and down the stairs to the production studio in the basement. He turned the corner and headed down the long hall that led to the set. From out of sight, Niko hollered out, "Cut! Everyone take fifteen."

Cat, Black Stallion's makeup artist, and all-around kick-ass woman, stood in the doorway of the makeup room, her shoulder against the jamb. Her face lit when she saw him. "I heard a rumor you're coming back."

Rose was many things. Discreet didn't look like one of them.

He wrapped Cat's curvy frame in a hug and pressed a kiss to the top of her spiked and gelled head. "Don't believe everything you hear."

From where they stood, Grant heard Niko roar, his words evaporating into the high ceilings, but that couldn't hide his ire. "He sounds pissed."

In the couple years Grant had worked with Niko, the director had always been even-tempered and as easy to work with as any perfectionist could be.

"It's been bad enough since he broke things off with Peter the Weasel, but since Sebastian screwed up Jacoby's contract, he's been a little bitch."

"Who's been 'a little bitch'?" Niko asked as he stormed down the hall toward them.

Cat folded her arms over her ample chest and stood as tall as a five-foot-four woman could. "*You* have. And we're getting sick of it. You don't pay us enough to put up with your crap. Go get drunk, or go get laid, but you need to get over yourself."

Niko shot an acknowledgment to Grant then returned his attention to Cat. He rested his hands on his hips and blew out a breath. "That bad?"

"So bad I've considered telling PornU I'll accept their job offer."

"You've got to be fucking kidding me," Niko spouted off. "They're a bunch of sniveling assholes over there."

Cat didn't back down. "Right now, that's an upgrade."

If Niko had been a sail, Cat had effectively stolen his wind, setting him adrift. "*Really?*"

Vin, Niko's number one cameraman, walked up. "Put it this way, boss. If you don't want the rest of the crew to mutiny, you gotta dial it back."

Vin had been a street urchin back in the day before Niko had put a roof over his head, stripped the paint can out of his hand, and replaced it with a camera. Maybe Grant could get Vin to talk to the kids at the Center sometime.

Vin thumped Grant in the middle of the chest with the back of his hand. "Niko's talking to you."

Grant shook his thoughts about the Center away. "I'm sorry, what?"

"Are you here to sign the contract?" Niko asked, the veneer of patience he'd slathered on running thin.

Over Niko's shoulder, Grant caught Sebastian's eye. Sebastian nodded, encouraging Grant to say yes.

"I'm... here to talk options," Grant hedged.

Vin clapped Grant on the shoulder and continued down the

hall. Cat did a little dance in place. Niko turned to Sebastian and said, "Don't fuck this one up."

———

SEBASTIAN USED THE SILENCE ON THEIR WALK BACK TO HIS OFFICE to think of all the different ways he could beg Grant to agree to do the scenes with Kattan.

All the while convincing his dick to forget what Grant's lips had felt like pressed against his.

Forget how Grant tasted.

Forget the press of Grant's cock against his hip.

A cock Sebastian had no difficulty imagining since he'd seen it on set—and in action—many agonizing times before.

Better get your brain right. Time to think with your big head, not the little one.

Sebastian ushered Grant into the chair in front of his desk and closed the door behind him with a definitive click. Sebastian thought about hitching a leg over the corner of his desk, but that felt too informal and intimate, but sitting behind his desk felt too sterile and far away.

And the two-seater couch... a definite no.

Don't be stupid. It doesn't matter where you sit. It only matters that he signs.

"Would you stop pacing," Grant said. "You're making me nervous."

Choosing the middle ground, Sebastian pulled his chair to the side of his desk and sat. "Before we get started, there's been a change in the shooting schedule. Originally, we were going to shoot all three scenes in one weekend, but Kattan had some things come up, so the scenes will have to be a couple of weeks apart."

"What about Jacoby Winters? Maybe now he can—"

"It still doesn't work. I've tried. Believe me."

"It's not like I don't have any obligations either. I've got a huge fundraising event scheduled for the Center a month and a half from now that's totally kicking my ass, and—"

"I'll help." *Like you have the time.*

He'd make the time.

Grant crossed his arms over his chest. "You'll help?"

The skepticism in Grant's voice should have been insulting, but Sebastian was clutching and grabbing at every straw, every remote possibility that would get Grant to sign with Black Stallion. If that meant he signed himself up as the chairman of the Center's fundraising committee, then he'd do it.

"I'm actually pretty good at it. I run Black Stallion's charity fundraiser every year, and I was head of fundraising for my high school theater. We had the best sets of all of the high school plays in the entire valley."

Grant wavered. Sebastian saw it in his eyes. He stuck out his hand to seal the deal.

"Not so fast. I could use some help in the afternoons. Vondra can cover some days, but she's in summer school at the community college, plus her real job. Leaves me grossly outnumbered by tweens on many nights."

"I've got a job, too."

Grant raised his brows, a smug grin turning up his lips. A grin that reminded Sebastian that he might *not* have a job if Grant didn't sign. Sebastian fought the return smile. You had to admire a guy who found a way to get what he wanted. "Seriously, you'd coerce me?"

"If that's what it takes. If it makes you feel any better, you can call your sudden interest in the Center altruism. Whatever helps you sleep at night."

"An I-stroke-you, you-stroke-me kind of deal?"

"I believe the word is 'scratch,' not 'stroke,' but that's the gist." Then Grant's smile faded. "To be clear, that kiss the other night... it didn't happen."

But the way Grant's eyes settled on Sebastian's lips, it most certainly *had* happened. Sebastian didn't see regret, or if he did, desire buried it deep. But if that's how Grant wanted to play things, Sebastian would deal. He raised his hands in surrender. "No one will hear it from me."

Sebastian opened the manila folder on his desk and pulled out the contract he'd already typed up, just in case he'd managed to talk Grant into doing the scenes. He slid the paperwork across the desk and held out a pen.

"Not so fast."

"What now?"

Grant scrubbed his hand across his jaw, tension stiffening his movements. "I need double my usual rates. And a five percent jump on the residuals."

The pen fell from Sebastian's fingers, and he didn't bother catching it when it rolled off the table and disappeared under the desk. "You know Niko's answer to that will be no."

"We won't know until you ask."

Grant stood as if he were about to leave, and Sebastian jumped out of his chair and caught Grant's arm. He would have thrown his body in front of the door if he thought it would help.

Grant eyed Sebastian's hand until he let go. "Double my rate is still less than what Niko would have paid Winters. That's no secret. And Black Stallion's audience has been jonesing for me to do a scene with Kattan for a year now. Niko will make his money back and then some. We both know it."

Sebastian stuffed the contract back into the folder. "Wait here."

———

SWEAT RAN DOWN GRANT'S BACK AS HE PACED SEBASTIAN'S office, waiting for Sebastian to return with Niko's verdict.

He hadn't come to the studios intending to up his rate, but if he wanted any chance of digging his grandmother's house out of foreclosure, he needed a hell of a lot more cash upfront and he couldn't wait around for the residuals to roll in.

No way could he get the money he needed if he didn't take a chance and be proactive about it. Especially when doing more scenes could jeopardize the Center if word got out. Frankly, he'd been surprised word of his illustrious time with Black Stallion hadn't already spread.

Grant stared out the window into the side yard that led to the pool and outdoor kitchen Niko liked to use when he had a house full of talent that needed to relax and get to know each other before the shoots.

Behind him, the door latch clicked. Grant's heart wedged in his throat, and sweat broke out along his hairline. He shoved his hands into the front pockets of his slacks and turned toward the door, going for the calm, casual look. "We have a deal?"

Sebastian walked over and held out his hand. "We have a deal. If you want to get with Rose, she can set you up with an appointment at the clinic to get your STI screening done."

Grant pulled a folded receipt out of his wallet. "I stopped by on the way over. Should have the results tomorrow."

STI screening was standard pre-shoot protocol. The fact that Grant hadn't been with anyone since he'd left Black Stallion more than a month ago, he kept to himself. Sebastian didn't need to know the pathetic state of his non-existent sex life.

In Grant's defense, the Center took up almost all of his energy. He hadn't had the time, or the inclination, to cruise the bars or find an anonymous one-night-stand on one of the dating apps.

And as careful as he'd always been with his hookups, the

risk of being outed, especially now that the Center had become a reality, made anonymous sex almost not worth the gamble.

You could blame it on that, or you could man the fuck up and admit to yourself that anonymous sex pales to the idea of having one man.

Of having Sebastian.

Which could never happen.

Sebastian was crap at keeping secrets, so Grant couldn't trust Sebastian with his. Not when he depended on discretion for his livelihood.

"I guess that's it then." Sebastian laid the lab receipt in the folder with the contract. "We have your scene scheduled for early Saturday morning. Kattan is flying in Friday afternoon if you want to come to the pool party with the rest of the talent."

"I'll be there. I might be a little late unless I can get someone to cover for me at the Center. We usually keep the doors open until seven on Friday nights."

"That's fine." Sebastian backed away. "I guess I'll see you then."

"Not so fast."

That brought Sebastian up short. "Am I forgetting something?"

"The fundraising for the Center?"

"Oh, yeah, about that. Um…"

"I'm holding my first meeting tonight with the committee members. Six-thirty. Be there."

Grant had no such thing planned, but a part of him didn't want the next time he saw Sebastian to be while he was fucking some other dude in front of the cameras.

"I might be late. The shoot isn't going the way Niko wants, and with having to drive across town during rush hour—"

Grant leveled him with a look. A look that said I-just-saved-your-ass. "Time to make good on our deal."

Sebastian blew out a breath and nodded. "Yeah, yeah. Alright. I'll clear it with Niko and cut out early if I have to."

"See you then."

As Grant drove away from the property, he wanted to kick himself. He should have come clean with Sebastian that the Center's committee for the fundraiser was a committee of one. Him.

Now the joke was on Grant.

He'd pulled off a lucrative deal with Niko. That had been the easy part. Now he had to get through the meeting at the Center.

With Sebastian.

Alone.

4

———

Niko hadn't been happy that Sebastian had to leave early, but his uncle's relief that Sebastian had signed Grant helped that bombshell land a little softer.

Sebastian glanced at his watch as he crossed the parking lot to the Center. Driving through the valley at rush hour had taken longer than he'd anticipated. Though, considering the jam-packed roads in California, being caught in traffic was usually a valid excuse for tardiness.

With his knuckles, he rapped on the glass of the locked door. He watched as Grant approached, dressed in jeans and one of the Center's polo shirts, the fabric stretching across his wide chest. Sebastian tried not to stare while Grant unlocked and held the door open with his body.

With chopsticks, Grant slurped noodles out of a white carton and muttered, "You're late."

"Traffic."

"That's no excuse." Grant stepped away from the door and locked them inside before heading back down the hall.

"It's the only one I've got."

Sebastian had only been to the Center once before, and that

had been months ago at the Center's opening celebration. He followed Grant and prepared to apologize to the rest of the committee for keeping them waiting, but when he turned into the kitchen, it was empty.

"Where is everyone?"

Grant held out his arms. "We're here."

Sebastian glanced from Grant to the assorted cartons of Chinese take-out sitting on the table. "A committee of two?"

"Looks that way."

"You should have told me it was only us."

"Would that have mattered?"

Yes. No. Maybe. Hell, Sebastian didn't know. A little warning to get his mind right would have been nice, though. The whole drive over he could have told himself *don't kiss him, don't kiss him, don't kiss him.*

Now, without the buffer of a room full of people to help him keep his hands, his lips, his *dick* to himself, the words wouldn't come.

Without waiting for an answer, Grant pointed his chopsticks at the food. "Help yourself."

Sebastian's eyes went straight to Grant's lips as they closed around another bite.

Grant bumped his chin toward the food. "I didn't know what you liked, so I got a little of everything."

With effort, Sebastian pushed thoughts of kissing Grant out of his head and picked through the cartons until he came up with the Sichuan chicken. Grant sat down and raised his brows at Sebastian's choice. "You like it spicy, huh?"

Sebastian swallowed hard and cleared his throat. "It keeps life interesting."

Grant chuckled and handed Sebastian a legal pad of paper and a pen. "Where do you want to start?"

At your nipples and work my way down to that magnificent cock,

Sebastian wanted to say. "Why don't you start by telling me your idea?"

"Invite lots of people and find a fun way to part them from their money."

"Great." Sebastian ladled on the sarcasm. "What's your plan to do that?"

Grant set aside the empty container of noodles and tapped his pen against the pad of paper. "That's as far as I've gotten."

Sebastian choked on a piece of chicken. "That's as far as you've gotten, and the fundraiser is eight weeks out?"

Grant's face scrunched up, in an adorably sexy way that said you're-not-going-to-like-this. "Six weeks."

"Fuck."

"I'm confident you can pull it off."

Groaning, because Grant clearly had no idea the amount of work and coordination it took to pull off a successful fundraiser, Sebastian took a fortifying breath and said, "Maybe it would help if we started with a theme."

"I'd like to involve the kids during the day as well as have something geared more toward the adults later that evening."

"We could do a carnival for the kids. You have plenty of space in the gym, and you could probably get permission from the city to use the empty field behind the Center for things like a dunk tank and sack races. Then for the adults... hmmm." They needed something that would attract a lot of money. "How about a masquerade ball with a bachelor auction?"

"You're kidding me, right?"

"In this town, you get the right guys, and the money will come. Trust me."

"I'm not going on stage and auctioning myself off to the highest bidder if that's what you're saying."

Shame. Sebastian would have paid a pretty penny for a romantic night alone with Grant. "We'll be too busy running the event to be in the auction ourselves, but Niko has connections. We might even be able to get some B-list actors or some local professional athletes."

"The Hawks," Grant and Sebastian said at the same time as the idea solidified.

The Hawks were the local Double-A baseball team. And since Alex Payne, one of their players, had worked with Black Stallion, they might have an in.

"Alex and I still keep in touch," Grant said. "And he's great about donating his time to community projects, when he's in town. I can check the team's game schedule and see if they'll be around."

"And I'll do some digging and see if there are any B-listers who want a little free publicity."

A grin spread over Grant's handsome face. He'd always been the quiet guy, the reader, the deep thinker type where the smiles seemed few and far between. His enigmatic undertone had always been something Sebastian had found exorbitantly attractive, and sexy as hell, but seeing that face... open, gregarious... *happy.* It tripped something in Sebastian's chest that made his heart stutter and his lungs refuse to expand.

"Did you hear that?" Grant asked.

Sebastian didn't want to admit that the sound Grant thought he'd heard was Grant's heart rattling in his chest, but then Sebastian heard the thump for himself. But it didn't come from his chest. It came from the front door.

Grant bounded out of his chair, and Sebastian ran toward the front of the Center after him. Grant fumbled with his keys and finally managed to shove them into the lock. A teen stood slumped against the glass, blood running down from his nose and into his mouth.

"Oh, my God," Sebastian said, "what happened?"

GRANT YANKED OPEN THE CENTER'S FRONT DOOR AND PULLED Tavi inside. "Who did this to you?"

Tavi nearly collapsed in the Center's lobby, and together Grant and Sebastian helped him to the couch in his office. Grant brushed the sweaty, leaf-littered bangs out of Tavi's face and watched as Tavi's eyes rolled around in his head. Conscious, but barely.

"Call 9-1-1," he told Sebastian.

Carefully, Grant stripped Tavi's backpack off his shoulders and laid it aside. Along with a bloody nose, Tavi's right eye had already swelled closed, and his jaw hadn't fared much better.

"No cops." Tavi shifted and grunted, hugging a protective arm around his ribs.

"Tough shit," Grant said. "You don't show up here looking like Tyson's punching bag and expect me to do nothing."

"They're on their way." Sebastian laid a hand on Grant's shoulder. "I'll wait for them up front. Unless you need me here."

"No. Go." Grant turned his attention back to Tavi, already lifting up the teen's shirt to get a look at his ribs. "Where else are you—*Fuck*. Tavi, look at me."

Grant held Tavi's chin and forced him look him in the eye. "What happened? There's a fucking boot tread on your ribs. Size thirteen from the looks of it."

Tavi jerked his chin out of Grant's hand, the sudden movement making him moan. "I was in the park..." Tavi met Grant's gaze but didn't finish the sentence.

He didn't have to.

From outside came the wail of sirens, and Sebastian called back. "They're here."

The paramedics arrived first and started assessing Tavi,

followed close behind by Officer Brewer. Grant stuck out his hand. "Connor."

Sebastian hung back, staying out of the way and taking it all in, looking a little shell shocked.

Connor pulled a flip notebook out of the breast pocket of his uniform. "What happened here?"

The paramedics held pressure on Tavi's nose and leaned his head back to help staunch the bleeding.

"He was in the park." Grant didn't have to say which park. "He got—"

"Mugged." Tavi's voice sounded thick and nasally.

Connor glanced up from his notepad. "What did the guy look like?"

Tavi's good eye drifted closed. "I don't know."

"You don't know?" Skepticism ripened Connor's words.

Tavi squinted and held Connor's assessing gaze. "I wasn't exactly looking at his face."

"Jesus Christ, kid." Connor stuffed the notepad back into his pocket. "You're gonna get yourself killed one of these days."

"What does it matter?" the kid shot back.

"Hey, tough guy." When Connor had Tavi's attention, he said, "It matters to me. That's why I'm gonna call CPS. I don't want—"

Tavi shoved off the couch—with more strength than Grant thought possible considering Tavi's current condition—knocking the two paramedics on their asses. Grant caught him by the shoulder and gently shoved him back onto the couch.

"Come on, kid," one of the paramedics said as he righted himself. "Let us do our job."

"I'm not going back into the system. You call child protective services, I'm just going to run away again."

Connor's exasperation might have looked comical if the situation weren't so dire. "Look, kid. I can't have these guys treat you and toss you back out on the street. Someone needs to look after you."

"I knew coming here was a mistake. I told you. I can take care of myself."

Connor crossed his arms over his chest. "Yeah. Clearly."

"We'll take him."

Connor turned around and leveled a steady gaze at Sebastian. "You?"

"Grant and I." Sebastian caught Grant's eye. "Right?"

"I—We—" Grant glanced from Sebastian's challenging and hopeful face to Tavi's swollen and dejected one. What the hell was he going to do with a kid? This couldn't end well. He blew out a breath. "Yeah. We'll figure something out."

———

As Grant pulled into his grandmother's driveway, Sebastian knew Grant had many things he wanted to say to him about his spur of the moment, coercive agreement into taking responsibility for Tavi.

A kid Sebastian knew nothing about.

But in that moment, Sebastian had seen the sheer terror on the kid's face when the cop mentioned CPS. Terror that said fending for himself on the streets and risking getting his ass kicked again was preferable to getting dumped into the system. He and Grant would have a conversation about it, he had no doubt, but Grant wasn't the type of guy who would do it in front of the kid.

Tavi roused when the engine cut off. He glanced around the older neighborhood, complete with street lights, sidewalks, and trees bridging the street. "The 'burbs? Fuck, man. Might as well take me out to the back forty and shoot me."

Grant turned in his seat and leveled a glare at Tavi that even had Sebastian sitting up straighter. "You say 'fuck' in front of my grandmother, and I just might."

Tavi grumbled. "Next, you're gonna tell me you know where to bury my body, so no one finds me."

"No, I don't." Grant grinned, then glanced at Sebastian. "But Sebastian does."

Tavi rolled his one good eye. "Are we going in or what?"

Grant popped his door. "Let's go."

Grant's grandmother met them at the door, a floral robe wrapped around her slight body. She had sharp eyes and a ready smile and hugged Sebastian and Tavi as if they were long, lost family.

"Call me Betty," she said to Sebastian as she led them down the hall. "I've set up the guest room."

She turned on the light to a room with just enough square footage for a twin bed and a dresser. She pulled a set of faded pajamas out of the dresser and handed them to Tavi. "These were Grant's when he was about your age. But I suspect they'll fit. The bathroom is at the end of the hall if you want to get cleaned up."

"Thank you," Tavi managed without tossing in an expletive. Sebastian had to give the kid points for trying. "I think I just want to go to bed."

He went to take off his torn shirt, but the movement hurt, and he grunted. Grant's grandmother helped, her eyes drawn to the bruising popping out along Tavi's left side. The kid stiffened as if expecting her to say something about it. Instead, she said, "I like your ink."

Tavi had 'Fear Nothing' tattooed on the inside of his left fore-arm, blocky and bold. Tavi's mouth gaped before he found his words. "It hurt like he—" He glanced at Grant. "Heck. It hurt like heck. And the letters are hard to keep straight when you're doing it on yourself."

"Wait. You did that?" Grant asked.

"Nice, dude." Sebastian held out his fist. Tavi grinned and pounded it.

"I got mine when I suspect I wasn't much older than you are," Grant's grandmother said.

Grant's jaw dropped, and Sebastian held a hand to his mouth, stifling his laugh. She reached for the flap of her robe.

"*Nana—*"

"It's just my side, dear. Don't be such a prude."

Sebastian chuckled, unable to keep it in. Tavi bent, holding a hand over his ribs and traced a finger over the portrait of a young sailor tattooed across her ribs.

"How did I not know this?" Grant finally found his voice.

She didn't bother glancing up. "You never asked, dear."

"That's so amazing and lifelike. Who did it?"

"A guy on Venice Beach back in the day. I..."

Grant touched Sebastian's shoulder, and his grandmother's voice faded into the background. Grant tossed his head toward the door. Sebastian followed him out, leaving Tavi and his grandmother to talk tattoos.

"You look traumatized," Sebastian said as they stepped into the kitchen.

Grant opened cabinet after cabinet. "You have no idea. I mean, more power to her, but I didn't need to see that."

"What are you looking for?"

"Her hooch. She thinks I'm still fifteen and that she has to hide the fact that she likes her bourbon."

"Oh, my God. I think I love that woman. That's not weird, right? I'm sure I could overlook the age difference and, you know, that she's a woman and all."

"Sorry," Grant said. "She only had eyes for my grandfather. He died twenty years ago, and she never dated again, though not for lack of prospects."

Under the sink, behind the dishwasher soap and a box of drain cleaner, Grant found the bottle he'd been searching for. Though half empty, enough remained for a couple long swallows, maybe more.

Grant pointed the bottle at the upper cabinet by the refrigerator. "Glasses are in there."

After picking out two mason jar style glasses, Sebastian followed Grant into the den and collapsed on the opposite end of the couch. Grant poured two fingers for each of them and set the bottle on the coffee table. "TV?"

They needed to figure out what they were going to do with Tavi come morning, but nothing said they had to figure it out in the next five minutes. A little TV and a little booze might be what they needed to take their mind off the sheer shittiness of the night and keep their thoughts from racing.

Sebastian wanted to scoot closer to Grant. Not for sex, but for comfort. A little intimacy would have gone a long way to settle his nerves, but this wasn't the time or the place. "TV sounds good."

5

___

Sometime after they'd nearly emptied the bottle and sometime before the second sitcom ended, Grant's grandmother came into the den. He'd never bothered with the overhead lights, so the glow from the television threw a bluish cast onto her skin.

"I think he's finally down for the night," his grandmother said.

Grant stood and folded her in his arms. "Thanks for taking him in tonight. I'm sorry it was so late."

She patted him on the chest and pulled away. "I'm an old lady. We don't sleep much anyway." She turned her attention to Sebastian. "It was nice meeting you, young man."

Sebastian stood as well, taking her hand in his. "Nice meeting you, too."

"Will you be staying?"

Sebastian stammered and glanced at Grant, looking for direction.

"We're probably going to hang out on the couch. We want to be here in case Tavi has any problems during the night. The paramedics thought everything was superficial, but I don't want to take any chances."

"Suit yourself. There's the bed in your grandfather's old office if you two change your minds."

Even in the shadows, Grant saw Sebastian's eyebrows raise. "We're fine out here." He kissed his grandmother on the cheek and sent her to bed before she could say anything that might out him in front of Sebastian.

Grant had come out to his grandmother when he was fourteen, back before he'd told his father, back before that explosive revelation blew up his and his father's already tenuous relationship.

He'd always been upfront with his grandmother, never expecting his real life and the carefully constructed lie that was his work life to collide.

If Sebastian thought anything about his grandmother's comment, he didn't say. Instead, he settled back onto the couch and took a sip of the bourbon he'd been savoring.

Grant kicked off his shoes and stretched out in the corner of the couch with his feet on the coffee table, his drink in his hand, and let the laugh track of the sitcom and the alcohol do their job. Sometime later, he heard a thump in the hallway and a muffled curse.

Sebastian sat up with a start, and Grant looked over his shoulder to see Tavi wrapped in a comforter, a pillow in one of his hands.

"What are you doing up?" Sebastian asked before Grant had the chance to.

Tavi's hair stood on end as if he'd tossed and turned. "Couldn't sleep."

"Come on," Grant said. "You can lay on the couch with us."

He tapped Sebastian on the thigh and motioned him to scoot closer to give Tavi some room.

After a brief hesitation, Sebastian complied. Tavi tossed his pillow against the opposite arm and reached for Sebastian's bourbon.

Sebastian pulled it away. "Get real, kid."

"I've been drinking for over a year," Tavi grumbled as he eased himself onto the couch.

"Still not giving you any." Sebastian scooted closer to Grant, their hips and thighs touching.

Maybe Grant should have thought the situation through before he'd invited Tavi onto the couch. But Grant was a big boy. He could keep his hands to himself.

Easier said than done.

They all drifted off into fitful sleep. Grant came awake as the newspaper hit his grandmother's front porch with a dull thud. His arm lay across the back of the couch, Sebastian slouched in the crook of his arm with his head on Grant's chest.

Grant's arm ached, but he didn't want to move it. He liked the feel of Sebastian pressed against him a little too much. Closing his eyes, he drifted off to sleep again.

The next time he opened them, Tavi sat in the club chair at the far end of the couch, the comforter around his shoulders, his ratty backpack at his feet, and his tongue sticking out the corner of his mouth as he sketched on a notepad resting on his upturned knees.

Grant glanced down. Sebastian had resettled onto his side, his head in Grant's lap, a slow, steady rhythm to his breathing. He caught Tavi's eye and made a let-me-see-it motion with his hand.

He'd expected Tavi to laugh at him and say, 'no fucking way,' but to his surprise, Tavi shucked the covers. He winced at the quick movement, but caught his breath and eased over to Grant, handing him the sketchpad.

It took Grant a second to focus on the sketch, on the depth of emotion, on the way his and Sebastian's bodies in the drawing had molded together.

Focused on the way Grant wished his life could be but knew it couldn't.

"Wow." The stricture in his throat made his voice squeak, and he had to try twice to clear it. He whispered because he didn't want to wake Sebastian. "You're exceptionally talented."

For the first time since Grant had known him, Tavi's smile landed in his eyes, shining bright with a pure joy that made Grant's eyes sting.

"May I?" he asked, before flipping the page.

Tavi's normal brash exterior turned shy. He shrugged a shoulder and sat on the coffee table, pushing the empty bottle and glasses aside. "Whatevs."

Grant started at the front of the tablet and flipped through the sketchbook. From the first drawing to the last, Tavi's gift shined on every page. He had a natural eye for perspective and for catching the rawness of each moment, from a beggar slumped in the doorway of a boarded-up business, to the hand of a toddler in the protective grasp of its father, to the lazy lull of a dog's tongue as it lay in the grass.

There were much darker images too, ominous clouds and lightning bolts, fierce warriors, and slain dragons.

Speechless, Grant went back to the last page. The page with him and Sebastian and a moment in time where everything seemed right with Grant's crooked world. "Can I have this?"

"Ah... Um..." Tavi stammered as if that had been the last thing he'd expected Grant to say. "I guess?"

"If you don't want me to, it's fine. I just—"

"No. It's all good."

The sound of the paper ripping out of the ringed sketchpad roused Sebastian. He sat up, his hair going every which way, a crease from Grant's jeans scoring his cheek.

"Look at this." Grant handed the drawing to Sebastian.

Sebastian rubbed the heel of his hand into his eye socket, then appeared to force himself to focus. He glanced from the sketch to Tavi and back again before handing it back to Grant.

"Christ. Cat needs to see this."

"Who's Cat?" Tavi asked.

"A makeup artist we know," Sebastian hedged, not telling Tavi they knew her from Black Stallion. "One of the guys she sees," which in Cat's world translated into 'hooked up with,' "is a tattoo artist here in the valley. Not too far from the Center, I think. Maybe she could introduce you two if that's something you'd be interested in."

Tavi tried to act cool and nonchalant, but with that smile, crooked as it was from the swelling on his jaw, it gave him away. "That would be dope."

Because Grant wanted nothing more than to pull Sebastian into his arms and give him a big fat smack on his lips for giving Tavi that kind of validation, he stood and stretched. "Who's hungry?"

"Me," Tavi said.

Sebastian followed them into the kitchen. "As long as you're cooking, count me in."

"You don't cook?" Grant asked as he pulled eggs and bacon from the refrigerator.

"I call out, and I cater. That's my skill set."

Which from the catered events Sebastian had set up at Black Stallion, Grant knew he excelled.

"Need help?" Tavi asked.

"You sit," Grant instructed as he dug into the freezer and set the container of ice on the counter. "And you," he said to Sebastian, "can refill the kid's ice pack."

"I'm fi—"

Grant cut Tavi off before he could finish. "Humor me."

In no time, Grant whipped up breakfast, set some aside for his grandmother, and scooted two plates across the island to where Tavi sat icing his face, and Sebastian scrolled through emails on his phone. Grant stood across the kitchen island from them as they all dug in.

Tavi's eyes went to the refrigerator, where Grant had tacked up the sketch with a magnet of his grandmother's that said, 'I may be old, but I got to see all the cool bands.'

Tavi made a motion between Grant and Sebastian. "How long have you two been a thing?"

Sebastian choked. Grant stilled, catching Tavi's eye. "We're not."

Tavi laughed. "I get it. Just fuck buddies, then?"

"I told you to watch your mouth." Not so much because he feared his grandmother would overhear, but because he wanted that and much more from Sebastian than he was willing to admit.

"Nana B is still asleep, she—"

"Nana B?" As far as Grant knew, he'd been the only one who'd called her that. Since when was some street kid calling his grandmother Nana?

One of Tavi's shoulders hitched up and down in that careless way he had about him. "She told me to call her that. That a problem? I know she's not my grandmother but—"

"No, it's fine. I was just surprised is all."

After they finished eating, Sebastian stacked the dirty plates and took them to the sink, refusing to make eye contact with anyone since Tavi's 'fuck buddy' comment. "You about ready? I need you to take me back to my car. I'm due across the valley soon, and I don't need to give Niko another reason to be pissed at me."

"Yeah, sure," Grant said and then turned to Tavi. "Pack up your stuff. I've got some work you can do for me."

"So, that's it?" Tavi stood and pushed in the bar stool. "You put me up for a couple of nights, and now I'm slave labor? Aren't there laws against that?"

Grant bobbed his chin toward the guest room. "Yeah, yeah. Go get dressed."

Tavi stopped on the way down the hall. "What about tonight?"

"What about it?"

"Are you bringing me back here?"

"I thought the 'burbs were social Siberia to a street kid like you."

Again, that shrug, like it didn't matter.

But it did.

Too bad Grant would have to disappoint him.

Grant blew out a breath and rested his hands on his hips. He couldn't impose on his grandmother like that. It wouldn't be fair to her. "Look, Tavi—"

"Of course you are, dear." His grandmother patted Tavi on the shoulder as she came into the kitchen.

Grant had to talk some sense into her. Tavi wasn't her problem. "Nana—"

"Hush, now." She patted Grant on the cheek, her arthritic fingers warm against his skin.

Grant grumbled but gave her a peck on the cheek. She had no idea what she'd signed up for. "We'll see you tonight."

———

It was Friday night and Sebastian felt as if he was drowning without a hot, ripped lifeguard to swim to the rescue.

At least that was how the past couple of days of work had felt. Besides getting everything ready for Black Stallion's pool party that night, he'd also been working his way down list after list, making sure he had everything set to go off without a hitch for the shoot between Grant and Kattan the next morning.

He didn't even want to think about the week-long shoot in the Bahamas coming up later that summer. Everything seemed to be going wrong, and while he might have managed to not get canned after the Jacoby Winters debacle, he may not fare so well with the Bahama shoot.

He didn't know what he'd done to deserve it, but karma was kicking his ass.

By the time Sebastian left his office, walked through the side yard, and stepped onto the pool deck, midnight had come and gone, as well as all the guests.

He'd been looking forward to seeing Grant again, but it looked like he'd arrived too late. The outside lights had already been shut off, and glancing through the sliding glass door into the living quarters beyond, it looked like Grant and Kattan had gone to bed as well.

Probably for the best.

The more Sebastian kept his work and personal life caged and locked in separate corners where Grant was concerned, the better.

In the glow of the underwater pool lights, Sebastian started stacking the discarded cups and plates and carrying them over to the overflowing trash cans. A cool breeze kept the California heat at bay, and the stars popped out, as much as they ever did in that part of the light-polluted world.

"There you are," Grant said from somewhere behind him.

Sebastian startled and almost dropped everything. He steadied the stack and turned. "You scared the crap out of me. What are you doing there? I thought everyone had gone to bed."

In the shadows, Grant brushed water out of his face and folded his arms over the lip of the hot tub. "Too keyed up to sleep, so I came back out. Where were you?"

"Working."

And yeah, he probably could have spared a few minutes, or even an hour or two, to go to the party, but on some level, he'd wanted to avoid the situation he currently found himself in.

Alone. With Grant.

"You gotta take a break sometime."

Sebastian blew out a weary breath. "There's no time."

"Take it now." The way Grant insisted, it came out more as a dare.

All day long, Sebastian had been on his feet fighting figurative fires. His soles ached as he walked around the pool deck. Kicking off his flip-flops, he plopped down at the edge of the hot tub and eased his legs into the hot water, not even caring that a puddle soaked through his shorts.

He sighed, the exhaustion creeping in and weighing him down. "Do you have any idea how hard it is being the family fuckup?"

"Everyone makes mistakes."

Grant eased to the far side of the hot tub and spread his arms out wide on the pool deck. Sebastian tried not to stare at the expanse of muscular chest and the smattering of hair he wanted to run his tongue through.

Sebastian chuckled. It came out dry and devoid of all humor. "My father warned Niko not to hire me. That's how bad it is. Who does that to their own kid?"

Grant treaded water across the middle of the hot tub and edged into Sebastian's personal space. "You want my opinion?"

Almost afraid to hear it, Sebastian braced for the verbal blow when he said, "What is it?"

"Black Stallion couldn't run without you, and Niko knows it. You work your ever-loving ass off every day. You made an honest mistake, and you fixed it as best you could. Any company would be lucky to have you on their team. If the Center had a guy like you working behind the scenes, we'd be able to do so much more for the kids."

"Is that a job offer?"

"I wish. I wish we could afford to pay someone with your kind of talent."

Sebastian didn't quite know what to say to that. For the most part, Niko treated him well, more like an associate, and less like the screw up he'd been in his late teens and early twenties. It had only been recently that Niko had been more volatile, and his mood swings more... *swingy.*

Ever since Niko had broken up with Peter.

That gold-digging, entitled, little shit of a boy toy.

Sebastian had wanted to dance a jig when the relationship dissolved, but Niko had been a bear.

Sebastian swirled his legs around in the water, the heat easing the soreness in his calves and the arches of his feet. He lay back with a groan, the no-slip surface rough against his back even through his shirt. "That water feels so good."

The surge of water came seconds before Grant's hands took hold of Sebastian's right foot, his thumbs working the ache in Sebastian's arch.

"Oh, sweet mother of baby Jesus, that's divine."

A low laugh rumbled through Grant as he put all those glorious muscles to work, easing Sebastian's pain. "Divine? I thought you were agnostic."

"Pretty sure I was just born again. There were lights. Angels sang."

Grant dropped Sebastian's right foot and started in on his left. Sebastian rose onto his elbows and, in the shadows, watched the play of Grant's muscles and tendons as he massaged the strain of the week away. "You could make good money doing that."

"More than porn?" Grant asked, his grin too delicious for

Sebastian not to want to take advantage of.

Sebastian sat up. Grant was much closer than he'd anticipated. "I'd pay."

Grant dropped Sebastian's foot and caged him in, his hands on the pool deck on either side of Sebastian's legs, his voice low when he said, "How would you pay?"

All the blood must have run south because Sebastian got hard, and all rational thought left his head. At least that's how Sebastian justified leaning down, taking Grant's face in his hands and covering that fuck-me mouth with his.

Grant grunted in surprise but didn't pull back. Instead, he leaned into the kiss, taking it deeper as Sebastian's heels locked behind Grant's thighs.

The word 'timid' wasn't in Grant's vocabulary. Sebastian knew that from watching all the scenes Grant had shot for Black Stallion—over and over again. Grant had taken charge in those scenes the same way he took charge now. Aggressive, possessive.

But all in a way that made Sebastian's breath hitch and his dick heavy.

All too soon, Grant broke the kiss, his arms shaking from the strain of supporting his body on the edge of the hot tub. He sunk into the water, his expression so damn enigmatic Sebastian had no fucking idea what thoughts rattled around inside Grant's head.

"You sure you're not gay?" Sebastian laid it out there, more of a statement than a question.

Grant's eyes flicked up to his and held steady as he shoved off the wall and drifted to the other side. "I can't be."

'Can't' and 'aren't.' Two *very* different things.

Sebastian cocked his head, trying to understand. Grant fidgeted under the scrutiny. Before Grant bolted—and by the cagey way Grant glanced around, he was searching for the escape hatch—Sebastian changed the subject. "How's Tavi?"

6

———

THE LAST THING GRANT WANTED TO TALK ABOUT RIGHT AFTER having his tongue down Sebastian's throat was Tavi, but it gave him something else to say instead of admitting the truth to Sebastian—that he was most assuredly gay, and wanted nothing more than to drag Sebastian back into his assigned room just beyond the sliding doors and show him exactly *how* gay.

One of these days.

But today wasn't that day.

"Tavi is good," Grant allowed. "The swelling is going down, and he's not so sore anymore."

"He still staying with your grandmother?"

"For now." Grant laughed. "Those two are thick as thieves already. I'm not sure who the bad influence is, but I went over to pick him up this morning to bring him to the Center, and they were both at the table having ice cream sundaes for breakfast."

"Sounds like Tavi is in a good spot. You're really making a difference in his life."

"I don't know." Grant eased closer again, not liking the distance between them even though he'd been the one to put it there. "So much is up in the air right now. He needs a guardian and someone to take him in. But he's resistant, and with the group home out of the question, that leaves the system. I think it's too soon to bring that up again. I believed him when he said he'd scram if he were forced back into foster care. And then where would he be?"

"Couldn't you be his guardian?"

Grant barked out a laugh. A laugh that would have woken all the talent and the neighbors if the house wasn't soundproofed and the nearest neighbor wasn't so far away. "I wouldn't pass the scrutiny of that kind of background check."

"You bury dead bodies under your grandmother's porch or something? Stuffed your freezer full of human livers?"

"You found my secret," Grant deadpanned. "But really, who's going to give a single guy who makes his money doing gay porn, an at-risk kid?"

"You're not doing anything illegal."

"No. But the optics aren't good. And I can't jeopardize the Center for one kid."

Sebastian shrugged. "I think that kid is worth the risk."

Fuck. The worst thing about what Sebastian said was that a not-so-small part of Grant agreed with him.

"You're a good man, Grant Hardy. Think about what I said."

All the thinking Grant had been doing recently made his brain hurt. Thinking about his grandmother, Sebastian, the fucking stifling closet, the kid.

"I don't need a kid. I don't want a kid." If he said it often enough, it might sink in and stick.

"I get it. I know what the Center means to you, but what if the Center isn't what was meant to come from Cory's legacy? What if you weren't supposed to save *all* the kids. Maybe you were supposed to save *this* kid."

Grant sank to the bottom of the hot tub, watching the bubbles rise and the ripples roll, as the quiet enveloped him. In truth, he questioned if he was doing right by any of the kids. He stayed beneath the water until his lungs burned and Sebastian reached a hand down for him to take.

He locked onto Sebastian's wrist and broke the surface. "Did that help?" Sebastian asked.

Grant blew out a long breath. "Not really."

The only thing that became clear to Grant at that moment was his need for the man in front of him. He grabbed Sebastian by the ankles and tugged. Sebastian squeaked, loud and high pitched and fucking adorable.

"What are you doing?" The mock fear turned Sebastian's grin lopsided.

"What I should have done the moment you sat down."

With one more yank, Sebastian splashed into the hot tub and came up spitting and sputtering. "You're going down."

Grant leapt back, out of Sebastian's reach. Scrambling out of the hot tub, he ran toward the pool and dove into the deep end, the pressure wave of Sebastian diving in after him hitting him from behind.

Grant surfaced with a laugh and swam for the far end, the rush of cool water on his over-heated body made goosebumps erupt all over his skin. Grant's lead was short-lived. Who'd have thought Sebastian would be a badass in the pool?

Sebastian caught Grant's ankle and dragged him under before letting Grant surface. Grant laughed and splashed a wave of water over Sebastian's head with a pool noodle.

"Okay, okay." Sebastian threw up his hands in surrender. "You win."

"I like the sound of that." Grant backed Sebastian against the side of the pool. Everything in Grant's brain told him to get the fuck out of the pool before he did something he couldn't take back, but for the life of him, his body couldn't give two shits.

A part of him felt like he was slamming his hand down on

the self-destruct button, while another part of him—the stupid, testosterone-soaked part—wondered if maybe his carefully constructed life needed exploding.

His body bumped against Sebastian's in all the best places. Then Sebastian reversed their positions, grinding up against him. The rounded edge of the pool rubbed the skin on his back, but the mild discomfort was worth the acute pleasure.

"I'm going to kiss you," Sebastian whispered, though no one was around to hear. "You need to stop me if that's not what you want."

The metaphorical bomb tick, tick, ticked—a deafening, resonating sound in Grant's head that nearly obliterated all thought, which in this case, was probably for the best. He didn't want to think.

He wanted to *feel*.

"I'm not stopping you." Grant leaned in, the chlorine scent clinging to Sebastian's skin.

"I thought you weren't gay."

"I'm not." The denial tasted like bitter ash on Grant's tongue. "But I'm kind of into you."

Shut up. Shut up. Shut up.

What the fuck was he saying? If he and Sebastian got caught, no way in hell could he stop the foreclosure.

"Look, Bass—"

Sebastian's mouth closed over Grant's exposed nipple, and whatever he had been about to say next tumbled from his brain. "Fuck, that feels good."

———

GRANT WAS MANY THINGS, MANY AMAZING THINGS...

Straight wasn't one of them.

No straight man moaned like that when another man's

tongue traced around his nipple. Or pulled him in tighter and held him in place instead of pushing him away.

Sebastian teased Grant with the tip of his tongue, the flat nipple peaking before he left the flat slab of pectoral muscle and sucked on the pulse point at the base of Grant's neck.

Sebastian's heart kicked up, matching Grant's rapid pulse. Yeah, Grant wasn't straight, which might explain why he'd always been *up* for his scenes with Black Stallion.

But right now, at this moment, the only thing that mattered was that Grant was *up* for *him*.

He kissed his way up Grant's neck and across Grant's jaw until he found those lips and dove in. Grant grabbed the hem of Sebastian's shirt and pulled and tugged and struggled with the clingy cotton until it came free and landed with a wet *splat* on the pool deck.

Then Grant's hands were on him, tracing the exposed ridges of his ribs and the long line of his spine as their tongues tempted and tasted and tormented each other.

Sebastian's lungs screamed. Coming up for air, he broke the kiss, his chest billowing and fighting for each breath.

"Christ, what are you doing to me?" A question? It sounded more like an epitaph. Grant's eyes drifted closed as his arms held on tight.

Flexing his hips again, Sebastian reveled in the way Grant's cock rubbed against his. All they needed to do was get rid of a couple of layers of fabric, and then Sebastian would be in heaven.

The fun, sexy version. Not the pearly gates, old men in robes version.

"What I'm doing to you is called frottage," Sebastian said as he reached for the waistband of Grant's swimsuit. "It's—"

Grant chuckled. "I know what the fuck frottage is. I meant—"

Sebastian nipped at Grant's bottom lip. "I know what you meant. And whatever the hell you think I'm doing to you, you're doing right back to me. He ground against Grant again, sucking in his breath and dropping his head on Grant's shoulder.

A week ago, if anyone had the audacity to tell Sebastian he'd be in a pool with his 'straight' man-crush, their bodies and their cocks aligned… he would have called bullshit. Not gonna happen. Too many planets and stars and comets would have had to align in perfect order.

He glanced at the sky, at the stars remaining wildly scattered above. So… not a cosmic intervention.

But Sebastian didn't have time to contemplate the cosmos. He needed in Grant's pants. He wanted to please Grant, and more than anything, he wanted Grant to want more. Pulling the tie on Grant's swimsuit, Sebastian slipped his hand down Grant's trunks and took that hard cock into his hand.

Grant's breath hissed in Sebastian's ear. "Fuck," Grant muttered at the same time his hand clamped down on Sebastian's wrist. "We can't do this. As much as I want you to jack me, you know Niko's rules the night before a shoot."

"No 'shooting.' Yeah, I know." Sebastian kissed his way up Grant's neck as his hand stroked Grant's cock. In Grant's ear, he whispered, "You don't have to come. I can take you to the edge. Again. And again. And again."

Grant's head fell back as he pulled Sebastian in tighter. "Fuck, that sounds amazing."

"Yeah?"

Grant grinned. "Oh, yeah."

"I could use my hands, or my mouth, or—"

The outside lights kicked on. One second Sebastian had Grant's dick in his hand, the next, his fingers closed around water.

Before Niko could open the sliding glass door, Grant had

swum to the far side of the pool and climbed out, wrapping a towel around his waist to hide his hard-on.

Niko stilled when he saw Sebastian in the pool. Then his gaze landed on Grant as he walked around the deck acting as if Sebastian hadn't almost given him a handy in the pool.

"Shouldn't you two be in bed?" Niko asked.

From the time Sebastian was a boy, Niko had always been an imposing man. That hadn't changed much since getting to know him as an adult. For a guy in his forties, he kept himself in shape and could have passed for ten years younger if he bothered to color over the gray creeping in at his temples and the scruff of a beard.

But that's how the boy-toys liked Niko, and he naturally played into that.

"We were just... *finishing*," Sebastian said. Grant cut him a what-the-fuck look, and Sebastian had to sink beneath the surface to hide his grin.

When he resurfaced, he found Niko digging through the smattering of forgotten items from the guests that someone had piled onto one of the patio tables. He reached under a towel and found his tablet. He tucked it under his arm and turned to both of them. "See you boys tomorrow."

"Night," Grant said.

"See ya."

Sebastian climbed out of the pool, water dripping at his feet, and borrowed a damp towel from the table from whoever had left it.

"*Finishing*," Grant practically growled. "Are you *fucking* kidding me?"

Sebastian grinned, then the smile slipped from his face. Grant wasn't kidding. He. Was. *Pissed*. "I—"

Grant leaned in, cutting off Sebastian's lame protest. For a moment, in the pool, Sebastian thought the two of them were getting somewhere. And he wasn't just talking about the sex. At one point, he'd felt Grant, not give *up*, but give *in* to Sebastian and the ecstasy.

"You don't know what you're playing with here. Is this all a big joke to you?"

Sebastian met Grant's steely gaze with a cutting one of his own. "No. I've never been more serious about something in my life."

Sebastian didn't back down or look away. He wanted Grant to see the truth of his words in his eyes and his soul. And yeah, maybe that was some stupid, high-school-level shit he pulled with the double entendre, he could admit that, but that didn't invalidate the feelings he had for Grant.

Even though Grant refused to admit he was gay, he'd freely admitted his interest in Sebastian. But now?

Grant gestured between the two of them. "This never happened."

Sebastian stepped back and made room for Grant to pass. "Yeah, sure." He waited until Grant had made it to the sliding glass door before adding, "Just like that kiss the other night never happened."

GRANT WOULD UNDERSTAND IF SABASTIAN NEVER SPOKE TO HIM again. After his shower—that had done nothing to ease his hard-on ever since he'd crawled out of the pool—Grant flopped onto his bed in his assigned room and pulled up Sebastian's name on his phone's messaging app.

I'm an asshole, he typed out. True, but it didn't change what he'd said. He hit backspace until it disappeared.

I didn't mean... to be a shit? He hit backspace again.

I'm sorry... also true, in so many ways.

He didn't hit backspace. He also didn't hit send.

Through the open blinds, he watched the shadows of the trees as they swayed in the breeze and realized for the first time since he'd come to Black Stallion that he dreaded the upcoming shoot.

It had nothing to do with not knowing Kattan beyond that night's meet and greet. He'd seen photos of the athletic, stacked Saudi, and of course, seen some of his work. At one point in his life, he'd have been eager to shoot that scene and bury himself balls deep.

Not anymore.

Kattan wasn't who he wanted.

Sebastian was.

He thought back to the pool, when Sebastian had Grant's cock in his grip, jacking him with long, slow, delicious strokes, and he'd been seconds away from saying 'fuck it all.'

Then Niko had turend on the lights, spotlighting Grant's utter stupidity. It horrified him that he'd almost thrown it all away—his chance to help his grandmother, the woman who'd taken him in and loved him when his father wouldn't—for what? A handjob?

For Sebastian.

For living your life with some personal integrity instead of hiding out in the dank, dark, closet and jumping at everything that goes bump in the night.

Reaching his hands down the front of his briefs, he took hold of himself, imagining the hand that gripped him wasn't his own, but Sebastian's.

He stroked himself to the brink until his balls drew up, precum slicked his hands, and the base of his spine tingled.

For the first time, he planned on breaking the Golden Rule.

Not *the* Golden Rule. The 'do unto others' bit.

Because he'd certainly love to *do unto* Sebastian what he currently was doing to himself.

No, he was about to break Niko's Golden Rule—no busting a nut the night before a shoot—because, by God, he was coming.

———

THE NEXT MORNING, GRANT'S ALARM WENT OFF WAY TOO EARLY. Despite blowing a load, not once, but twice, Grant barely slept.

He dragged himself out of bed and poured himself into the showers at the end of the hall, prepping for the shoot, but even that didn't help wake him. He rolled into the kitchen area and found Kattan sitting at the counter with a cup of coffee in one hand and a folded newspaper in the other.

"The world still spinning?" Grant asked as he filled a mug with coffee.

Kattan set the paper aside, a sardonic tilt to his lips. "For now."

Grant leaned against the counter across from his scene mate, afraid if he sat down, even on an uncomfortable barstool, that he might fall back asleep.

"Is it always this quiet here?" Kattan asked.

"Hah. No."

The residence area of Black Stallion had a chef's kitchen and a long dining table to accommodate all the talent at one time.

Down the hall were the dorm-style rooms that the guys usually shared two per room, but Niko had wanted to focus on him and Kattan. More men were expected, but they weren't due until later that night.

Hopefully by then, Grant would be long gone and would have rescued his grandmother from Tavi. Or Tavi from his grandmother. He wasn't quite sure who would need rescuing most.

"You lucked out," Grant said. "Usually, it's like a frat party in here, only wilder, and with more naked bodies."

"I'd heard Black Stallion was different."

"In a good way. All these guys are like brothers now. And there are times when Rose is more of a mother to them than their own."

Grant stared across the counter, at all the sexy brown skin and all the long, lean muscles of one of gay porn's top stars, and waited for that attraction, that zing, to hit his gut and for his dick to wake up, but... nothing. *Shit.*

He slugged back the rest of his coffee, almost burning his tongue. "I guess I'll see you down there."

Kattan picked up his newspaper. "Sure, man."

Grant poured himself more coffee before he headed to the studio downstairs. Cat would be waiting to give him his clothes for the scene as well as prep him for the cameras.

He met her with a hug in the doorway of the makeup room and slumped into her chair. She pumped the chair up higher and met his gaze in the mirror. "Fucking hell. You're gonna make me work today, aren't you?"

"I don't look that bad."

"Keep telling yourself that, pretty boy." She put away the concealer she normally used sparingly and brought out her 'big guns'—the concealer she only used when Niko shot the daddy porn, and all the over-fifty guys lined up down the hall.

Cat sighed and went to work. By the time she'd finished, she'd trimmed his stubble down to an acceptable five o'clock shadow instead of the three-day-drinking-binge-vibe he'd been rocking.

Magically, the bags and dark circles under his eyes had disappeared, and his cheeks no longer looked hollow or his skin tone sallow.

He almost looked like himself again.

"Smile, Hardy." Cat lowered his chair and unsnapped the drape from around his neck. "You get to fuck Matek Kattan today. If that were me going out there in thirty minutes, my grin would wrap all the way around my face."

"He's straight." Grant glanced at Cat's curves, the long dark hair, and the dragon tattoos that normally left all the guys who sat in her chair drooling and begging for her number. "I'm sure you could have him any time you wanted."

"Yeah, but it would be so much more fun in front of the cameras with everyone watching."

Grant barked out a laugh and brought her in for a hug. "Thanks. I needed that."

She tilted her head and looked at him again. "Everything okay?"

He hesitated only a fraction before forcing a smile and lying to her face. "Sure, why wouldn't it be?"

7

———

SO FAR, THE ONLY THING GOING RIGHT WITH THE SHOOT WAS THAT the set Sebastian had designed and had built, totally rocked.

Niko had Grant and Kattan doing a camping scene. Complete with a tent, a realistic campfire, a hammock that would be used as a sex swing, and trees so real Sebastian had considered adding a bottle of bear spray, just in case.

That's where the good parts ended.

Over an hour into filming, if they had more than a few minutes of usable footage, he'd count that as lucky.

Grant's natural on-camera chemistry he usually had with all his co-stars, came off as lackluster. His usual charisma and way he played up to the camera came across as anemic. From watching the scene, you wouldn't know that Grant had been the top stud of Black Stallion's impressive stable.

Sebastian stepped back into the shadows, well behind Niko and the set where Grant and Kattan kissed and groped, but instead of their scene being hot, it looked sophomoric and... well... *blah.*

Vin, Niko's right-hand cameraman, looked away from his viewfinder long enough to catch Niko's eye and shake his head.

Sebastian had hoped the scene read better through the camera and that it was only his imagination that things were off.

"Cut!" Niko called out.

Vin lowered the camera and stepped away from the set. Niko stood, hands plastered on his hips, his words halting and catching. "That... That was..."

"Crap," Grant said. "Yeah, I know. I'm trying. I don't know what's up today."

Vin backed up next to Sebastian and whispered, "I know what's *not* up today."

Sebastian rapped him on the bicep with the back of his hand, trying not to smile. "Stop."

"Sorry." Though Vin didn't look the least bit contrite.

"You're enjoying this."

Through the grin Vin tried to hide, he said, "I'm not. It's just nice to know that Hardy is human like the rest of us."

"He's never claimed he's perfect."

"I know. That's why everyone loves the guy."

Rose handed Kattan and Grant their robes, and Niko turned, dismissing the two men. "Fifteen minutes, everyone."

Grant disappeared off set while Kattan settled into one of the camping chairs, striking up a conversation with Rose, the robe carelessly lumped in the middle of his lap, hiding his junk, but little else. If a modesty gene were such a thing, Kattan was missing his.

But Sebastian noted it wasn't Kattan's thick thighs, his bulging biceps, or the wide expanse of his muscular chest that Vin couldn't keep his eyes off of, it was Niko. Vin watched Niko as he, too, stalked away and disappeared around the corner.

"You know," Sebastian said, "if you would just suck Niko off and put a smile on that man's face, the rest of us would totally appreciate it."

The laugh and the shove that Sebastian expected never came.

Vin's gaze held Sebastian's with a frank openness he'd never witnessed from the cameraman before. "It's not me that Niko wants. He's made that perfectly clear."

Wait. What? "You're into Niko?"

"Forget I said anything."

"You ever told Niko you're interested?"

"Not in so many words, but..."

Vin let the sentence drop. When he started to walk off, Sebastian caught his arm. "Spill."

"This isn't high school."

Sebastian raised a brow at him, keeping his hand on Vin's arm to keep him from escaping. "You mean a lot to Niko. You're like the son he never—"

Vin's expression went flat, and he pulled his arm free. "Not helping." Then the tips of his lips curved up—a forced, stiff plastic smile that didn't come close to real. "Besides, he's already seeing someone. Everyone knows that."

"Since when?"

Vin shrugged. The motion said that he didn't know, didn't care, but the expression on Vin's face said that he knew *exactly* when. Probably down to the hour, minute, second. Vin had it bad for Niko. How had Sebastian not seen it before?

"I don't know. Niko's been seeing the guy a couple of weeks now, maybe."

"Who?"

"Rick Holland."

A laugh bubbled up, and Sebastian didn't even try to hold it back. Rose and Kattan stopped talking long enough to glance their way. "No way. He's older than Niko. That's not Niko's type."

"And what's Niko's type?"

"The young, fit, brooding artistic type. You know. *Like you*."

"Still not helping." Vin crossed his arms over his chest. "Anyway, I think Peter cured him of his infatuation, fascination, obsession, or whatever the hell it was, with younger men. He's sworn off them."

When Vin started to leave, Sebastian said, "Where are you going?"

Vin inclined his head toward the stage. "To go talk with Kattan. This conversation isn't going anywhere."

Niko returned in time to see Kattan's eyes light when Vin walked on set. Niko grumbled out, "Don't you have camera shit you should be doing?"

Vin spared Niko a glance. "Not without Grant, I don't."

For the first time, Niko looked around. "He's not back yet?"

Rose put down her clipboard. "Want me to get him?"

"I'll get him," Sebastian said. If he'd sounded too eager to run into the Ready room and maybe catch Grant fluffing himself, no one seemed to notice.

He checked his watch on the way to get Grant. Twenty minutes had already passed since Niko had called for a break. Despite wanting nothing more than to see Grant's cock in his hand, Sebastian rapped his knuckles on the door of the Ready room before opening it.

With one hand gripping the jamb, he leaned into the room. Grant was sitting on the couch, the sash of his robe tight around his waist, his elbows on his knees and his head in his hands.

"You don't look ready to go back out there. You okay?"

Grant leaned back. "Sure. I'm..." he motioned toward his lap, "... all up in my head. I just need a few more minutes. Tell Niko—"

"Forget Niko. I'll handle him." Trying to take the focus off Grant and his underperforming dick, he said, "Speaking of Niko, did you know Vin is into him?"

Cat brushed past Sebastian into the Ready room. "Vin's into Niko?"

"Shh..." Sebastian glanced down the hall, but they were alone. "It's a secret."

"If it's a secret," Grant said, "why the hell would Vin tell you?"

"What do you mean?"

"Dude, you're so adorable when you're clueless," Cat said.

Sebastian turned his attention to Grant. "What is she talking about?"

"Everyone knows not to tell you anything unless they want the world to know. A word of advice: If you're contemplating new career choices, don't send the CIA your resume."

"I didn't mean—"

Cat stood on her toes and kissed his cheek on her way out the door. "It's okay. We won't tell anyone."

Sebastian plopped on the armrest of the couch. "Fuck. I was only trying to distract you from your dick."

"It's all good. Just give me a minute." Grant unlocked his phone, the straight porn he'd been watching started playing on mute.

Standing to leave, Sebastian said, "No one knows what erotic script you've got rolling through your head. You can think about whatever you have to think about to crank yourself up." Then he leaned in and whispered, "Even if that's me."

———

FUCK IF SEBASTIAN WASN'T RIGHT.

Normally when Grant did a scene, he was all in the moment. He enjoyed a wide variety of men and their bodies. He didn't think he had a type, and while he still found other men attractive, Kattan included, the junk wanted what the junk wanted and what *his* junk wanted was Sebastian.

Closing the door, Grant shut down the porn site on his phone and clicked over to what he knew would get him hard.

Sebastian's private social media account.

He scrolled through his favorite photos. A video icon showed up that he hadn't noticed before. He clicked on the video and waited for it to load.

In the video, Sebastian was lying naked on his bed, his fist wrapped around that glorious dick. Seriously, why wasn't *Sebastian* doing porn?

It didn't take more than a few seconds of imagining that it was his hand on Sebastian's cock for Grant to pop wood.

He couldn't even thank the Viagra he'd taken when he'd come back to the Ready room because there hadn't been enough time for the medication to be effective.

Reaching a hand beneath his robe, he stroked himself, Sebastian's words from the night before, rattling around in his head.

I can just take you to the edge. Again. And again. And again.

Fuck.

Grant jacked himself at the same pace that Sebastian stroked himself in the video, almost coming when Sebastian squirted a load on his abdomen and chest.

He tossed his phone into a locker and headed for the set.

They got right to filming, taking full advantage of his erection while they had the chance. Physically, Kattan was larger and more muscled than Sebastian, but as Grant bent Kattan over the hood of the Jeep they had on set, he imagined it was Sebastian's fine ass beneath his grip, not Kattan's.

Later, after several changes of position, Kattan laid crossways in the hammock, their bodies slick with sweat, and Grant's condom-sheathed cock lubed and ready to go.

Kattan was relaxed and ready for him as he placed his cock at Kattan's entrance and pushed inside. Even though he'd already fucked him several different ways, his gaze locked on Kattan's, checking in and making sure everything was okay.

He liked Kattan. He seemed like a good man. A couple of months ago, Grant would have loved every second of his time in front of the camera with Kattan, instead of hoping like hell he could keep his erection long enough to finish the job.

As soon as Kattan came, Grant could come as well, and the longest shoot of his life would be over.

Kattan groaned for the cameras as Grant sunk balls deep and lifted Kattan's legs over his shoulders. Vin moved in close with the camera, but Grant ignored him.

Closing his eyes, Grant skimmed back through the video files in his memory banks, hitting Play on Sebastian's jack-off video that he'd had on repeat in his head since they'd restarted filming. You'd think he'd grow tired of it, but no.

All it made him want to do was get Sebastian in his hands and satisfy him.

"Jack yourself off," Niko instructed Kattan as Grant fucked him harder and harder.

Precum dribbled from the tip of Kattan's dick in a steady stream, his balls drawn up tight. He writhed beneath Grant, his breath coming short and fast, as Grant also fought for air.

Grant felt the first shudder of Kattan's release, and he imagined that was Sebastian's tight ass clamping down around him. When he opened his eyes and stared into Kattan's, his mind overlaid Kattan's dark brown eyes with Sebastian's lighter ones.

After Kattan came, he pulled Grant in close, bringing him in for what should look like a passionate, heated kiss. Then Kattan broke the kiss and whispered in Grant's ear. "Hurry up. My ass is on fire."

Grant hid his chuckle beneath another kiss, giving himself

up to the moment and for once, allowing himself just to feel. He straightened again, plowing himself into Kattan, reaching for his elusive release.

Then a soft scuff of shoes on concrete and a groan caught his attention. Off set, through the branches of the fake trees, he caught sight of Sebastian. He couldn't see Sebastian's hands, but from the exquisite torture on his face, Grant knew exactly where they were.

The thought of Sebastian jacking himself while Grant pounded into Kattan made Grant's stomach tight, and his nerves zing.

Sebastian's eyes fluttered open and locked on Grant's as the first pulse of Grant's impending climax hit. He pulled out of Kattan, slipped off the condom, and stroked himself for the camera, vaguely aware as Vin and his camera closed in.

Grant shifted his full focus to Sebastian and what he wanted to do to him. Everyone else in the studio ceased to exist as Grant's climax ripped through his body, as his cum mixed with Kattan's on his scene mate's abdomen.

Kattan pulled him down for a final camera kiss. "That was fucking hot as hell."

"Yeah," Grant agreed as his lungs billowed. "It was." Though he had a feeling he and Kattan weren't talking about the same thing.

"Cut!"

Rose appeared on set and handed them their robes and a couple of cum rags to clean up. They wiped themselves down, and Grant held out his hand to help Kattan up.

"Thanks, man. Catch me after a shower, and I'll buy you a beer."

"Sounds good."

Kattan walked away while Grant slipped on his robe, his eyes darting back to the spot between the branches where he'd last seen Sebastian, but he'd vanished.

———

On the backside of the set, Sebastian stared at his cum covered dick in his hand and rolled his eyes at himself. He just fucking jerked off at work. What the—

"Oh, sorry," Cat said as she walked down the alley behind the sets and bumped into him.

"What are you doing here?" Sebastian fumbled with his still-hard dick, trying to stuff it back into his pants.

Cat laughed, that low, throaty laugh that always got the straight boys all hot and bothered. Her eyes went to his crotch and back up again, a light in her eyes and a grin on her face. "I'd ask you the same, but I'm pretty sure I know."

She pulled a small rag out of the apron she wore and handed it to him.

"Sorry," he said as he cleaned himself up.

"Don't apologize. One of the perks of the job, right?"

"Yeah, but—"

She leaned in close as he finished tucking himself away and zipped up his pants, her voice low and conspiratorial when she said, "Who were you jacking off to?"

The heat crept up the back of his neck. Being caught with his dick in his hand didn't make him as uncomfortable as the question did.

"Come on." Cat nudged him with her shoulder. "You can tell me. Unlike you, I can keep a secret."

When he went to step around her, she put her hand in the middle of his chest and pushed him against the back wall. He wasn't leaving without telling her unless he went through her. And while she wasn't a big woman, she was scrappy as hell. He wouldn't win, so he might as well tell her and save himself the embarrassment of her kicking his ass.

"Grant."

"Wow."

Wow? "What?"

"I had no idea. This day is just full of surprises. First Vin, now you and Grant."

"There's no *me and Grant*." As much as he wished it were true, it didn't make it so. "Nothing but an unreciprocated man-crush. No big deal."

"Right," Cat said as if she had hip waders on and could slog through all his bullshit. "It doesn't make you jealous?"

"What?"

"Watching the man you have the hots for plow some other dude?"

"No. It's fucking hot. Besides, as I said, Grant's not mine. And even if he were, I wouldn't want to stop them. I'd want to join them."

"You want my advice?"

There was no correct answer to that question because the determined look on Cat's face said she planned on telling him either way. "You need to stop jonesing for the straight dudes. Knock it off, get your gay on, and go get laid. What has it been, two years?"

"Hardly." But long enough.

8

———

It was after ten that night at the Center when Grant's cell phone rang, and he glanced at the screen. *Sebastian*. Grant had expected a call from him at some point, though he hadn't yet decided if he would answer.

He couldn't quite wrap his head around what had happened back at the studio. He'd never had to take Viagra before, unlike some of the other guys. And he'd never needed to look at one man to get off while he fucked another.

What the hell was wrong with him?

The phone stopped ringing, and before he could decide if he would call Sebastian back, it rang in his hand again.

Grant hit the green button and put the phone to his ear. "Hardy."

"Seriously? You're going to answer the phone like you have no fucking idea who's on the other end?"

The headache Grant had been fighting all afternoon thumped behind his eyes, and Grant pinched the bridge of his nose to stave off the white spots at the periphery threatening to overtake his vision.

"Sorry." He opened the top drawer of his desk, thumbing the

top off a bottle of analgesics and tossing a couple into the back of his throat. Grimacing, he washed them down with a convenience-store beer that had long since gone warm.

Merry fucking Saturday night.

"Where did you disappear to so fast? I thought you were having a beer with Kattan after the shoot."

"I got a rain check. I had stuff at the Center that needed attention."

"You still there?"

"Where else would I be?"

"With Tavi and your grandmother."

Grant laughed. "They're going to the midnight showing of that new horror movie that just came out. He's staying the night with her, and I'm supposed to pick him up in the morning."

"So, you're alone then." Sebastian's voice dipped low, and the seductive pull made Grant ache for what he couldn't have.

"Look, I'm busy here. Can I—"

"You working on the fundraiser? I could come over and help."

Grant rubbed at the grit in his eyes and slugged back another swallow of tepid beer. As much as he wanted to say yes, Sebastian had already blown Vin's secret. He couldn't take the chance Sebastian would blow his. After all, it wouldn't be Sebastian who would have to tell his grandmother she was homeless when Grant got fired and couldn't make the required minimum payment to the bank.

"Maybe you helping me with the fundraiser isn't such a good idea."

The silence drew out so long that Grant glanced at his phone's screen to make sure the call hadn't dropped. "Bass? You still there?"

"I'm not going to screw up your fundraiser if that's what you're worried about."

"What? No." Grant sucked in a breath and blew it out. When the hell were those analgesics going to kick in? "I don't think you're going to screw anything up."

"Then why don't you want my help?"

Now it was his turn to let the silence drag out. Finally, he said, "You know why."

"Yeah. Sure. If that's how you want to play it. I can respect that. You have a good night, okay?"

Fuck. *Tell him to come over. Tell Sebastian you want him.*

"Yeah. Night."

Hanging up, he grabbed his bottle of beer. Instead of bringing it to his lips, he threw it across his office. It shattered on contact with the wall, a beer and glass bomb.

It should have made him feel better, but all it made was a giant mess.

Tossing his phone on his desk, he went to the utility closet and got the mop and broom. As he swept up the shards of glass and cleaned up the spilled beer, his anger grew. He wouldn't be in this fucking mess if it weren't for his father.

If it weren't for that selfish bastard, he wouldn't need to do the extra scenes with Black Stallion or keep Sebastian at bay.

And if he didn't need the income from Black Stallion, he could step out of the closet. He was so sick of living his life in the dark.

If you want out so fucking bad, what are you gonna do about it?

He could start with his father.

He dumped the glass shards in the trash and threw the bag in the dumpster out back so none of the kids would accidentally cut themselves. When all evidence of his temper tantrum had been cleaned up, he plopped into his chair behind his desk and scrolled through the contacts on his phone.

There was no name above his father's number. Just two words: *Don't answer.*

If only he'd listened to that prophetic warning and never answered the call that had essentially invited the deadbeat back into his and his grandmother's lives, things might be different between Grant and Sebastian.

And while he'd tried getting hold of his father since his grandmother had dropped the foreclosure bombshell, he hadn't tried too hard. As much as he wanted his father to make good on the loan, he hadn't wanted to deal with his utter bullshit.

He hit the call button, and as he waited for his father to pick up, he tossed another analgesic into his mouth and crunched it between his molars like a Tic-Tac, willing the pain in his head to go away.

Without voicemail set up, the phone rang and rang. Grant almost gave up. Then he heard someone pick up. There was fumbling and cussing, and a woman's voice said, "Ouch, that was my boob, you idiot."

Grant's thumb hovered over the 'end' button, but then he thought about the shit show that was his non-existent sex life and held on.

"What?" His father finally said, somehow managing to slur even that one word.

"It's me." And then because Grant wasn't entirely sure his father would recognize his voice even if he had been sober, he added, "Grant."

"Yeah? What do you want, kid?"

"I want the money you stole from your mother. The bank is going to foreclose on her home. What I *want* is for you to make it right." As soon as the words left his mouth, he knew how idiotic that sounded. His father wasn't capable of taking care of himself, much less the problem he'd created.

"About that..."

This should be good.

"Look, I'm just a little short. But there's this thing, you see? If you could spot me about five Benjamins, then—"

Grant launched to his feet and started pacing, his chair toppling to the floor. "Are you fucking kidding me right now? You want me to give you five hundred dollars?"

"Clint said it's a sure thing."

Grant thumped his head against the wall. It already hurt like hell. Maybe a couple knocks would make it feel better. "You can't believe your bookie. You're un-fucking-believable. You're seriously going to screw over Nana?"

Silence. Well, not complete silence. Somewhere in the background, the woman complained about not being able to find her underwear, which Grant tried hard not to think about.

His father cleared his throat, and instead of an apology, he said, "You ain't no saint either. At least I'm not whoring myself out."

No. Daniel Hardy just hired them. Grant pitied the unsuspecting woman who'd pulled *that* short straw. "I'm not a whore."

And even if he were, so the-fuck what. There were worse things in life he could be, like a deadbeat, misogynistic, homophobic, racist piece of shit.

"You're humiliating." *Humiliating.* That his father knew that word and could use it in a sentence coherently almost made Grant laugh. "Everyone I goddamn know, knows you're a buttfucking cocksucker. I should have disowned you from the start."

So, dumping Grant on his grandmother's doorstep when he came out to his father wasn't disowning him? "I'm not getting into this with you."

Now that his father was on a roll, he couldn't shut him up. "Your mother... now there was a smart lady. Got out while she still could. Before you could make her a laughingstock."

"Stop. Just... stop." His father had always blamed Grant for his mother running out when he was a little kid, saying she must have known he was a fairy before everyone else. It had never occurred to Daniel Hardy that his mother might have left because he was an abusive, alcoholic, shitbag. "Look, I thought maybe—"

Grant cut himself off. He'd thought what? That maybe his father would wake up and suddenly care about someone other than himself? No. The world didn't work like that.

There was no arguing or reasoning with a man like his father.

"Never mind," Grant said. "Forget I called. Have a nice life."

And then Grant did what he should have done years ago. He blocked and deleted his father's contact from his phone.

———

Sebastian knocked on the Center's door. When no one answered, he scanned the parking lot and found Grant's Civic. He knocked again, harder this time.

Beyond the light in the lobby, Grant emerged from the hallway and froze. His hands went to his hips, and he glanced back behind him down the hallway. Sebastian wondered if Grant would go back to his office and pretend Sebastian wasn't standing at his door.

What are you doing here, anyway?

You can't pretend his reaction isn't unexpected. He told you not to come.

But a guy could still hope. Right?

"Open up." Sebastian infused as much authority into his words as a rejected man could muster.

Grant scrubbed a hand down his face, turned his keys in the lock, and opened the door enough to stick his head out. "I told you not to come."

"Yeah? Well, I'm not here for you. I'm here for Tavi and all the other kids at the Center. Now, are you going to let me in, or are you going to let the fundraiser and the kids suffer because you're inept?"

"Inept?" The scowl on Grant's face softened.

"Your entire fundraising plan was to invite lots of people and try to get them to hand over their money. That doesn't scream competent to me."

"Fine. Get your ass in here." Grant took hold of Sebastian's shirt and hauled him through the door, the lock twisting home in the door behind him.

He followed Grant into his office, the scent of beer heavy in the air. Grant grabbed his office chair and righted it.

"What the hell happened here?"

Grant dropped into the chair. "I'd rather not talk about it."

Sebastian looked Grant over. From the rumpled Cory Center golf shirt to Grant's hair that stood on end, to his hollow cheeks, to the tension at the corners of his eyes. "You okay?"

"Why wouldn't I be?"

"You tell me."

They stared at each other, each waiting for the other to break. Grant crossed his arms, looking content with the drawn-out silence.

"Look, if it was about me jacking it at your shoot, I'm—"

"It's not that."

"Then what?"

"I thought you were here to work." Grant changed the subject entirely.

If that's the way he wanted to play it... okay. "Sure. Where do you want to start?"

After they'd developed their plans for promoting the event, decided on the carnival games for the kids, and made a solid list of local celebrities they wanted to contact for participation in the live auction after the masquerade ball, Grant bumped Sebastian's arm.

"What?" Sebastian straightened at the table in the kitchen, papers and lists all around him, and wiped the drool from the corner of his mouth.

"You were snoring," Grant said.

"Sorry." He stretched the kinks from his neck and rubbed the grit out of his eyes. "Where were we?"

"I think it's time we called it a night."

Sebastian couldn't say he was sorry to hear that. "I guess we can work on this tomorrow night, or the next."

He pulled his keys out of his pocket, stumbling when he stood. Sebastian caught himself on the table as Grant stripped the keys out of his hand.

"What are you doing?"

"You're not in any condition to drive this late at night."

"Just get me another cup of coffee, and I'll be good."

"No." Grant pocketed the keys, his gaze stern until it dropped to Sebastian's lips for a beat. "You're going home with me."

As much as Sebastian wanted nothing more than to spend the night at Grant's apartment, even though he knew the invite wasn't a booty call, he said, "I don't think that's such a good idea."

"Better than you driving home and running off the road. Niko would kill me if something happened to you."

Sebastian swallowed hard, scared to hear the answer to the question he wanted to ask.

Again, that flick of Grant's eyes to Sebastian's lips. Grant wanted more. He couldn't hide that. But wanting Sebastian and doing something about it were two different things. "Is that the only reason you don't want me driving home?"

Grant blinked at him, but no words came. Sebastian was too

exhausted to push him any further. Sebastian did have *some* pride.

"Fine," Sebastian allowed. "I'll stay at your place, only because I don't want to drive across the valley."

Besides, as tired as Sebastian was, he doubted he could get it up even if Grant wanted him to.

Grant was an idiot.

That assessment wasn't even up for debate.

Taking Sebastian to his place, while it had seemed smart at the time, was proving to be a big mistake, because two hours after he'd left Sebastian on his couch and gone to his bed like a good little boy, he couldn't get any sleep.

Not with Sebastian only a cheap, hollow-core door away.

His stomach grumbled. Between the fucked-up shoot and working his ass off at the Center well into the night, he'd hardly had a chance to eat.

Quietly, he slipped through his bedroom door, not wanting to wake Sebastian, and padded toward the kitchen. His hand skimmed along the wall to keep from bumping into things in the dark.

He opened the fridge and rummaged around, coming up with an apple and several individually packaged slices of American cheese.

As the refrigerator door closed and his eyes readjusted to the darkness, he turned and bumped into Sebastian. He slammed a hand on the light switch. "What the hell, man, you scared the shit out of me."

"Sorry." Sebastian blinked at the brightness and took one of the cheese slices from Grant's hand, peeling away the wrapper and stuffing the cheese into his mouth. "I'm starving."

Grant leaned against the counter in nothing but his boxer briefs and took a bite of the apple then held it out for Sebastian.

Grabbing Grant's wrist, Sebastian steadied the apple and took a bite, the juice running down Sebastian's chin. Before he could wipe it away, Grant swiped it with his thumb, licking the sweet juice from his skin.

"What are you doing?"

"I wish I knew."

Grant didn't know if it was the crummy shoot with Kattan, or writing his father out of his life, or the exhaustion and the stress of trying to hide who he was from a man he could see himself with, that made him want to spill his guts. Whatever the reason, he couldn't lie to Sebastian anymore.

But really, who had he been kidding anyway?

"Actually," Grant said. "I do know."

He backed Sebastian up a half-step until the counter stopped them and took Sebastian's chin in between his thumb and forefinger.

And that dick of Grant's that hadn't been able get hard without a little pharmaceutical help, now had no difficulty popping wood.

Leaning in, he kissed Sebastian, their lips brushing, and his tongue tracing Sebastian's bottom lip until he opened up and let Grant in.

He tasted the apple's sweetness on Sebastian's tongue and took the kiss deeper, loving the way Sebastian's hesitation gave way to unabashed eagerness, not questioning, just accepting.

But would Sebastian accept him if he knew the truth about what a horrible human he'd descended from? Would he always wonder, the way Grant did, if there was a part of Daniel Hardy in his makeup that he could never escape?

Grant pulled away and pressed his forehead against Sebastian's, his heart rattling around in his chest, refusing to settle.

"I want you. Beneath me. On top of me. Inside me. Or me inside you. Whichever way you want me, you can have me."

A grin flashed across Sebastian's face, turning sad before it fell. "*Any* way, huh?"

"That's what I said."

"I want you out."

Grant pulled back. It was *his* apartment. Not Sebastian's. "What do you mean?"

"*Out*, out. Out of the fucking closet."

As much as Grant didn't want to let Sebastian go, he stepped away. "I can't be out. Not now. Not yet."

Sebastian folded his arms across his chest, looking like something Grant wanted to devour as he watched the play of muscles across his chest and the ripple of his abdominals. A smattering of hair arrowed down beneath the briefs that molded to Sebastian's every fucking nook, cranny, and hard cock.

"Why not?"

"It's complicated."

Grant wanted to spit it all out, but the heat of humiliation stopped him. What did it say about Grant that his homophobic, asshole of a father dumped him on his grandmother's doorstep when he was barely a teen? That his father wouldn't think twice about stealing her money, her house, her sense of security, her faith in her family?

What did it say that Grant came from *that* kind of man?

Yeah, he could admit he was gay. The other stuff? That was too painful, too humiliating.

"Your family doesn't know?"

"They know. My grandmother doesn't care. My father..." Grant shrugged, hating the bitter taste that calling that man his father left in his mouth. "He can't accept it, but that's on him, not me."

"Then I don't understand what the big deal is. Is it the Center?"

"Some, but not all." Grant blew out a breath. The basics he could admit. The rest, he would keep to himself. "I need the money."

Rocking back on his heels, Sebastian said, "So, it's Niko who can't know."

"And I can't take the chance of anyone else knowing and risk word getting back to Niko. Is that going to be a problem?"

"I have one rule when it comes to sex. Something I've had to learn the hard way."

Grant raised a brow, afraid to come out and ask what it was, because, from the expression on Sebastian's face, Grant wasn't going to like what he heard.

Hopefully, Sebastian would speak loudly because with the rush of blood going past Grant's ears, and the *thud-thump* of his heart in his chest, he doubted he'd hear a tornado if it came barreling down on them.

"Rule number one," Sebastian finally said. "No sleeping with closet cases."

Figures.

Grant had been prepared to hear it, but that didn't make the slam of those words hurt any less. "I get it. You're out. You don't need me dragging you back in and making you police what you say and to whom. It's not a way to live. No hard feelings, yeah?"

Grant slapped his hand on the light switch, pitching them into darkness and effectively ending the conversation. He didn't want to see the pity in Sebastian's eyes because Grant chose to live in a world that made his skin feel a size too tight.

One of these days, things will be different.

Maybe then he and Sebastian could circle back around—if they were both still single—and try to pick up where things left off.

Sebastian reached out and took one of Grant's hands, his thumb sweeping across the top of Grant's knuckles. He waited for Sebastian to let go, to return to the couch so they could both get some much-needed rest.

But instead of dropping his hand, Sebastian tugged.

"What are you doing?" Grant asked.

"Breaking my rule."

9

———

"Are you sure about this?" Grant asked as Sebastian led him into the bedroom.

No. Sebastian wasn't sure about anything, other than he wanted Grant. *Had* wanted him for too long, and he wasn't going to be the one to deprive either of them any longer.

Tomorrow he might regret it.

But not tonight.

Light from the master bathroom shined through the partially opened door, illuminating the bedroom enough for Sebastian to shove Grant down on the mattress without missing it entirely.

Sebastian moved to the nightstand as Grant settled back on his elbows. "Your stuff in here?"

"Yeah."

Digging through the drawer, Sebastian came up with a condom and a bottle of lube and tossed them on the bed.

"What do you want?" Grant asked, his voice a gruff whisper.

"You," Sebastian said, "in me. I want you to take me the way you took Kattan."

Kneeling on the edge of the mattress, Sebastian crawled up

Grant's long body and straddled his hips. "I want you to take me with the same power, the same passion, the same force."

He shoved Grant back against the mattress, hooked his fingers beneath the waistband of Grant's briefs, and freed that colossal cock. "But first, I'm going to take you to the edge, like I'd promised you I would."

And because he wanted to make sure he and Grant were on the same page, he added, "That sound good to you?"

"Shut up and suck me already."

Sebastian grinned as Grant's fingers threaded through Sebastian's hair, the gentle tug steering Sebastian to his rigid dick. Whatever problem Grant had getting hard earlier that day, certainly wasn't an issue now.

Shucking his underwear before settling between Grant's legs, Sebastian ignored Grant's dick and nibbled his way along the tender skin of Grant's inner thighs. Sebastian licked and sucked Grant's balls and grazed his tongue along Grant's taint, loving the way Grant squirmed and shuddered beneath him.

When Sebastian finally took Grant in his hand, the hiss of breath Grant sucked in sent a zap to Sebastian's dick. He couldn't wait to climb on board and have Grant inside him. He'd been celibate too long for a guy like him and, as much as he wanted to torture Grant with the tease his mouth and his hands could give, the torment was also his.

Slowly, he worked his tongue along the underside of Grant's shaft, Grant's fingers fisting in Sebastian's hair, the flash of exquisite pain across his scalp egging him on.

Grant grunted when Sebastian skimmed his thumb across his slit, the dab of precum slicking the head. "Don't tease me."

"You want my mouth?"

Grant lifted his head, locking eyes with Sebastian. Even in the shadows, Grant's brewing need turned his eyes dark with an intensity that made Sebastian's dick throb. "And your throat. Then I want to plow that fine ass."

Sebastian almost forgot all about the face fucking and went straight to giving them what they both wanted, but Sebastian was determined to bring Grant to the bitter edge at least once before they did.

Rising on one elbow, Sebastian took Grant in his mouth, inch by slow inch. Grant's eyes fluttered closed, and his head fell back as that glorious cock bumped the back of Sebastian's throat, threatening to gag him.

"Fuck that feels good," Grant muttered, his hands going to Sebastian's ears, using them like handholds and taking over the pace and depth of the thrusts.

Sebastian relaxed his throat, enjoying Grant's salty-brine flavor, leaving him dying to taste Grant's cum. But he'd save that for another time.

If *there's going to be another time.*

This could be your one shot with Grant. What do you think your chances are of getting another? He already said he wasn't coming out of the closet, and your willingness to bend your rules this once doesn't mean you should do it again.

Grant pulled Sebastian off his cock and stared down at him. "Where did you go?"

Sebastian wasn't going to let his doubts get in the way of his pleasure. "Nowhere. I'm here."

Then Sebastian went back to work, adding his hands and more saliva, giving Grant a wet, sloppy, blowjob using everything he had—lips, tongue, throat, hands, and the occasional light scrape of teeth that made goosebumps flash across Grant's flesh.

Grant's grunts and groans and 'fuck, yeahs' when Sebastian unexpectedly took Grant deep again, lit Sebastian's nerves. Grant's hips thrust into his hands and mouth, the aggressive, possessive grip he had on Sebastian's head made Sebastian's gut twist in the most erotic of ways.

Fuck, this man's going to be your undoing.

Grant's balls drew up tight, and when Sebastian cupped him and stroked his knuckles across Grant's taint, Sebastian felt the first pulse of Grant's impending release.

Sebastian pulled off with a pop.

"Asshole. I was so fucking close." The whine in Grant's voice made Sebastian chuckle.

Reaching for the condom, Sebastian said, "You're not getting off that easy."

Grant jacked himself in slow, languorous strokes. Sebastian had to tear his eyes away from the glorious sight. He could have spent half the night watching Grant jack off, but his own need for release had him ripping the condom wrapper with his teeth.

"Can I put it on you?"

Grant dropped his hand. "All yours."

If only that were true.

Stop.

Get out of your head.

Or leave.

You can't spend the entire time you have with him second-guessing your decision and hoping for more than what he can give you. He told you his truth, and you dragged him to bed anyway.

When he breaks your heart, that's on you.

Slowly, Sebastian rolled the condom down Grant's shaft, leaning forward when he finished, going in for a quick kiss. When he pulled away, Grant slung an arm around his neck and pulled Sebastian in for another, their tongues meeting and mating.

Sebastian pulled back, catching his breath, and Grant said, "I love tasting myself on your tongue."

Groaning, Sebastian went in for another kiss. "Shut up and fuck me already."

Grant grinned, with mischief in his eyes. "Gladly."

"Where do you want me?"

"On your knees."

———

GRANT'S HAND BUMPED DOWN EACH VERTEBRA IN SEBASTIAN'S spine as Sebastian settled near the edge of the bed on his hands and knees.

"You've got the sweetest ass," Grant said as he bent and bit each cheek. He couldn't wait to taste him.

Running his hands up the back of Sebastian's thighs, Grant kneaded Sebastian's ass and parted his cheeks. Sebastian dropped his head and groaned as Grant's tongue darted down the middle, teasing that tight bunch of muscle.

Sebastian rocked back against Grant's tongue, encouraging Grant to go deeper. He didn't disappoint—Sebastian's musky flavor arousing him even more.

Reaching for the lube, Sebastian handed it over.

Grant could take the hint. "Now, who's the impatient one?"

"Just hurry it up."

After pouring lube into his hand, Grant slicked the condom and Sebastian's hole. He leaned over as he slowly slid one finger in, holding tight to Sebastian's shoulder for leverage and whispered in his ear, "You ready for me?"

Sebastian blew out a breath as he drove back against Grant's finger. "Always."

Then Sebastian twisted, catching the back of Grant's head with one of his hands and drew him in for a kiss. Grant swallowed Sebastian's sweet, dick-hardening cry when he added a second finger.

Sebastian's breaths came in short, harsh pants, and he nipped at Grant's lip.

Grant pulled free, and raked his teeth over his lip, the lick of pain only making him harder.

"Fuck me already, Hardy. I'm not some porn noob who just discovered anal. Trust me. I can take you."

Grant chuckled. "You think so, huh?"

"I know it. And if you'd stop fucking around, I'd prove it to you."

The challenge in Sebastian's eyes and the wicked desire on his face had Grant reaching for the lube again. But as much as they both wanted this, and as sure as Sebastian was that he could take all of Grant, Grant wasn't the kind of asshole who'd shove it in a guy and not give him a chance to adjust.

Grant stood and pulled Sebastian to the edge of the bed by his hips and pressed the tip of his cock to Sebastian's hole. At this rate, the condom would fill with precum before Grant got inside him.

Sebastian sat back, sinking on Grant's hungry cock.

With his hands on Sebastian's hips, Grant stilled him. "Holy hell, you're tight."

Sebastian blew out a couple of deep breaths, and second by excruciating second, his muscles relaxed around Grant's shaft. Leaning forward, Grant licked and chewed his way up Sebastian's back in a series of open-mouth kisses trying to distract himself from the driving need to ram himself home.

"More." Sebastian's voice came out gruff as his eyes squeezed shut. Grant eased in, his hands skimming through the beads of sweat balling up on the lean muscles bracketing Sebastian's backbone.

"Like that," Sebastian grunted. "Fuck yeah."

Grant would have said something, but as he buried himself balls deep, all rational thought left his head. All that he could think about was the tightness around his dick and the man on his knees in front of him, taking and demanding more.

If Sebastian expected him to last the way he normally did on set, the man was going to be sorely disappointed, because this wasn't the set. This was real life. This was Grant fucking the man he'd been fantasizing about since he'd signed on with Black Stallion.

His late-night fantasy with his right hand.

His never-gonna-happen.

Except it was happening.

As Grant pumped in and out of Sebastian to the sound of flesh slapping flesh, the room filling with the scent of musk and sweat and sex, Sebastian's little moans and shivers driving Grant faster and faster.

Sebastian hadn't lied. He took every bit of Grant, matching him stroke for stroke as they both chased their climax. But this wasn't how Grant wanted it to end.

This wasn't one for the cameras.

This was personal.

Because Sebastian mattered.

Man, you are so fucked.

That realization should have made him go soft, but it only spurred him on. When he felt the first tinglings at the base of his spine, he slowed his thrusts.

Sebastian whined, not from pain, it seemed, but from disappointment. "Why the fuck did you stop? I was almost there."

Grant pulled out and with a hand on Sebastian's hip, rolled him onto his back. He dropped down, his hands on either side of Sebastian's head, and he locked on Sebastian's accusing, heated gaze.

Even though Grant knew this time with Sebastian would be a one-off, Sebastian wasn't an anonymous hookup. "Because I want to watch you jack yourself and see your face the first time I make you come."

Sebastian's hands snaked between their bodies, taking both of their dicks in his hand, rubbing them together. "Fuck yeah."

Grant pressed his chest to Sebastian's, loving the pull and slide, the tightness and tug of Sebastian's ministrations. With his free arm, Sebastian wrapped it around Grant's neck and pulled him in for another kiss, taking it from hot and heavy to so sweet and tender it made Grant's chest tight, bringing him to a place where words, and thoughts, and hopes all jumbled up in his head until something gave way and words spilled out.

"You make me want more."

The way Sebastian's expression softened, he knew Grant wasn't just talking about the sex. "Is that good or bad?"

"I don't know yet," Grant admitted with great reluctance. "It feels... dangerous. Like a ticking time bomb that I can't diffuse."

"There's time on the clock for that," Sebastian said with an understanding and grace that Grant didn't deserve. "But for now, I want you to finish getting me off."

Grant grinned. "You have a way of digging through the bullshit to get to what matters."

"Damn straight."

After adding another dollop of lube to the condom and spreading it around, Grant draped Sebastian's legs over his arms as Sebastian squirted lube into his hands and slicked up his dick, his hand already rubbing his knob and stroking his shaft.

"Don't keep me waiting," Sebastian said.

"You're so fucking sexy, Bass," Grant said as he slid home again.

Grant had been with many men, but never had it been like this. Less rutting and more connection. Less pure lust and more focused passion.

He'd told Sebastian that he wanted to watch him masturbate, but stroke after stroke, he couldn't take his eyes off Sebastian's face. Loving the way his eyes fluttered closed, his face contorting as his moans turned to groans.

Even if he hadn't felt Sebastian's ass tightening around him as the waves of his climax pulled him under, Grant would have known Sebastian was jumping off the cliff by the way Sebastian's head fell back, his jaw going slack as his hand furiously worked his shaft.

Grant went harder and faster, his rhythm going erratic as the pressure wave built. Then Sebastian's muscles tightened around him, and the long, deep groan clawing up the back of Sebastian's throat made Grant's balls tighten.

With a shout, Sebastian hit his release, his spunk spilling out between his fingers and squirting across his abdomen. Grant had never seen anything as beautiful as that.

Three more pumps and Grant followed Sebastian, his back arching as he emptied himself. Knees weak, Grant fought for every breath as Sebastian went limp beneath him. Over the thundering beat of his heart, Grant almost didn't hear Sebastian's low laugh. "Niko would have loved to have had a camera on that."

Grant pulled out and tossed the condom in the trash can beside the bed and ran his hands up Sebastian's thighs. "That was too good for the cameras."

Then he caught a drop of cum as it dripped over Sebastian's side and brought it to his mouth for a taste. "That was only for us."

Sebastian's eyes darkened as Grant pulled the finger out of his mouth. Reaching out, Sebastian pulled Grant in for a kiss. "You do that again, and we'll have round two before morning."

Grant groaned. "Don't remind me of the morning. It's going to come all too soon. What time do you have to be at the studio?"

"Not until ten. Rose is picking up one of the guys from the airport in the morning, so we have a late start. What time do you have to pick up Tavi?"

"Nothing set in stone. After breakfast." With a pat on the leg, Grant said, "Wait here, I'll get a washcloth."

Minutes later, he returned with a warm washcloth and wiped Sebastian's hand and cleaned the spunk off his abdomen, wishing their time together didn't have to end so soon. He gave Sebastian a hand up, and they trudged into the shower, too exhausted to do anything but get clean.

Back in the bedroom, Sebastian reached for his underwear, but Grant stripped them from his hand. "Where do you think you're going?"

"The couch?"

Grant tossed the underwear over his shoulder and planted his hands on Sebastian's hips. "You think I want you on the couch? After what we just shared?"

The surprise on Sebastian's face made Grant's chest tight. Despite what he'd told Sebastian in the kitchen, did Sebastian think all he wanted from him was a fast fuck?

"I didn't want to assume."

Grant pointed to the rumpled sheets. "Bed. Now. We can still get a few good hours of sleep before we have to wake up."

When Sebastian just stood there, indecision written all over his face in big, bold letters, Grant took him by the hand and dragged Sebastian to the mattress with him. He settled in behind Sebastian, lifted the sheet over them, and snugged Sebastian against him, his back to Grant's chest.

Sebastian reached down and linked his fingers with Grant's as Grant pressed a kiss to Sebastian's shoulder.

"How's your ass?"

Sebastian chuckled. "Sore. But in the best possible way."

SEBASTIAN DRAGGED HIS ASS INTO THE STUDIO WITH ONLY MINUTES to spare. He sneaked into the makeup room and stole a cup of coffee from Cat.

Her eyes narrowed at him. She probably noticed that he hadn't had time to fix his hair or even run to his house to change clothes. "What happened to you?"

Besides having his ass fucked, his world rocked, and his heart completely busted in his chest? As much as he wanted to tell Cat everything, the way he always did after a hookup, he didn't dare. "Nothing. Where is everybody?"

"Already on set." Cat sat in her makeup chair and used one foot to twist back and forth. "For the record, I'm not fooled, but I'm going to let it go for now because Niko will have your ass if you're late this morning."

He held up the mug. "Thanks for the coffee."

"Come see me after the shoot so we can talk."

Sebastian made a zipper motion over his mouth.

Cat's jaw dropped. "You banged a celebrity, didn't you?"

"I'm not saying anything." Sebastian backed out of the room and started down the hall.

Cat gave chase. "Just tell me, A, B, or C list?"

"Stop it." Though Sebastian couldn't help but laugh. If she only knew. And because she was on the wrong scent, he led her on. "You know how those guys like their privacy."

A normal person would have let it drop, but Cat wasn't normal. "It was Tom Hutchens, wasn't it?"

"What? The guy in the last Star Crypt movie? No. He's straight."

"That's not what the celebrity rags say."

"And he's not that hot."

"I'd still bang him," Cat said as they rounded the corner.

The New York skyline set was already lit, and Vin was busy checking his light levels. Hearing Cat, who didn't always know when to use her inside voice, Vin glanced up and with a laugh, said, "Cat, you'd bang just about anybody."

"It's my superpower." She grinned. "If you want, you can be next."

"I'm gay," Vin said, not that it was any news.

"So was the last guy, but that didn't stop him from leaving with a smile on his face."

"You guys finished messing around, or can we get started here?" Niko's scowl might have been scary if Sebastian hadn't been too exhausted and too well fucked to care.

Grant showed up at his grandmother's later than he'd planned, half asleep as he sipped coffee from his travel mug.

But damn, spending the extra time that morning with Sebastian had been worth every exhausting second he suffered after.

Walking up his grandmother's steps, he entered without knocking and followed the voices to the kitchen.

"There you are, dear boy." His grandmother smiled when she saw him.

Grant stopped, his chest threatening to crack when he looked from Tavi—who sat at the kitchen table with his tablet and what looked like a new set of charcoal pencils—back to his grandmother, who wore the same flat-billed baseball cap with a local rapper's logo that Tavi wore. Both at the same awkward angle.

He stepped into the kitchen and pulled his grandmother in for a hug, his voice rough when he said, "You're the best, you know that?"

She patted his back, and he kissed her soft cheek. When he pulled away, she gave him a wink that made the back of his eyes misty.

"Let me fill that for you, dear." She took his travel mug and refilled his coffee, giving him a second to compose himself before he turned to Tavi.

"You about ready?"

"Can't I just stay here?" Tavi asked. "Nana B's cool with it."

"Yeah, well, *Nana B* has her own life, too. Besides, I've got a surprise for you."

Tavi gave him the side-eye as if Grant were trying to pull a fast one on him. "This isn't a trick to get me back into the foster system, is it?"

"What? No. This is a good surprise. Promise."

His grandmother handed Grant his coffee then laid a hand on Tavi's shoulder. "You're not going anywhere you don't want to go."

She shouldn't be saying those kinds of things, making promises that they might have to break. "Nana, you can't—"

She leveled a piercing gaze at Grant—one she hadn't used on him since she'd caught him sneaking into the gay bars while still in high school—that shut him up.

His grandmother was sweet, kind, loved unconditionally, and was generous to a fault. And—except where his father was concerned—she wasn't a pushover.

The last thing Grant ever wanted to do was disappoint her.

But Tavi wasn't a stray puppy. He was a kid, and they couldn't lose sight of that.

"It's okay," Tavi said to his grandmother, which only made Grant feel like even more of an ass than he already did. "I get it."

Tavi packed his things into a new backpack his grandmother must have bought for him and slung it over his shoulder. "I'm ready."

Grant kissed his grandmother goodbye. "Thanks, Nana, I'll call you later tonight."

Tavi slumped in the car seat, quiet on the drive as he stared out the window at the cars and shops and people that passed by in a blur. He didn't even pester Grant on where they were going.

"Look, kid—"

"You don't have to say anything." Tavi pulled his blank gaze off the passing scenery and met Grant with a fierce determination. "I survived before you guys. I'll survive after."

"I'm not looking for a way to dump you. I'm trying to do what's right by you. I just don't know what that looks like yet."

Tavi continued staring out the windshield, not looking the least bit mollified.

"Living on the streets is a tough life. Especially for a kid."

Tavi shrugged. "The hardest part is trying to figure out which john is going to pay you, and which one is going to kick your ass, but other times, it's not so bad."

Tavi pointed to his face. Much of the swelling had gone down around his eye, but the bruising had turned his face multiple shades of black, blue, purple, and yellow. "Even this isn't as tough as being in the closet."

Grant's head popped back with the direct hit, even though Tavi had no idea Grant had been a target. "Is that why you ran away?"

"I didn't run. I was kicked out. But I'd much rather live out there than live a lie. I don't understand why everyone doesn't come out."

Grant remembered a time in his life when things had been that black and white, that right and wrong with no nuances of gray or room for the thin spaces in between. "It's not always that simple. You can't judge anyone on their chosen path out."

Tavi gave him a look that said he *could,* and he *did.*

Which made Grant feel like a coward.

Here he was shutting down a relationship with Sebastian because, as an *adult,* he refused to come out. And here was this kid who'd rather survive by his sheer wits than not be his authentic self.

It was kind of scalding to be schooled by a kid.

But life could be a complicated mess, and everyone did what they could to come out the other side alive and in one piece.

But between wanting what he couldn't have and sitting next to a kid who'd risked his very own survival to be himself, Grant's closet grew even more stifling.

Grant stuck a finger in the neck of his golf shirt and gave it a pull, but the feeling of suffocation came from within.

He pulled into a parking space in a strip center. "We're here."

Tavi glanced around. "Where's here?"

Grant popped his door. "Come on. I'll show you."

Tavi shouldered his backpack and followed. Glancing up, he read the name of the business. "Pigment of Your Imagination? You're getting a tattoo?"

"No. Better than that, I think." And hoped.

He held the shop door open for Tavi, and the kid spun in a slow circle taking in all the original artwork on the bright red walls.

Nobody sat up front, and it looked like Grant and Tavi were the only people there.

A man emerged from the back room, all tatted up, looking like he rode with the Hells Angels for kicks and picked fights with demons for fun. He leaned his meaty paws on the counter. "What can I do for you guys?"

Tavi hung back, and Grant said, "I'm looking for Truman. Cat sent me."

A grin broke out on the man's face, and he flicked his lip ring with his tongue. "I'm Truman." He turned his attention to Tavi, cataloging the bruising, but not commenting. "This the kid?"

"Yeah. Tavi, this is Truman. A friend of a friend. If you guys get on, he's got an opening for an apprenticeship."

Tavi cocked his head. "What's an apprenticeship?"

Truman leaned heavily on the counter. "It's where you do scut work around the shop, and if you work hard and pay attention, we'll teach you how to become a tattoo artist. *If* you have the talent, and if that's something you wanna do."

Grant could tell Tavi fought his grin, trying not to geek-out and maintain some sort of cool-kid street cred. "Possibly."

Truman bumped his chin toward the ink on Tavi's arm. "You do that?"

Holding out his forearm, Tavi said, "Yeah."

Truman held it up to the light for a closer inspection. "Your line work's not too shabby, and that script is pretty killer. Where did you find it?"

"Uhhh..." Tavi seemed at a loss for words. "I didn't find it. I just made it up."

"You made that up?" Truman crossed his beefy arms over his barrel chest. It should have been intimidating, but the lopsided smile and the pop of gold tooth softened the look. He glanced up at Grant. "I think the kid and I'll get along fine." Then he turned his attention back to Tavi. "As long as you don't sit around on your phone all day."

Tavi laughed. "Yeah, no phone."

Clapping Tavi on the shoulder, Truman said, "Put your backpack behind the counter. There's a mop in the back with your name on it."

Grant held out his hand for Truman to shake. "Thanks, man." He handed over one of his cards. "If he's a problem, call me. Let me know when you want me to pick him up. I can come whenever."

"Cat said you're at The Cory Center, right?"

"Yeah. We close at five today, but I'm usually there late."

"I can drop him off by then," Truman offered.

Tavi dumped his bag. "I'm not some five-year-old that the

grownups have to pick up from a play date. The Center's less than a mile from here. I can walk."

"We'll see," Grant said. When Tavi's eyes rolled, Grant said, "Later, kid."

The rest of the morning and early afternoon zipped by. For a Sunday, the Center had a ton of kids come through. Luckily Vondra was there to take up the slack so Grant could get some work done in his office.

Then Grant did something that he'd been avoiding since his grandmother came to him about the bank issue—he sat down and really worked the numbers, and what he found terrified him.

Even with his doubled rate per scene with Kattan and the upped percentage of his residuals, he would fall way short of the money he needed before the deadline.

Fuck. Grant knew what he had to do, even if he hated the idea of doing it. Especially after that fiasco with his last shoot with Kattan. But it wasn't like he'd have to keep doing porn forever.

Just until he saved his grandmother's house.

With a renewed determination, Grant worked his way through the Center until he found Vondra with a group of teens in the gym.

A tall, athletic black woman, Vondra had a rag-tag group of guys and girls around her as she showed them how to serve a volleyball. She demonstrated with a jumping serve that smashed down on the other side of the net.

"Whoa, dude," one of the teens said. "She's badass."

"I didn't know you knew how to play volleyball," Grant said.

"She don't," another one of the teens said. "We looked it up on YouTube."

Off to the side, Vondra had her laptop open with a video cued up. She had a way of connecting with the kids and engaging them in learning new things that Grant admired. The teens thought they were just goofing around, but they were learning how to teach themselves new things.

A lifelong skill that everyone could benefit from no matter their background.

"I've got a favor," Grant said. "I need to run across the valley for a meeting. You think you can hold down the fort? Tavi is at Pigments and should be showing up here in a couple of hours."

"I've got it. The kids are thinning out, and it should be pretty quiet for the rest of the afternoon."

"Thanks, I owe you one."

And it looked like Grant was going to owe a lot of people before the day ended.

———

Niko stepped into Sebastian's office between scenes, the frenetic energy rolling off him in waves threatened to swamp anyone in his path. He got like that when he worried.

Sebastian glanced up from his computer. "What's up?"

"I just wanted to check in with you on the Bahamas shoot."

"That's almost two months away."

Niko didn't bother to sit. "Humor me."

"I've got the talent lined up. The airfares booked. The rooms reserved. Still verifying passports as they come in."

"Sounds like you're on top of it."

"I am. Stop fussing."

Sebastian sat back, trying not to let it show that Niko's micro-management and lack of confidence in his ability to do his job was not only a blow to his ego, it hurt. Not that Niko had been trying to ruffle him, but after the screwup with Jacoby Winters, it seemed like Niko had been on his ass more than normal. Sebastian couldn't remember being this closely supervised even when he first hired on at Black Stallion.

Niko swiped a hand through his hair and blew out a caustic breath. "Yeah. Sorry. We've got a lot riding on this. The Bahamas is our most expensive location shoot to date, and we need to end up in the black on this. You're sure about the rooms?"

"Checked and double-checked. We've rented out the whole facility, but the numbers worked out. With their private beach, we should be able to film a scene or two out there as well."

"Good, good."

"Between you and me, are you okay?"

Sebastian only asked because Niko was the least okay that he'd ever been since Sebastian had joined the company, and that Niko had seemed off ever since his breakup with Peter came as too much of a coincidence not to be part of the problem.

For the blink of an eye, Niko's guard dropped, and Sebastian's chest went tight at the flash of pain. "Is there something I can do?"

Niko's smile came across as more of a grimace. "No. A relationship blowing up is never fun. I need to focus on Black Stallion and ride the rest of the bullshit out. But thanks."

A knock came on the open door, and Sebastian's heart slipped and fell on its ass when he glanced up and saw Grant.

"Am I interrupting?"

"I was just leaving," Niko said. "Don't keep him too long. We start filming again in fifteen."

"I'll be quick."

Niko left, and Grant closed the door behind him, taking a moment before he turned and leaned against the door.

"You think that's a good idea?" Sebastian asked. "You and me behind a closed door?"

Grant smiled, but his eyes didn't brighten. "I've got a situation."

Sebastian stood. "Is it Tavi? Did the cops pick him up again?"

"No, nothing like that." When Sebastian gestured toward the chair in front of his desk, Grant remained standing, not venturing any closer, as if he needed the physical distance between them to spit out what he had to say.

"I need more work," Grant finally managed. "A lot more work. Even at my old rate, if you can swing it with Niko. I just... *fuck*."

Grant massaged the muscles at the back of his neck, his grip so tight he left red marks on his skin. "I'm in a bind, and I need a way out."

Coming around his desk, Sebastian said, "I've got money—"

Grant held up his hand, whether it was to fend off Sebastian's offer or whether it was to keep Sebastian from getting any closer, he wasn't sure, but he shut up and held his ground.

"I don't want your money or your handouts. I want the work."

"I thought you were getting out of the business."

"I am. Or was. Fuck, Bass, can you help me out or not?"

Sebastian leaned a hip against his desk. "Why don't you tell me what's going on?"

Grant locked his hands behind his head, his eyes closing. Sebastian wanted to move closer, to lay a hand on Grant's shoulder and tell him whatever the problem was, they could face it together, but that kind of intimacy and dependency might make Grant run.

A fast fuck didn't a relationship make.

As much as Sebastian wished otherwise.

"Just lay it on me." Sebastian snuck a glance at his watch. He didn't want Niko to come barging back in when he didn't show up on set in time.

Grant slid down the door until his ass hit the floor. He laid an arm across his knee and said, "My father swindled my grandmother, and if I don't pay back the home equity loan she took out on time, they're threatening to foreclose. She's on a pension. She's got nowhere else to go, and it's not like I've got another room at my place or that I can afford a bigger apartment."

The defeat in Grant's eyes nearly undid Sebastian. Here was a man who was doing everything he could to help the community and take care of his grandmother, and the universe kept coming at him with one fat sucker punch after the other. He didn't deserve that.

At a loss for words, Sebastian sat beside him and leaned against the wall. He could talk Niko into something, but would it be enough? And really, how many scenes could one man shoot?

Could Grant really fuck his way into solvency?

It didn't seem likely.

Sebastian took Grant's hand when what he wanted to do was wrap Grant in his arms and tell him everything would be okay. "I'll talk to Niko tonight. See what we can work out."

Grant stared down at their joined hands as if memorizing how well they fit together. "I'd understand if... you know... you don't want anything to do with me after this... I—"

"What the hell are you talking about?" Sebastian's heart didn't know whether it should skip along with glee or drop in his chest. On the one hand, it sounded like Grant wanted more, that maybe their one night together could become something. On the other, the defeat, the self-loathing, in Grant's voice, weighed heavy on Sebastian's heart.

Grant turned and looked at him. "My parents are..." It seemed that Grant had to search the memory banks to find the right descriptor. "...not good people..."

From what Sebastian had heard, that was likely a gross understatement, and if Grant needed help, Sebastian would be happy to come up with better, more fitting words.

"I come from them. I've gotta think that somewhere inside,

there's a part of my parents in me that's waiting for the right time to come out and destroy the ones I love the way they've tried to destroy me."

Sebastian tightened his grip on Grant's hand. "I don't care who or what your parents are, you're not that guy. Your grandmother is as much a part of you. She's goodness and light the same way you are."

"Yeah." Grant glanced away. The single word lacked conviction.

Sebastian stood and pulled Grant to his feet. "Go on. I'll talk to Niko and give you a call later tonight."

11

———

GRANT CUSSED THE TRAFFIC ON THE WAY BACK ACROSS THE VALLEY. On a Sunday, the traffic shouldn't have been that bad. He made it back to the Center to find the front doors locked, but the lights on in the back.

He had a niggling in the pit of his gut. The tattoo shop had closed by the time he got on the road, and the last time he'd talked to Vondra, she hadn't seen any sign of Tavi.

He knew he should have arranged to have Tavi picked up from the shop.

You know the kid lived out there on the streets until a week or so ago, and now you can't let him walk a mile by himself?

It wasn't the walk that concerned him. It was Tavi cruising one of the parks and running into another one of those assholes who got off on using Tavi as their personal punching bag.

He went into the Center, locking the door behind him. "Anybody here?"

"Art room," Vondra called out.

Striding to the back, he said, "Have you seen—"

He turned the corner and found Vondra, Tavi, and another kid he'd never seen before crowded around one of the art tables.

His stomach unknotted, and a sliver of anger slipped in over the relief. "Why didn't anyone tell me you were back?"

Vondra dipped her brush into the blue paint and leveled a gaze at Tavi. "I thought you said you called him?"

"I did, or I was going to, and then Remy showed up and..." Tavi glanced up at Grant, shrugging one shoulder. "Sorry, man."

Grant blew out a breath, letting the frustration dissipate. "You worried me."

Tavi went back to his painting. "You don't have to worry, I ain't even your kid."

"About that." Vondra dropped her brush into a cup of water and gathered her things. "Grant, Officer Brewer came by looking for you. Said he'd try to catch you after his shift if you're still here."

Grant immediately looked to Tavi, who held up his hands. Paint dripped onto the linoleum from his paintbrush. "I didn't do anything, I swear."

Remy laughed. "At least not that anyone can prove."

Tavi gave him a playful shove. "Shut up."

Vondra backed out of the room. "See you guys on Tuesday."

They all said their goodbyes, and Grant asked Tavi, "You going to introduce me to your friend?"

Tavi didn't look up from the poster board, his concentration on outlining the letter A with paint. "That's Remy."

The beefy black kid in a T-shirt, basketball shorts, and a ratty pair of sneakers a couple of sizes too big held out his fist for Grant to bump.

"I'm Grant," he said after rapping knuckles. "You new around here?"

Remy was quick to smile. "No, man. Tavi and I roomed together at the group home. Before they kicked him out."

Grant took Vondra's vacated seat and focused on Tavi. "You never did tell me why they kicked you out."

Remy's grin spread over his face, and he crossed the first two fingers of both hands, making a hashtag. "Hashtag, epic night."

A knock came on the door jamb, and Grant looked up. Connor stood in the doorway. "Vondra let me in. I hope that was okay?"

"Po-po's here. I'm out." Remy's mock horror made Tavi laugh.

As the teen passed by Connor, Connor said, "Keeping your nose clean, kid?"

"Clean enough," Remy teased.

Connor leaned into the hallway and called out after Remy. "I'm still waiting for that invite to one of your pickup games. I've got moves I can show you."

From the lobby came Remy's mocking laugh. "Old white dudes don't have game."

"Old white dude, my ass," Connor said as he stepped into the art room. "I don't know who he's calling old. I'm twenty-seven. I'm not even old enough to be his father."

"But twenty-seven is almost thirty and then..." Tavi's hand flew through the air in a steep, downward dive that ended with an epic explosion.

Connor chuckled. "Thanks, kid, you're great for my ego." Then he bumped his chin toward the posters. "What are you working on?"

"The Center's having a fundraiser." Grant handed Connor one of the fliers from the shelf behind him. "Carnival for the kids and a masquerade and bachelor auction for the adults. The kids from the Center are making posters to hang around town."

"I'll post this at the station. A lot of the guys have kids who'd enjoy it." Then Connor caught Grant's eye. "You got a minute?"

"I know you guys are gonna talk about me," Tavi grumbled. "You don't have to hide it."

"You keep painting," Grant told him. Vondra hadn't said what Connor had wanted to talk to him about, but the surprise on Connor's face said Tavi wasn't wrong. "And figure out where you want to go eat. We'll call Nana B and have her meet us for dinner."

Grant had left his keys in the door. On their way to his office, he relocked the door behind Remy. Dressed in his street clothes with his off-duty weapon under his shirt at his hip, Connor closed the office door behind them and took a seat in front of Grant's desk.

"What's up?"

"How are things with you and the kid?"

"You seem pretty invested in Tavi." Some of the cops in the area either turned a blind eye to the homeless kids or actively gave them a hard time. Grant found it refreshing that one took a personal interest.

A shadow flashed in Connor's eyes. "I'm invested in all these kids. My older sister's kid ran away. They found his body a month later. I try to take them under my wing when I can."

"I'm sorry to hear about your nephew."

"Thanks. Tavi reminds me too much of him, and I can't get him out of my mind. Have you thought any more about looking into fostering or petitioning the court for guardianship?"

Even though Grant knew the door was closed, he couldn't help glancing at it to be certain. "It's a big step. A huge commitment. I just—"

"But he's a good kid, right? I mean, some of them out there, I think they're too far gone, but Tavi is different. He's something special."

"He's been great, and he and my grandmother have hit it off. She's always been a go-getter, but he brings a spark to her life that I didn't know she lacked."

"That's good. See? Everyone wins."

If only Connor knew the truth, he might not be saying that. Not because Grant was gay, he didn't think Connor would have a problem with that. He certainly didn't seem to have a problem with all the LGBTQ kids he interacted with. But Grant wasn't going to get into the nitty-gritty of all the reasons why becoming a parent to a teen at this stage in his life wasn't the best idea.

Money—and the lack thereof—and his grandmother's housing situation, and Grant's deep dive back into porn notwithstanding.

"It's not that simple. If it were, I'd have gone to the court-house already."

Connor stood. "Well, think about it, will you?"

"Trust me, that's all I've been thinking about lately."

Grant showed Connor out, shaking his hand before he left. "Thanks for taking the time to check on us on your off time. I appreciate it."

"No problem. See you around."

He almost had the door closed when a voice said, "Hold up."

Sebastian jogged toward him. Grant held the door open, trying to ignore the way his breath caught when he saw Sebastian. "What are you doing here?"

Once inside, Sebastian slapped a hand over his chest. "*Jesus.* I either need to take up jogging or stop running."

"Why are you here?" It came out more accusatory than Grant had intended. When Sebastian raised a brow at him, Grant added, "I wasn't expecting you is all."

"I wanted to let you know I talked to Niko. He's going to get back with you in a few days and let you know what kind of work he can get for you."

"You could have called and told me that." Which sounded crappy, too. What the hell was wrong with him? Here Sebastian had driven across town to give Grant the good news, and he was being pissy. "Sorry. That didn't come out right."

What he wanted to say was 'In my office, now.' Then he'd tell

Tavi to turn the radio up, and he could do something about the ache in his balls and the stutter in his heart.

"Thanks," Grant said at last. "I appreciate you going to bat for me."

Sebastian took a step closer, and Grant couldn't take his eyes off the man's lips. Tavi came out of the art room. He and Sebastian jumped apart.

They must have looked as comical as it felt because Tavi grinned and said, "Am I interrupting?"

Sebastian recovered first. "You look better than the last time I saw you."

"No kidding." Then Tavi turned to Grant. "Is he going to dinner with us?"

"Umm..." The less time Grant and Sebastian spent together, the better. Grant couldn't be around Sebastian and not want a repeat of the night before.

A repeat of the mind-blowing sex, and so much more.

Sebastian waited for Grant's answer, a guarded expression on his face.

"Where we going?" Grant asked Tavi.

"Pizza. The one on Garza Street. Nana B's gonna be there in ten."

"Pizza?" Grant asked Sebastian. "Romano's is the best this side of the valley."

"Sure, why not."

"Awesome," Tavi said as he pushed through the door, "then you can tell me what Connor said about me."

———

Sebastian had expected two things when he'd walked through the Center's door, either Grant would tell him to beat it, or he would drag him into the office and pick up where they'd left off that morning.

He hadn't anticipated the invite to dinner.

Now, already on his third slice—because it *was* the best pizza that side of the valley, maybe even in the *whole* valley—he was having the best time.

Some of it had to do with sharing the narrow booth with Grant, their thighs glued together as they ate. The other had to do with the company in general. They laughed, they joked, they gave each other a hard time.

Like a real family.

If not an unusual one.

But he had learned early in his *out* life, that there were two kinds of family. Your biological family and, as Armistead Maupin said it, your *logical* family. The family you put together piece by piece until it was whole.

Sometimes there was overlap. Other times, there was none.

This isn't your family.

Didn't stop him from wanting it.

Tavi sucked on his straw, slurping up the last of his soda. The waitress came by with a refill, and after she left, Tavi said, "Are you going to tell me what the cop said about me?"

"Oh, dear," Nana B said, "what cop?"

Grant shoved the bite of pizza into the corner of his mouth. "Connor Brewer. He's the guy who brought Tavi to the Center."

"Well?" Tavi prodded.

"What did he say?" Grant's grandmother already had six crusts on her plate and went in for another slice. Where the hell had she put it all?

Grant dropped his pizza onto his plate and wiped his hands and mouth. Only the point of Grant's slice remained since he ate it crust first. Crust first? Who did that? Was he a closet psychopath as well as a closet gay?

A psychopath who'd given you the best dicking you've ever had.

"Okay." Grant's level gaze hit Tavi. "You say you're not a kid, so I'm going to respect that and not treat you like one."

Tavi stopped drinking his soda, the joviality at the table gone. "*Okaaay.*"

"Connor wanted to know if I was going to seek guardianship."

"You said yes, right?" Sebastian asked before he thought better of it. When Grant cut him a look, Sebastian said, "Sorry. Not my place."

"No, it's not that."

"Then what is it?" Tavi may not have been a kid by a lot of people's standards, the streets aging him more than the average fifteen-year-old, but in those four words, all the shellac of toughness vanished, and all of Tavi's vulnerabilities and insecurities welled to the surface.

Grant went silent as if trying to gather what he wanted to say in the most concise way. His grandmother nodded her encouragement.

"That's what I need to talk to you two about," Grant said, directing his words at Tavi and his grandmother. "I would like to seek guardianship, but there are some practical issues that could be a problem."

"Like what?" Sebastian asked because Tavi dropped eye contact and slumped in the booth.

"He can't live at my place because I don't have a bedroom for him—government rules—and I can't afford a bigger place."

"I have room," Nana B said. "Room for you and Tavi."

Grant pushed his plate away, the partial slice remaining. "Unless you lose the house. Then we've got nothing."

"Why would you lose the house?" Tavi asked.

Nana B patted Tavi's hand. "Nonsense. We're not losing the house, right?"

"Not if I can help it, Nana, but..." Grant cleared his throat.

"But I may not be able to pull it off. We have to prepare for that eventuality."

Sebastian didn't have a lot by California standards, but Niko paid him well. He had savings, and what was the purpose of having them if he couldn't spend the money how he chose? "I want to help. I have a rent house you can stay at, some money, and—"

Nana B sat back. "No, young man. We appreciate your offer. This mess is my doing, and I won't have you sacrificing your house and wasting your money on us."

"It's not a wa—"

Grant clamped a hand on Sebastian's knee, the grip firm enough to shut him up. But fuck it, he had a right to offer what he had.

"I won't take charity." Grant's ire clashed with his own. "I'm working on a fix. Right, Sebastian?"

Sebastian didn't know how much money Grant needed—a detail Grant refused to divulge either out of stubbornness or embarrassment. But in the time frame Grant had, even with the extra scenes he might pick up from Black Stallion, Sebastian didn't know how it would be possible.

Was it so wrong that Sebastian wanted to keep Grant and his family off the streets?

But pressuring Grant now wouldn't get him to change his mind. Changing the subject, Sebastian turned his attention to Tavi. "I heard you were at Pigments today."

The tension fell from Tavi's face, and Grant's grip on Sebastian's knee relaxed.

"How did you hear that?" Tavi asked.

"Truman is Cat's... boyfriend," Sebastian said. Lacking a more PG way of describing Cat's relationship with her Dom. "He told her you were there."

"What did you do today besides mop the floors?" Grant asked.

"I had to wipe down all the chairs, and Truman showed me how to clean some of the equipment, and how to run the autoclave. After lunch, he didn't have any appointments, so he asked to see my portfolio."

"Portfolio." Grant grinned. "Already picking up the lingo?"

Tavi rolled his eyes.

"Don't keep us in suspense. What did Truman think?" Nana B reached for the last slice. Sebastian almost looked under the table to see where she was putting it all.

"He almost busted a nu—" A swift kick under the table from Grant cut Tavi off. "I mean, he loved my dragons. Thought my geometric patterns on the scales rocked, and then he said he'd pay me to develop an exclusive script for the shop."

"Nice," Grant said. "I knew you had talent."

Nana B hugged him to her side and planted a smacking kiss to his cheek that he pretended not to like, but that stupid grin on his face told Sebastian otherwise. "I'm so proud of you."

Tavi wiggled out of Nana's clutches, the red running up his cheeks. "It's not like I cured cancer or sent a man to Mars. It's just pen and ink."

"Don't underestimate the power of art, Tavi," Sebastian said. "It's a gift you need to share with the world."

"There's only one problem." Tavi sank deeper into the bench seat and started playing with his straw wrapper. "Truman said I could only apprentice at the shop if I got back into school in the fall."

"Let me guess. You hate school," Grant said.

"It's not that." Tavi tapped his temple. "Not stupid, remember?"

Grant chucked a balled-up napkin at Tavi that landed in his lap. "Yeah, yeah."

"I couch surfed in the fall and stayed in school, but when my friends' parents got tired of me hanging around, I split. Haven't been to school since Christmas. I'm crazy far behind."

"I can help with that," Grant said.

"You gonna do my work for me?"

"Nice try, kid."

Grant's grandmother pushed her plate away, finally full. She leaned into Tavi, her voice a stage whisper. "Trust me, my Grant's a smart boy, but you're better off doing your own work if you want to pass."

"*Nana*."

She patted Grant's hand. "No one has a bigger heart, but let's face it, you almost didn't make it out of high school."

"I made up for it with perseverance."

Beneath the table, Sebastian threaded his fingers between Grant's. "I have a feeling the Center wouldn't be here without it."

"Who was this Cory dude, anyway?" Tavi asked. Sebastian was glad Tavi brought Cory up. He'd wanted to ask but didn't think it was his place, though he might have found a more delicate way of putting the question.

The mood at the table shifted, and under the table, Grant's fingers tightened around Sebastian's at the same time he heard Grant's sharp intake of breath.

Nana picked up the menu. "Who wants dessert?"

"I don't want dessert, Nana B." By the way Tavi refused to break eye contact with Grant, the only thing the kid wanted was answers.

"I hear their cherry pie is—"

"It's okay, Nana," Grant said, "It's a fair question."

Grant stirred the ice in his soda that had all but melted as he gathered his thoughts. "He was a kid a lot like you, in a way. Bold. Brash. A righteous sense of self. No closet was big enough to hold him, so he'd never even tried. He lived on the streets when his parents kicked him out and did what he had to to survive."

"It ain't easy," Tavi allowed. "But if you can find a group, it helps keep you safe."

"Cory never found that group. No one had his back, and when he wanted to get off the streets, he had a hard time finding a safe space or anyone willing to help."

Grant's voice faltered, and he swirled the straw faster and faster. Tavi's expression tightened, and darkness settled in his eyes. Cory's story probably wasn't much different than a lot of the street kids whose parents had disowned them.

Tavi rubbed at the vestiges of the bruise on his jaw but didn't interrupt the story.

"I ran into him at the park. The same night he disappeared. He was pumped. He'd met a guy who'd promised him a way out. It sounded too good to be true. But Cory wouldn't listen. He never did. Despite what his parents had done to him, he always saw the good in people. That naivete got him killed."

Nana swiped at her red-rimmed eyes with a napkin, and it looked like Tavi had forgotten how to breathe.

"They found his body two days later in an alley off Cardinal and Lark, behind a dumpster, buried under a pile of fu—" Grant winced and glanced at his grandmother. "...freaking garbage bags.

"Someone beat him so badly, he was unrecognizable. But when I saw the news report, I *knew*. I went down to the police station to identify him because his parents refused to, saying Cory was already dead to them. Dental records later confirmed his identity."

"That sucks," Tavi said, with an understanding and maturity that shouldn't have surprised Sebastian.

The look that passed between Grant and Tavi said they

understood each other on a level that should never have been possible if only the world were a better place.

"Check?" The waitress asked as she came by.

"Yeah," Grant said. "I'm done here." The way he said it, Grant didn't sound like he was talking about dinner.

Sebastian picked up the tab in the end. No way was he allowing Grant to pay when he knew the dire circumstances of Grant and his grandmother's finances. Not that a fifty-dollar meal would make or break them, but it was the only way Grant would allow Sebastian to help financially, and even then, it had been a fight.

They left the pizza joint and walked out to the parking lot. Tavi crawled into Nana B's passenger seat. Grant held onto the door and leaned in. "Before you go to Pigments in the morning, I'll give you a list of online high school programs that you can choose from that will help you get back on track with your schoolwork. Sound like a plan?"

"Yeah, tomorrow." Before Grant could close the door, Tavi said, "Thanks."

"You going back to school is thanks enough."

"That, too. But I was talking about... You know..." Tavi inclined his head towards the restaurant. "I get it now. Why you do what you do."

Nana volunteered to drop Tavi at Pigments the next morning, so Grant was off the hook for kid duty until the next afternoon.

Sebastian had followed Grant to the restaurant in his car. Grant walked him to his driver's side door, his mood dark and distracted as if his mind was still on the kid he hadn't been able to save.

Sebastian leaned against his car and pulled Grant between his legs, half expecting resistance, but found none.

Grant pressed his forehead to Sebastian's and said, "Come home with me?"

The request wasn't about sex. It was about comfort. "Don't want to be alone?"

"Not if I can help it. That okay?"

"That's more than okay. I'll meet you there."

12

———————

GRANT WAITED ON THE STEPS TO HIS APARTMENT FOR SEBASTIAN. Time ticked by, but still Sebastian didn't show. Had he changed his mind? Wouldn't be a surprise. It wasn't like Grant had been the best company that night. He wouldn't blame Sebastian one bit if he'd thought better of it and bailed.

He'd about given up when headlights turned into his complex. Grant stood and waited, feeling that little flip in his chest that was becoming all too familiar every time he saw Sebastian.

Sebastian parked and trudged up the steps with a paper bag tucked against his side. When he got even with Grant on the steps, he rubbed his thumb across the crease between Grant's brows.

"What's the matter? Did you think I ditched you?"

"Of course not." Grant climbed the stairs before Sebastian read the lie on his face.

"Wait." At the door, Sebastian stopped him with a hand on his arm. Grant turned to him. "You thought I wouldn't come when I said I would?"

"I wouldn't have blamed you if you hadn't."

Sebastian fisted his free hand in Grant's hair, the light bite of pain getting his attention before Sebastian's lips fell on his. Just a brush, and a hint of what they'd shared before. "I wanted to be here. I wouldn't have come otherwise. Okay?"

"Yeah. Sure. Whatever."

Again, that lick of pain at the back of his head. "I mean it."

Reaching up, Grant took Sebastian's hand and led him into the apartment where they collapsed on the couch. Only the kitchen light was on from when he'd left that morning. Sebastian dropped the bag on the coffee table and pulled out a couple of beers. He twisted off the top on one and handed it to Grant before opening his own.

"Trying to get me drunk?"

"It's not *the* answer," Sebastian allowed, "but it can be *an* answer. Drink up."

Grant didn't feel like talking, and Sebastian seemed content to let him be. Somewhere near the bottom of his third beer, Grant said, "Stay the night?"

"That sounds good." Sebastian stood and held out his hand.

"Now?"

"It's late. We both have an early day."

They abandoned their empties on the coffee table for the night, and Grant allowed Sebastian to drag him into the bedroom. With care, Sebastian helped Grant undress.

When Sebastian had stripped him down to his underwear, Grant said, "Those, too."

"We don't have to do anything."

"What if I wanna?" The petulance in his voice couldn't be helped after downing three beers in the time it had taken Sebastian to drink part of one.

"I'm not sure you're in any shape to—"

"I'm buzzed, but it's not like I'm too far gone to give consent."

"I'm not so sure about that."

Because the room swayed, Grant plopped on the bed and watched Sebastian strip. Maybe the beer had gone to his head more than he'd thought. Not enough to not want Sebastian, just enough to push the maudlin thoughts to the back of his mind. They could be paralyzing if Grant allowed it, and he thanked whatever gods that be that Sebastian—a very naked, very aroused, Sebastian—was there to take his mind off his failures.

Grant reached for Sebastian's dick, wanting it in his hands, his mouth... his ass, but Sebastian batted his hand away.

"Hey."

"Hey, what?" Sebastian tugged the covers from beneath Grant and planted his hands on his hips.

"I wanted that."

"Yeah? Well, that's not why I'm here."

"Why *are* you here?"

Instead of answering, Sebastian allowed Grant to pull him onto the bed. "I'm here for you."

"That the only reason?" Grant held his breath, waiting for the response. Wanting more than he cared to admit for the answer to be 'no.' He wanted Sebastian to be there because he *wanted* to be there, not because Sebastian felt like he had to be there.

Sebastian's answer was to wrap his arm around Grant's waist and pull him flush to his body, Sebastian's hard cock neatly settled in the crack of Grant's ass. Grant wiggled and settled deeper against Sebastian's groin.

Sebastian grunted. "Be good."

"Where's the fun in that?" Grant rolled to his back, loving the way Sebastian's leg fell across his hips, trapping his hard-on against his abdomen.

"What are we doing, Grant?"

The mellow buzz in Grant's head made it impossible to define. "Does it have to be anything other than two guys enjoying each other's company and giving each other satisfaction?"

The spark of what Grant thought might have been hope, dimmed. "No. I guess not."

Sebastian ran his fingers through the mat of hair on Grant's chest. The slow and deliberate slide south made Grant's abdominal muscles quake and his dick pulse beneath the confines of Sebastian's thigh.

Trailing a finger through Grant's precum, Sebastian sucked the tip of his finger clean. *Fuck, that was hot.*

So hot, that Grant forgot about Sebastian's PG-rated plans for the night and pulled him in for a kiss. His tongue snaking into Sebastian's open mouth, teasing and taunting him for more.

Way more.

Shifting, Sebastian rolled on top of Grant, taking the kiss deeper as their dicks aligned. Grant eased a hand between them, gripping them both at the same time, loving the contrast of having another guys dick in his hand. Breaking the kiss, Sebastian sucked in a breath, his breathing rapid as he rested his forehead on Grant's shoulder.

Grant stroked them both, and Sebastian shuddered. "Christ, that feels good. I can't get enough of your hands on me."

"My hands like being on you. There's no place they'd rather be."

Sebastian raised his head, that same spark of hopefulness there that Grant had seen before. Too bright and too hot to be mistaken for anything else.

Sebastian shifted away.

"Where do you think you're going?"

"I've got something to say, and I don't want you thinking I'm saying it because my dick is in your hand."

Folding a hand behind his head, Grant waited him out, not

sure if what Sebastian had to say would be anything he wanted to hear.

"I'm here in whatever capacity you'll have me. I'm into you." Sebastian glanced down at his own impressive hard-on, a self-deprecating smile on his face. "I can't hide that, even if I wanted to. But I know you have things going on. I may not like what that means about your ability to be out, but I'm willing to live with it if it means I can be with you."

"I can't ask that of you. You may not think so now, but you'd suffocate if I dragged you into the closet with me. I'm not worth it."

"Bullshit. And that's not your call to make. That's mine."

"So, what does this mean? You my boyfriend or some shit? Can we even call it that if no one else can know?"

"What we are to each other doesn't need defining for anyone else but us."

Grant let the word 'boyfriend' roll around on his tongue, decided he liked the taste of it. He'd never had a boyfriend before, only tricks, fuck buddies, and the straight guys at Black Stallion, who were great, but didn't count.

"Boyfriend?" Grant asked at last.

"Yeah."

"Then, as my boyfriend, there's something I want you to do for me."

Sebastian grinned when he caught the lascivious look in Grant's eye. "Name it."

Grant leaned in and whispered in Sebastian's ear. A grin split his boyfriend's face. "If that's something you're into."

"Oh, hell yeah."

———

If Sebastian had ever been that hard before, he couldn't

remember a time. Grant rolled onto his stomach, his whispered words played on repeat in Sebastian's head.

I want you to fuck me.

In all the scenes Grant had shot with Black stallion, he'd always been the top. Sebastian had assumed his boyfriend—what a trip *that* was, calling Grant Hardy his boyfriend—didn't bottom. Which had been fine with Sebastian. He preferred bottoming himself, but he had a touch of *top* in him that made him cum-drunk thinking of fucking Grant.

He couldn't dig the lube and condoms out of the bedside table fast enough.

Dropping the supplies on the bed beside Grant, he laid out on top of Grant's amazing body, with the long line of muscles bracketing his spine and the two perfect globes that wiggled beneath Sebastian's crotch. Sebastian ran his hands across both shoulders and followed the play of bulging muscles down Grant's arms until he linked his fingers with Grant's.

The muted mutter and soft sigh when Sebastian nuzzled Grant's neck and traced the curl of Grant's ear with the tip of his tongue sent tingles down Sebastian's spine. He wanted Grant more than ever, but he didn't want to rush it.

"If you don't hurry," Grant pressed that fine ass against Sebastian's dick, "I'm gonna—"

Sebastian bit the soft spot at the nape of Grant's neck. Grant yelped, but the rash of goosebumps skittering across Grant's skin told Sebastian how much it turned him on.

The warm chuckle deep in Grant's chest made Sebastian want to bundle him up, take him home, and never let him out of his bed...

Or his life.

But Grant wasn't his prisoner... He was Sebastian's boyfriend. The man he wanted to cherish and protect any way he could, but even as he thought that, as he eased down Grant's body, tattooing him with open-mouth kisses and nips and nibbles that made Grant grunt and groan, a part of him knew Grant wouldn't allow him that privilege.

Grant must have sensed a change in Sebastian's touch because he braced his weight on his elbows and glanced over his shoulder. "We don't have to do this. If you don't want—"

"*I want.*" Sebastian shook off the remains of his melancholy and focused on Grant, and the here and now, knowing what might happen later was completely out of his control.

What he could control was Grant's pleasure, and he intended to leave him spent and well sated.

With both hands, he kneaded the taut ass, running a finger down the crease. Grant flexed his hips as Sebastian's fingers skimmed over Grant's hole.

"Right there." Grant groaned. "Fuck me."

Sebastian nipped one cheek. "I plan to, but you're going to be begging for it first."

Whatever Grant's response was, Sebastian tuned it out as he spread Grant's cheeks and flicked his tongue across that tight bunch of muscle. Grant bucked up, pressing his ass against Sebastian's tongue, his hands fisted in the sheets, his body demanding more.

Raising to his knees, Grant allowed Sebastian easier access to his ass, his taint, his balls, his cock. Sebastian didn't leave an inch unlicked, untasted, the soft cries and muttered curses making his own dick weep with precum. Grant's balls drew up after Sebastian sucked them into his mouth, first one and then the other.

Going back to Grant's hole, he fucked him with his tongue and with a free hand, jacked him with the same force and rhythm.

"Jesus fucking Christ." Grant writhed, his hand covering Sebastian's as it gripped his cock.

Sebastian chuckled, loving Grant's response to him. He'd seen him in front of the cameras many times, had dreamed of bringing Grant to the edge and hearing that soft muttered curse and wanting to be the one who brought those words to Grant's lips.

Now, those pants, those cries, those curses were his own doing, and it almost brought Sebastian to the brink being the man giving Grant so much pleasure.

"Now." Grant shoved Sebastian's hand away from his cock.

"Are you begging, or are you demanding?"

"Both."

Sitting back on his haunches, Sebastian rolled the rubber down his dick and slicked himself, as well as Grant, unable to wait any longer.

He pressed his tip against Grant's entrance and sucked in a breath as he slowly eased inside.

Grant groaned, and it was the most glorious sound Sebastian had ever heard. It sounded like a prayer that had been answered, or maybe that was Sebastian projecting because all he wanted was the man beneath him.

This was where he was meant to be.

This was home.

Before he went balls deep, he pulled out almost all the way, drawing out his gratification, and by the way Grant reached a hand back and urged Sebastian on, drawing out Grant's as well.

Grant, the greedy bastard, couldn't wait. He slammed back, seating Sebastian to the hilt. They both groaned, and Sebastian hugged Grant around his waist, laying over the top of him.

"Fuck, I've missed that," Grant muttered.

Beads of sweat popped out over Grant's skin. Sebastian went in for a taste, the salt and sweat fueling his fire. "I love how you taste."

Grant didn't answer, but then he didn't have to. Sebastian

went in for another sample before rising on his knees and taking Grant's hips in his hands, the need to drive overwhelming.

"You ready?" Sebastian rubbed his hand over the two dimples at the base of Grant's spine.

"Been ready."

Before Sebastian could thrust into him again, Grant pushed back, again and again, not waiting for Sebastian, but taking what he wanted.

Sebastian wasn't content to let Grant have all the control. Gripping Grant's hips, Sebastian took over, quickening the pace and setting the rhythm.

"Fuck yeah." Grant matched his strokes, the pounding he took shook the bed and stole Sebastian's heart.

Sebastian would top all the time if it meant he could be inside Grant. The tight ring of muscles around his dick pulsed, drawing a long, low groan from Sebastian.

Grant was close, but the tingling at the base of Sebastian's spine said he was even closer. When his hips developed an erratic rhythm, Sebastian gave himself up to the ecstacy.

"Come," Grant demanded as he reached a hand between his legs and started pumping himself.

Two strokes later, Sebastian succumbed, shooting his hot load deep in Grant's ass, wishing they were fluid bonded and didn't have to have the barrier between them.

The thought of leaving his load, leaving a piece of himself behind to claim Grant as his was a dream too far.

Maybe. Someday.

Grant panted as he jacked himself furiously. Sebastian didn't want Grant to waste his load in his hand. Easing out, Sebastian flipped Grant onto his back and brushed Grant's hand away, taking him deep to the back of his throat as the first pulses of Grant's release hit.

Grant's hand went to the back of Sebastian's head, holding him in place, but Sebastian wasn't going anywhere.

Not now. Maybe ever.

Grant stiffened and cried out, and Sebastian glanced up to witness the ecstasy on Grant's face as Sebastian swallowed the salty load.

Sebastian pulled off before Grant got too sensitive, kissing his way up Grant's limp, sated torso, a mumbled word fell from Grant's lips that sounded remarkably like, "Mine."

Exhausted, Sebastian ditched the condom and collapsed against Grant's body as their breathing slowed. Sebastian had given up on his heart rate ever being normal again, since every time Grant looked at him it became erratic—Just this quivering ball of muscle in his chest pumping inefficiently, making his head light and his thoughts unclear.

From the vicinity of the floor and their tangled pile of clothes, a phone dinged. *Niko.*

"That mine or yours?" Grant managed, sounding half-asleep, though the lazy circles he traced on Sebastian's hip with his fingertip said otherwise.

"Mine," Sebastian grunted and pushed off the bed.

"Where you going?"

"It's Niko. If I don't answer, he's going to stay at it until he gets me. I've learned it's much easier to answer than go dark."

In response to the simple *call me* text, Sebastian dialed Niko's number. It wasn't often that Niko needed Sebastian that late at night.

His stomach did a slow noxious roll. What had he screwed up?

He waited for the call to connect, pacing the room naked, the sweat drying on his skin. The musk in the air made him want to crawl back into bed and take Grant all over again.

Racking his brain for what ball he might have dropped, he

came up with nothing, which should have made him feel better, but it didn't.

Niko picked up without so much as a hello and started in on some nonsense about the upcoming shoot in the Bahamas. Sebastian listened with half an ear because he'd been over and over everything they needed for the shoot, down to every last seemingly insignificant detail. The Bahamas was covered. Niko was just having one of his bouts of needless worry.

In all the right spots, Sebastian said, "uh, huh," and "yeah, sure," his attention falling away from the conversation and focusing on Grant.

Instead of lying there sated and satisfied and dozing through Sebastian's conversation, Grant covered his eyes with his arm, his body tense. Finally, Grant got up with a huff and disappeared into the bathroom, not meeting Sebastian's eyes and ignoring the hand he'd held out in passing.

What just happened here?

"Hey, Niko, I need to let you go."

"What about the catering?" Niko continued as if Sebastian hadn't spoken. The shower taps turned on in the bathroom, and the shower door opened and closed. "You know Hayes is vegan, and Preston has issues with gluten. And—"

"I've already got it sorted. Don't worry. I have to go. We can go over this first thing in the morning, promise."

Sebastian leaned against the door jamb to the bathroom, his eyes on Grant as he stood beneath the hot spray, head bent, hands on the tiles, steam billowing up.

All Sebastian could think was that he'd done something wrong or hurt Grant somehow, and he couldn't get rid of Niko fast enough to find out what it was so he could make it right.

"I'm hanging up, Niko. I'll talk to you tomorrow."

Niko was still talking as Sebastian hung up. He half expected Niko to ring him back, but his phone remained silent.

Sebastian climbed into the shower behind Grant, the hot water already turning cold. If they stayed in much longer, they'd freeze.

"Everything okay?" Sebastian placed a hand on Grant's hip. Grant jumped as if he hadn't noticed Sebastian slipping in behind him.

He reached for the soap, not bothering to turn around. "Why wouldn't it be?"

Stripping the soap out of Grant's hands, Sebastian scrubbed Grant's back like a nursemaid instead of a lover. "You tell me."

Grant turned around, his broad back blocking all the spray, but it wasn't the wetness of Sebastian's skin that brought a chill to his body. It was the bleakness in Grant's gaze. "This whole boyfriend thing? It's a big mistake."

As much as the wounded part of Sebastian wanted to slink away, he wouldn't let what could be a great thing with Grant go without a fight. Sebastian hitched his chin up and forced Grant to meet his eyes. "I don't agree."

Grant's expression soured. "Yeah, well, if this goes tits up, all you're out is a boyfriend."

But it was a big deal to Sebastian, and the way Grant's voice came out unsteady, it was a big deal to him, too.

"I'm the one who'll pay with my job at Black Stallion and with the banks. It's not worth the risk."

What Sebastian heard was, *You're not worth the risk.* Sebastian wasn't going to beg, he had more pride than that, but that didn't stop him from one last try. "I wouldn't say anything to Niko. You know that, don't you?"

"Not on purpose, maybe." But that was all the ground Grant gave. "I wish things were different, but they're not."

The sharp, jagged bone Grant threw Sebastian cut as he swallowed it.

"But they will be soon. Get things sorted with the bank, help your grandmother get back on track, and then you can forget about Black Stallion, about the fucking closet, and all we'll have to focus on is you, and me, and Tavi."

Grant blew out a breath, resting his forehead against Sebastian's. "Tavi, huh?"

Sebastian leaned back, swiped the wet hair out of Grant's eyes. "It looks like the two of you are going to be a package deal."

"It's looking that way, isn't it? I can't leave him on the streets. Not this kid. And you're okay with that?"

"I don't want him out there either."

Grant pulled him in for a scorching kiss that the cold shower had no chance of putting out. His dick responded as if it hadn't been in Grant not thirty minutes before.

"I—" Grant started. Sebastian didn't breathe, waiting for Grant to finish that sentence. "I think you're something special."

It wasn't the 'I love you,' Sebastian had thought might tumble from Grant's lips if the heated, possessive way Grant had looked at him were any indication. But it was something.

"I think you're something special, too."

13

———

GRANT ROLLED INTO THE MAKEUP ROOM AT BLACK STALLION A week and a half later, excited to see Darius Williams and Reynaldo Reyes sitting in Cat's chairs.

"The stud has returned to the stable." Darius jumped up from his seat, already finished with makeup, and pulled Grant in for a one-armed bro hug.

"Hey, man, good to see you."

There was a time not too long ago when Grant, Reyes, and Darius had shot many scenes together, and today would be a nice change from shooting with strangers—some of the young up-and-coming pups Niko had worked hard to cultivate.

A studio like Black Stallion relied on a constant influx of new blood, but luckily for Grant, demand remained high for him and the studio's favorites.

Reyes started to stand, as well. Cat clamped a hand on his arm and said, "You move, you die."

Sitting back, Reyes held up a fist for Grant to bump. "I've been in this chair since last week," Reyes grumbled as Cat pushed his head back and started plucking his brow.

"If you would quit being a baby, we'd be done by now."

"Ouch," Reyes hollered. "Be gentle with me, *chica*."

"You should have done this ahead of time, so I wouldn't have to."

Reyes waggled the brows Cat was trying her hardest to wrangle. "My girlfriend likes the natural look."

That didn't bode well. "Your junk better not be natural or Niko's going to have your ass."

"Me too," Darius said, "I'm not going to suck you off if you're so hairy I can't find your dick without a machete."

"Relax," Reyes said as Cat finished plucking and started styling his hair. "My lady likes everything high and tight down there. She's the one that shaves me."

Darius slapped his forehead with his palm. "I'm not gonna be able to get that image of Reyes's girl all up in his junk with a hedge trimmer out of my head. Where is one of those MIB dudes with the brain zapper when you need one?"

"Has anyone seen—" Sebastian came up short as he walked into the room. "Oh, hey." The wattage on his smile could have lit up the Las Vegas strip at night, and damn if Sebastian didn't make Grant feel eleven feet tall knowing he was the man who'd put that smile there.

Darius held a hand in front of his eyes. "Damn, dude, that smile's blinding. You off your fucking meds or something?"

"Can't a guy be in a good mood without being accused of being manic?" Sebastian tried to rein in his enthusiasm, but Grant knew how his boyfriend felt.

They hadn't seen each other over the last ten days except for a few stolen moments at the studio. Grant had been so busy with the Center and the upcoming fundraiser, and Niko had Sebastian working from sunup to late at night.

They'd texted, called, and jacked off together over video chat, but it wasn't nearly as good as seeing Sebastian in person.

What Grant wouldn't give to shoot with Sebastian instead of Darius and Reyes.

He thought back to the shoot with Kattan and how Sebastian had gotten off watching him fuck another dude. Maybe if things went south in the dick department today, the way they had with Kattan, Grant could get turned on thinking about Sebastian getting off watching him work.

"I need everyone on set in thirty," Sebastian said, going back into producer mode. "Hardy, if you could see me in my office beforehand, I've got something I need to go over with you."

Grant cleared his throat, going for his professional demeanor, but the smile he couldn't quite hold back kept returning. "Sure thing."

Sebastian left, and Darius glanced from the empty doorway to Grant. "Oooh, man. I think Sebastian took the one-way train to crush town."

Grant let the stupid smile he had for Sebastian slide off his face and took the seat Reyes abandoned. "I don't know what you're talking about."

"You're dreaming, dude." Reyes dropped trou right there in front of everyone and reached for the same name-brand, high-end business suit Darius wore. In the upcoming scene, Grant would be called in to 'service' the two businessmen.

Reyes was on the shorter, stockier side, while Darius was long and lean. Both sexy as hell in their own way, and Grant had fed off their sexual energy in the past. But neither one of them did it for Grant the way they used to.

Maybe Sebastian ruined you for other men.

Reyes buttoned up the dress shirt Grant would soon be ripping off. "Sebastian doesn't go after straight dudes. Not after Chucky boy left a boot tread on his heart."

"Charles wasn't straight." How Darius knew that, Grant had no idea. "He was a closet case."

"Same thing," Reyes said. "Neither is anything he wants."

How had Grant not heard about this? "I guess you two are the experts on Sebastian's love life?" Grant said, his words coming out chiding.

Reyes shouldered into his suit coat. "Yeah, well, Sebastian doesn't exactly make it a secret."

Grant met Cat's eyes in the mirror. She'd been oddly quiet. She couldn't hold his gaze, and at that moment, Grant's heart flatlined. She *knew*.

Or suspected.

Which was just as terrifying.

———

After Cat finished with him, Grant dressed in a pair of work coveralls, and popped a second Viagra for good luck, practically running the whole way to Sebastian's office knowing he only had a few minutes before he had to be on set.

He knocked on the closed door. It opened immediately. Had Sebastian been standing next to it the whole time? Waiting? Sebastian gripped Grant's arm, yanked him into the office, locking the door behind him. "Hello."

"Hi, yourself."

That's as far as Grant got into the room before Sebastian pressed him into the wall and devoured him with a kiss, their tongues fighting for dominance. When they came up for air, Sebastian grinned up at him.

"You called me in here for that?"

"No." Sebastian unzipped the work coveralls, and seconds later had Grant's dick in his hand.

Grant's head fell back and thudded against the wall, the sweet pain a welcome contrast to the intoxicating bliss of Sebastian stroking him.

Then Sebastian sank to his knees and took Grant into his mouth. All rational thought fled. As much as he wanted Sebastian to stay on his knees all day sucking him off, he had work to do. But he couldn't bring himself to make Sebastian stop.

Best fluffer ever.

"Fuck me," Grant said as Sebastian pulled off with a *pop*.

"No." Sebastian tucked Grant away and zipped him up, his hard-on spilling out of the *King Dong* jock he wore for the camera. "Next time, you're fucking me."

Oh hell yeah.

Grant reached behind his back and unlocked the door. "Can I see you tonight?"

Sebastian pulled a face. "I hope so, but with the uptick in production, I'm having a hard time staying ahead of Niko's shooting schedule."

Grant gave him a quick peck on the lips, wanting much more, but knowing he'd have to wait. "Call me."

"I will."

Opening the door, Grant backed out and bumped into a solid wall. Hands grabbed his arms to steady him.

"Oh, hey, Niko..." Grant's heart slammed into his chest, and the raging hard-on Sebastian had given him, vanished. "... I was just..." *Letting your nephew suck me off.*

This was why you didn't take your boss's nephew as your boyfriend when your livelihood depended on you being straight. It was just a matter of time before you got caught.

THE SHOOT WENT... WELL, IT WENT. THAT'S ALL GRANT COULD say about it. And now it was done. *Thank fuck for that.* And despite the double dose of Viagra that made Grant worried about all those things the fast talkers in the commercials warn users about, he'd survived.

With all the scenes he'd been shooting lately, and his long hours at the Center he tried to chalk up his dick's performance issues to exhaustion, but deep down, Grant knew better.

The only way he'd been able to maintain an erection was when he thought back to Sebastian's mouth around him in Sebastian's office. Even then, they'd had to stop filming multiple times.

Still in his robe, Grant sat at the back of the studio, his elbows on his knees, his head hanging, trying to gin up the energy to follow Darius and Reyes up to the showers.

Sebastian, Vin, and Rose set up for another shoot between a couple of guys Grant had seen around before but didn't really know.

A hand lightly clapped him on the shoulder. He must've dozed off because he glanced up to see Darius and Reyes return to the studio freshly showered and dressed and headed straight for the refreshment table, laughing and cracking jokes the way they always did.

Beside him, Niko took a seat. "Everything okay?"

Though far from okay, the only answer he could give Niko that was closest to the truth was, "Why wouldn't it be?"

"You tell me. I want to help if I can."

If Niko only knew the truth, he wouldn't feel the same way. He'd be the first one showing Grant the door. As generous as Niko had been scheduling Grant more work, he felt guilty taking advantage of Niko's generosity. Over the years, the director had always been good to him.

"You've helped plenty. I appreciate it. I'm sorry for all the..." Grant waved vaguely at the set and then at his lap.

"The limp dick?" Darius supplied, walking by with a devilish grin.

Niko glared. "Not helpful."

Reyes elbowed Darius in the ribs. "Dude, everyone is entitled to a one-off bad day."

Only Reyes didn't know the truth of it. Grant's limp dick issues were becoming the norm, not the exception, and chasing them seemed self-defeating.

"Will you idiots leave him alone?" Sebastian walked over, followed closely by Vin.

Great. Just what Grant needed was half the studio standing around discussing his dick.

"Uh, oh." By the devilment on Darius's face, Grant knew he wouldn't like the next thing out of Darius's mouth, but like an impending train wreck, Grant seemed powerless to stop it. "Looks like Sebastian is going all mama bear. You got a secret thing for our boy, Sebastian?"

"I'm out of here." Grant stood as the rash of heat crawled up the back of his neck.

He left the others arguing behind him without a backward glance, too afraid his face would give him away if he stayed. He wanted to tell Sebastian to drop it, because the more he argued with Darius, the more into Grant Sebastian seemed.

Or maybe it didn't.

Hell, Grant didn't know anymore. His paranoia of their relationship being discovered only intensified with the due date on the upcoming bank loan.

He might pull off the impossible if he could make it to the last scene with Kattan. If the numbers were right and he kept his expenses in check, he'd have just enough to pay back the past due payments plus penalties and save his grandmother's house.

Voices rose. Grant turned. Darius and Sebastian were chest to chest, all humor and teasing gone, Sebastian red in the face, and as close to coming to blows as any man he'd ever seen.

Vin grabbed Sebastian's bicep and said something Grant

couldn't hear. Sebastian got impossibly redder and shoved Vin back a step and turned his frustration and animus on one of his closest friends. "At least I don't have a secret hard-on for my boss."

Vin stilled. Darius glanced from Sebastian to Niko and back again. "Oops. *Awkward.*" Reyes elbowed him again.

Sebastian slapped a hand over his mouth, but the words were already out and had inflicted their damage.

"What the actual fuck, Bass?" Though Vin didn't deny a word of it.

"Vin?" Niko put a staying hand on Vin's arm.

Grant didn't stick around for any more drama. This was why he should have called things off with Sebastian from the start. The man couldn't keep a secret. It was only a matter of time before Sebastian blurted out theirs.

Sebastian found Vin in the production room later that evening, leaning back in his chair, his eyes closed, his hands behind his head. All the lights were off, and the video he'd been editing paused.

Normally, Niko could be found in the room with Vin, making sure the cuts were to his satisfaction, but it was Vin's genius editing and his camera work that made the productions shine.

Niko should have been there, but he'd left right after their last scene of the day with a muttered excuse about some meeting Sebastian knew he didn't have.

Unless Niko had some hot new Grindr hook up, but that wasn't usually Niko's style unless he was desperate.

Sebastian knocked on the open door. "If I come in, are you going to deck me?"

Vin didn't even spare him a glance. "I should."

Taking his chances, Sebastian squeezed past Vin's outstretched legs and plopped into Niko's chair.

"I'm really sorry."

The glow from the video monitor cast harsh, cutting shadows across Vin's face. "I deserved it. That 'puppy love' comment I made was outta line."

"You still didn't *deserve* it. I can talk to Niko—"

"No." Vin sat forward. "It will be awkward for a bit, but we're all adults here. Once he sees I'm not perving on him, things will go back to normal."

"Is that what you want? Things to go back the way they were?"

Vin went off somewhere in his head, and it took a nudge from Sebastian's knee to bring him around.

Finally, Vin said, "It's not what I want, but Niko's never going to see me as anything more than that snot-nosed street kid he pulled out of the alley ten years ago. In his mind, I'll always be off-limits."

Vin's smile fell short, but he looked like he'd given it considerable effort. He clapped Sebastian on the arm. "Who knows, maybe this is the kick in the ass I need to put him behind me and move on."

"So, he's not 'the one?'"

"I don't believe in 'the one.' There's plenty of men out there that are close enough that I can round the fuck up to *one,* and hopefully they can do the same for me. I've just got to make my peace with what will never be and get out there and find him."

"You will. You're a fucking catch."

Vin's eyes rolled as if he thought otherwise, but he turned and pressed play and went back to work, cutting off further conversation.

Sebastian stood to leave. "So, we good?"

With a dismissive wave of his hand, Vin didn't bother taking his focus off the screen. "Yeah, we're good. Though I'm taking a rain check on that offer to deck you."

"Fair enough."

In the hallway, Sebastian checked his phone, but the text and the call he'd sent Grant had gone unanswered. Even if Grant hadn't wanted to text while driving, he'd had plenty of time to get back to the Center and respond to Sebastian.

The cold cut sandwich Sebastian had scarfed down between shoots churned in his stomach, leaving no doubt in his mind that Grant had heard him blurt out Vin's secret during a brain fart moment. Knowing Grant's fear of him reveiling their secret relationship, Sebastian kept an eye on his phone, expecting the worst.

But no response was almost worse than a bad response.

Sebastian drove home, every turn, every mile, a damn battle not to head straight to the Center and confront Grant, but if Grant needed his space, he'd give it to him.

Grant knew where to find Sebastian when he wanted to talk.

14

———

The next day, Grant stared at Sebastian's text from the previous night: *Can we talk?*

They could talk, but to what end? Too much rode on the secrecy. As much as he wanted Sebastian, not just for a midnight booty call, but as a man, a boyfriend... a life partner, Grant's heart, and his intimate relationships must take a backseat.

He had his grandmother depending on him. And now Tavi as well. Because as days went on, Tavi no longer loomed as a question, he'd become a done deal.

Just not legally yet.

But Grant had a lawyer friend working on that pro bono.

Until then, it was imperative they had a place for them to live. It did Tavi no good if Grant couldn't provide shelter.

A Nerf ball landed in his lap. Grant glanced up to see Tavi standing at his office door.

"You didn't hear a word I said, did you, old man?"

"*Old man.*" Grant fired the ball at Tavi's head. Tavi ducked behind the jamb at the last second, laughing his ass off.

He popped his head back into the office. "Too old. Too slow."

It felt like ages since Grant had cracked a genuine smile, but

Tavi always seemed to drag one out of him. As each day passed, as Tavi's self-esteem and confidence grew, he bloomed, smiling and laughing more, acting like a big brother and mentor to some of the younger kids that came through the Center.

A day didn't go by that Truman at Pigments didn't send a text or photo showing Tavi hard at work.

Tavi was making a place for himself in the community, building his logical family where his biological one had failed him.

Tavi walked into the office. "Why do you have that sappy look on your face? Have you been watching those stupid kitten videos again?"

"No videos," Grant allowed. "I'm proud of you is all."

The red bloomed on Tavi's cheeks, but Tavi being Tavi, he didn't quite know how to hold on to the complement, so he deflected. "You been drinking? It's not even five o'clock."

"No, but I'm sure you'll drive me to drink eventually."

Tavi grinned, cheesy and chipper as if making Grant an alcoholic was a good thing. "Grab a chair. I want to go over the different high school programs you emailed me."

Grant pulled up the email and links to Tavi's top three online high school programs he'd selected from the possibilities Grant had given him. They clicked through all the links and Tavi showed Grant his top choice. It was the lowest-rated, the cheapest, and the most basic of all the programs.

"You sure that's the one you want?"

"Something wrong with that?" The smile vanished, and Tavi leaned back, the gears clicking, clacking, and churning as Tavi cranked up his guard. "Besides, it's all I can afford on what Truman is paying me."

"Truman's paying you?"

"He said I worked so hard I deserved something. But it's not much."

Wait. Tavi thought he'd have to pay for the program? Then again, Grant had never made it clear that he would foot the bill. The Center's scholarship programs weren't in place yet, but somewhere along the way, he'd assumed financial responsibility for Tavi. He wanted to slap himself for the miscommunication.

But if Tavi knew the truth, that Grant would pay, would he tell Grant the one he preferred? Probably not.

Grant came at it from another direction. "If money wasn't an issue, which would you choose?"

Tavi pointed to the last link. "That one."

"Why's that?"

Taking the mouse, Tavi clicked on the link. "A lot of their classes you can also get college credit for, and here…" Tavi clicked on a list of coursework, clicking through to the art department and their figure drawing classes. "This class can count as one of my humanities credits."

"You should sign up. If that's what you want, I'll spot you the money."

"Seriously?" Tavi looked dubious and excited all at the same time. "I can pay you back. I can come here after Pigments closes and mop for you, and do the evening cleaning, and—"

"You already do most of that. If you did more, when would you do your classwork?"

"For those classes, I'd find the time."

"Let me worry about paying. You worry about getting good grades. Deal?"

Tavi bumped Grant's fist, fighting his over-sized grin to keep his cool-teen cred intact. "Deal."

Tavi glanced at the clock on the wall. "Shouldn't Sebastian be here by now?"

Grant's heart staggered, then ran at the mention of Sebastian's name. He willed it to slow, but it refused. "What are you talking about?"

Beneath raised brows, Tavi stared at him with benign patience as if Grant had gone brain dead, and he was waiting for what few neurons that remained to kick in.

Fuck. Was it Thursday already? Grant groaned. "The fundraising meeting is tonight?"

"Yeah." Tavi dragged out the vowels, the *you dumbass* clear even if Tavi didn't utter the words. "I wanted to show him the signs Remy and I made for the carnival games, and we're supposed to start decorating the masks for the masquerade. Vondra even skipped class tonight to help, and Remy got permission from the home to stay out past curfew. Nana B promised she'd drive him back after."

The more Tavi's excitement grew, the more Grant's stomach floundered until the lunch he'd had threatened to come back up. How was he supposed to break it to Tavi that Sebastian wouldn't—

The bell clanged on the front door, and Sebastian called out. "Where is everybody?"

Tavi jumped up and stuck his head around the door jamb. "Office."

By the scuff and tap of Sebastian's dress shoes on the floor, he was already headed their way, greeting Tavi with some convoluted, complicated, crazy handshake Grant couldn't possibly memorize. "Hey, kid."

"The art room is set up as soon as you're ready."

"Be right there. I need a word with your fearless leader."

Tavi made tracks, and Grant said, "Leave the door open."

Sebastian closed the door and leaned against it. "Not until we talk."

"*Bass.*" A warning and a plea.

Sebastian crossed his arms over his chest but didn't move any closer. Grant almost reached behind him and turned on the fan on the wide windowsill behind him. Where had the air gone? Maybe he needed to get the Center's AC serviced again.

"You don't get to *Bass* me. Not when you're not even talking to me."

Somewhere between Black Stallion and the Center, Sebastian had lost his tie, if he'd had one to start. His collar lay unbuttoned with the sleeves rolled up his forearms, looking as fuckable as ever, even with a disapproving scowl on his face and the trace of dark circles under his eyes.

"Maybe you should call it a night. Go home. Get some sleep. Looks like you could use it."

Sebastian approached, and Grant backed up in his rolling chair until the wall blocked his escape. Sebastian leaned in, his hands on the chair's armrests, his voice ball-tighteningly low. "Niko's not the one making me lose sleep."

Grant caught himself before he could admit the same. Sebastian straightened and took a step back. A nanosecond longer and Grant would have pulled Sebastian onto his lap and considered never letting him go.

Sebastian sat on the edge of the desk, close enough for Grant to reach out and ruin everything with a stray touch.

"Maybe you should go." Those words ripped up the back of Grant's throat, and he wanted them back as soon as they were out because, in reality, he wanted the exact opposite. He wanted Sebastian to stay and never leave.

"Not here for you. I'm here for the kid and the fundraiser. You don't want to talk to me? Fine. Don't talk. I know you're scared."

"I'm not scared. I'm *terrified*."

But just when he was about to tell Sebastian he couldn't take them being apart, that he'd take the chance on him because he *was* worth it, Sebastian said, "I know. I get it. I fucked up. I lost my cool and Vin's secret slipped out. I'll always regret putting

Vin and Niko in an awkward spot. You and Tavi and Nana mean too much for me to risk exposing you, too. So, I'm staying away. For now. Except for the fundraising and your shoots at Black Stallion, I'll stay out of your way."

Grant nodded.

At least one of them was thinking clearly. Sebastian leaned in, touching his lips to Grant's, too fleeting for arousal and too damn depressing as a goodbye. "Call me when this is all over if you're still interested."

Grant closed his eyes, his throat constricting. It wasn't that Grant wasn't interested. He was falling headlong for Sebastian—pitching, plunging, fumbling, stumbling, tumbling.

A disorienting, humbling realization.

Grant opened his mouth to tell Sebastian so, but that's not what came out. "I've got an old set of clean gym clothes you can wear. I don't want you getting paint, glue, and glitter on your good clothes."

———

SEBASTIAN WALKED INTO THE CENTER'S ART ROOM, TIEING THE strings on Grant's athletic shorts. They were a size too big and threatened to swallow him whole.

It took everything in his power not to bring his face to the sleeve of the Nirvana T-shirt he'd borrowed and try to get a good whiff of Grant's intoxicating scent. Even though the clothes were clean, he could still smell Grant on the fabric, making what he'd told Grant back at the office even harder to take.

Sebastian had been the one who'd fucked up, and he couldn't blame Grant for not trusting him to keep their relationship a secret.

Just as well. Keeping his emotions in check at the studio and holding back in public had been increasingly harder to control as his infatuation with Grant grew into this tangible, all-consuming need to have him in his life.

Sebastian was bound to destroy it, no matter how well-intentioned.

Sebastian found Tavi and Remy alone in the art room with no sign of Grant or Vondra. "What's that you're working on?"

Tavi turned his sketchpad around and slid it across the five-by-five work surface. It stopped within Sebastian's reach.

"Truman called a friend at the SFV art museum. They're sponsoring an art contest during the masquerade judged by their curator. Winner will get their art framed and hung in the gallery for a month. The theme is 'family.' It's not done yet, but that's going to be my entry."

One glance at the drawing and Sebastian's heart stopped, his gaze flicking to the AED device mounted on the wall in the hall. He just might need it to jumpstart his heart.

His fingers ghosted over the page, not wanting to touch, but to feel the emotion in each fluid stroke of the charcoal pencils, the scene a snapshot of him, Grant, Nana, and Tavi that night at the pizza joint—a fly on the wall view.

Even Remy was there, though he hadn't been there at the time. Artistic license that conveyed so much.

What that fly would have seen was Grant's head thrown back and laughing, the indulgent smile on Nana's face, Tavi's happiness in the upward slash of his grin, and the tight grip he had on Remy's hand. But what confounded Sebastian the most was Tavi's depiction of Sebastian, the obvious love in his eyes as he stared at Grant. Even back then. How could Tavi have seen that, much less captured it, so clearly in black-and-white?

Could everybody see the emotion there, playing on his face, or was he reading into what he'd just come to realize he felt?

But perhaps the most profound discovery was that Tavi considered *him* part of his new-found family. Throat tight, he glanced up at Tavi, at the shy smile on the teen's face, and the unguarded expectation in his eyes. "Beautiful work."

"No kidding?"

"Totally serious. You amaze me."

Remy nudged Tavi with his shoulder. "Told you it was fly."

Sebastian bumped his chin at Remy. "What about you? You have an entry?"

"I can't even draw a stick figure."

"Yeah, but you should read the stories he writes. Dude's gonna be famous one of these days."

"You guys ready to get some work done?"

Everyone turned as Grant and Vondra walked into the room.

Sebastian rubbed his hands together. "Let's do this."

Several hours later, when they were elbow deep in glue, masks, paint, and sequins, Nana let herself into the Center, carrying a bag of late-night Chinese take-out.

The same take-out Grant had bought Sebastian when he'd come to the first fundraiser meeting. It seemed forever ago.

Sebastian glanced at Grant and caught him staring at the containers. Was he, too, remembering that kiss, the way their bodies and their attraction couldn't be denied?

They washed up as best they could and settled in the Center's kitchen to eat. Sebastian had detoured to the restroom, and when he returned to the kitchen, all the seats were taken. Tavi jumped up. "Sit here."

The kid took his food and boosted himself up on the counter leaving the seat next to Grant empty.

If this were some evil plot by Tavi to get them closer together, his expression didn't show it.

Sebastian remained suspicious even as he sat down and dished out his food.

Nana ate a piece of sweet and sour chicken with her chopsticks then waved them between Grant and Sebastian. "What's the matter with you two?"

"Nothing," Grant responded all too quickly.

And Sebastian's silence said too much.

"Lover's spat." Tavi giggled, not knowing he'd stomped all over the truth.

"You wish." Remy saved Sebastian from answering while Grant choked on his udon noodles. "Wanting a family doesn't make it so."

"Har, har. We're not together." At least that was Sebastian's assumption. Shortest relationship of his life, but it had still been the best because it had felt real and genuine. Neither of them had intentionally played any head games, which had made their epically short time together that much more refreshing.

The sex didn't suck either.

Grant grunted in agreement, or because the slap of the words hurt, Sebastian couldn't determine. Remy continued to eat like a kid who didn't know when he'd have such a treat again.

Nana took it all in, the awkwardness, the furtive glances Grant shot Sebastian's way.

"We just have a lot on our plates." Which, in Grant's defense, wasn't a lie even if it wasn't the truth.

"It's my fault," Nana said. "You're working too hard because of my mistakes and—"

"We've been through this, Nana." Grant's sympathetic eyes belied his harsher tone, and Sebastian blamed himself for only adding to Grant's stress.

Everyone around Grant kept screwing up, and he barely had his head above water while everyone dragged him under.

No doubt, Grant would go down before he would let go and let anyone drown.

All the more reason to give Grant his space.

———

IT WAS AFTER MIDNIGHT, ON WEDNESDAY—ACTUALLY, EARLY Thurdsay morning—his final shoot with Kattan hours away.

And the day before the bank payment was due.

Sitting in his apartment at his kitchen table, with a stack of scratch paper, a calculator, his bills, and his bank statements, Grant had gone over the calculations.

Again.

After Niko paid him, and he paid the bank, he'd have two hundred dollars to his name. Maybe he shouldn't have let Tavi pick the most expensive high school curriculum.

Grant couldn't sleep, could hardly eat. He set his money issues aside and ran through some of the last-minute checklists for the fundraiser coming up a week from Saturday.

The games for the kids had been finalized, the always brilliant Vondra had started a social media campaign that had netted the Center some print and television attention, and it was looking like the carnival, the masquerade, and the live auction would be a big draw—thanks also to Sebastian and Niko's connections in the film industry helping to pull some of the B-listers in.

Sebastian...

Fuck if he couldn't get that man out of his head.

Maybe if you stopped jacking off to every memory you have of him, it might help.

While he told himself his countdown to repaying the bank would give him the breathing room he needed to get his grandmother's housing secure, the truth was, while he hadn't lost sight of securing his Nana's future, the biggest reason for that countdown in his head was Sebastian.

He'd vowed to stay away from Sebastian until the bank

papers were signed. Then he was coming out. No more closet. No more denying his true self.

No more life without Sebastian.

Who's to say he'll still have you?

Besides a nod of acknowledgment when you showed up for the shoots, you've had no contact.

And certainly no back office, pre-shoot blowjobs.

Grant scrubbed a hand down his face. His corneas felt like someone had poured a bag of gravel under each eyelid. Even his whiskers hurt as they scrunched beneath his fingers.

He glanced down at the countdown app on his phone. The one that ended when he walked into the bank at nine on Friday morning.

Thirty-three hours, twenty-six minutes, and nineteen seconds until he could beg Sebastian to take him back. He tossed down his pen.

Fuck it.

He couldn't wait until then.

15

———

"COMING!" SEBASTIAN DIDN'T KNOW WHO STOOD ON HIS FRONT porch pounding on his door in the middle of the fucking night, but someone was about to get their ass kicked.

He swiped his phone off his nightstand and checked for an emergency call or missed message, but nothing on his screen explained the racket at his door.

Flicking the hall and porch light on, he stared through his peephole.

Grant.

The knocking stopped, and Grant spun away from his door only to come back again.

"Open the fucking door." Grant's voice carried through the door, but barely, as if he knew Sebastian stood just on the other side with his heart rate jacked, his nerves on edge, and his emotions in an impossible tangle.

Sebastian put his hand on the lock, knowing if he opened it, he might be making the biggest mistake of his life.

This wasn't like the time in high school when he'd gotten blotto drunk and called the school's football team a bunch of homophobic cocksuckers to their faces.

The bruises then had healed, even if he did still have the small scar on his chin where the quarterback's punch had knocked him to the ground.

This time, if he went against his better judgment and opened that door, he might not survive it.

The deadbolt clicked to unlock, though he hadn't made the conscious decision to let Grant in.

The knob turned in his hand, and the door banged into Sebastian, his body-blocking it from opening.

"Let me in." Grant's chest and feet lay bare. He came dressed in only a holey pair of sweats that should have made a one-way trip to the dumpster a decade ago.

"Not a good idea."

As much as he wanted to throw the door open and invite Grant in, he moved to close it. It hurt too damn much to be living in that limbo space between being in Grant's life and being out of it.

He should have listened to Grant when he said Sebastian would suffocate being pulled into the closet.

But Sebastian hadn't been thinking straight.

Having Grant drill your ass would screw up anyone's sense of self-preservation.

"Please?" With his hair sticking up, the multi-day rash of stubble on his face, and the bags under those bloodshot eyes, Grant looked about to break, and Sebastian didn't have it in him to stand there and watch him shatter.

Sebastian stepped back, following Grant back into his den, scooping up the two-day-old pizza box and the empty beer-can pyramid he had working on the coffee table.

But the den was as far as he was willing to let Grant into his home.

And into his life.

Sebastian crossed his arms over his chest, only now becoming aware that he stood before Grant buck-ass naked.

Grant scanned Sebastian's body, taking in every inch of him, his perusal more wistful than superheated.

Sebastian planned to brazen out his nakedness. After all, it had been Grant who'd barged into his space in the middle of the night, silent and brooding.

But... Even as Sebastian stood there stewing in his hurt and dismay, his body stirred, and it pissed him off that Grant continued to have that effect on him despite the rift between them.

"I—"

Sebastian held up his hand, and Grant swallowed whatever he'd had in his mind to say next. "Wait here."

He waited a beat for Grant's nod before disappearing into his bedroom and scrounging around for his cutoff sweatpants, finally digging them out of his hamper, giving them a cursory sniff, and slipping them on.

The sight of Grant sitting on his couch, his elbows on his knees, his head in his hands, had Sebastian pulling up short in the doorway of his bedroom, not even willing to let his mind question what Grant was doing there.

Because to question was to hope.

And hope brought heartache.

He had half a mind to tell Grant to fuck the fuck off and shove him out the door.

But that wasn't possible.

And not only because Grant had the advantage of height and muscle.

All those glorious muscles.

Stop. It.

No matter how difficult it would be, Sebastian decided to hear Grant out. Clearly, they were both hurting, and the fact that

Sebastian wasn't blameless in their dilemma had him walking down the hall and sitting in the opposite corner of the couch.

Grant sat back. Sebastian's brain couldn't tap into all the scorched feelings and knowing that he'd played a part in his own misery by being unable to keep his fucking mouth shut.

Methodically, his reptile brain clocked and cataloged every fine detail of Grant's exposed torso from the cut of his ribs, to the hard planes of his pectoral muscles, to the baby smooth skin on his chest that he must have freshly shaved for the shoot with Kattan in the morning.

Grant caught his eye... And him staring. A dimple flashed with the half-smile before vanishing again.

Sebastian grabbed the T-shirt off the back of the couch that had probably been there for a day or so and tossed it to Grant.

"Put that on."

Grant turned it right side out and fingered the tag. "It's not my size."

"Just put it on." The 'please' unsaid but flashing in bright neon with his tone.

Doing what Sebastian asked, Grant slipped the shirt over his head. Sebastian had to lean over and tug the back of the T-shirt down because it fit so tightly.

Sebastian's T-shirt hugged Grant the way Sebastian wanted to.

Every crease.

Every curve.

Every cut.

Fuck.

"Better?" Grant flattened the wrinkles over his chest and lifted his brow, that damn dimple teasing Sebastian in all the worst ways. Sebastian put his hands in his lap because the cut-off sweat pants hid *absolutely* nothing.

"Yeah," Sebastian croaked.

Grant's knowing gaze called Sebastian a fucking liar.

"Well?"

Sebastian couldn't take the weighty silence, and he willed himself not to fidget. Or say fuck it and peel the too-tight shirt off Grant's body, pull the sweats down his hips, and do something useful with his mouth besides apologize again.

Leaning forward, Grant planted his elbows on his knees and stared at or through the television hanging above the fireplace. "I love you, Bass."

If Sebastian had a set of jet packs or one of those jettison buttons the fighter planes had, he couldn't have launched any farther out of his seat.

"The fuck?"

Sebastian landed somewhere over by the front windows, the blinds open, the sky still dark beyond. He assumed the earth still spun because the ground beneath his feet tilted precariously, threatening to dump Sebastian on his ass. Though he doubted the fall would hurt, not when those words made his nerves zing and his mind numb.

Maybe he should click on the news. Maybe the earth shaking was the 'big one,' and Grant and Sebastian and the rest of California were about to disappear beneath the ocean in one horrific, catastrophic slide.

He stood stock-still, waiting for the ground to open and swallow him whole, but when that didn't happen, he had to face the brutal reality of Grant's admission. "Why would you say that?"

Grant's declaration of love didn't change anything. Did he think it would make Sebastian feel better about their breakup? Well, it didn't. It felt like Grant had dangled the biggest, juiciest, fattest fucking carrot in front of his face and yanked it away at the last second.

Grant eyed him as if he feared Sebastian would run out the

door, leaving a human-sized hole through the solid core door. "Because it's the truth."

The statement came out more like a question.

No long ago, Sebastian would have welcomed the revelation, but now? It felt like Grant had reached inside his chest and ripped his heart out for shits and giggles.

"Would you say something?"

How could he say something when there was this huge fucking hole in the middle of his chest?

Sebastian did the only thing he could. He went to his front door and held it open, his words a harsh, scraping whisper. "I think you should go."

"That what you really want?"

Sebastian only nodded because if he opened his mouth, he feared the truth, a 'no,' would tumble out.

Grant stood and stepped to the door, obeying. But instead of walking out, Grant reached past Sebastian, placed his palm on the door, and eased it closed. The latch clicking into place clanged as loud as a church bell in the silence.

Caging Sebastian in, with his hands on the door on either side of Sebastian's head, Grant stood as close as he could without actually touching.

Sebastian had nowhere to run, nowhere to hide from Grant's piercing gaze. "Look at me."

Sebastian could no more ignore that order than if Grant had gripped his chin and forced his gaze upward.

Grant waited until he had Sebastian's full attention before he said, "I'll leave..." Sebastian locked his hands behind his back to keep from putting them on Grant and preventing him from walking out that door.

His leaving was for the best.

"... if you tell me you don't feel the same."

That close, Sebastian smelled the heady trace of sweat on Grant's skin. Felt the warmth of Grant's breath on his neck.

Sebastian closed his eyes, his head falling back and thunking against the wall, the lick of pain bringing him back to himself enough to say, "Don't do this."

The words came out as a plea. Sebastian didn't care. Grant had stripped him to his bones. He had nothing else to hide. There came no shift in air pressure, no let up on the zap Grant's closeness put on Sebastian's ability to think straight and defend himself against what he wanted more than anything.

But Grant didn't play fair. He hadn't budged an inch. Sebastian opened his eyes. Grant gazed down at him as if Sebastian were his entire world, his everything.

Ducking his head a fraction—which was all it took when two people practically occupied the same space with only a few scattered electrons, protons, and neutrons keeping them apart—Grant kissed the corner of Sebastian's mouth.

A breath, a whisper of a touch, almost heartbreaking in its tentativeness and tenderness.

A sound ripped from the back of Sebastian's throat, and whatever control he had escaped his body with it.

When Sebastian reached for him, Grant cuffed Sebastian's wrists with one large hand, and pinned them to the door over Sebastian's head.

Grant took the kiss deeper, Sebastian going where Grant led, the tether light, intangible, but nearly stronger than titanium steel. Their bodies only touched at their hands and their lips, but Sebastian had never felt so connected.

Sebastian's lungs labored, and his dick grew heavy. He was *so* gone for this man that the next sentence came out of his mouth before he had a chance to censor it. "How long have you known?"

"Had an inkling for a while now." Grant's words came out low and intimate. A shiver skittered across Sebastian's skin even as sweat broke out over his brow. "Not only because of the way you've welcomed Tavi and Nana into your life but because of the way you make me feel, the way you've wormed your way under my skin—"

Sebastian chuckled. "You make me sound like a parasite you can't shake."

"I'm trying to be serious." But Grant couldn't hide the grin.

"Sorry."

Taking one of Sebastian's hands, Grant flattened the palm on the center of his chest. "You're in here, too. That beat you feel? You're the only one that trips it up and makes me feel crazy unsteady and categorically unbalanced and stone-cold centered all at the same time."

That was all fine and good, and poetic as fuck, but what did that mean? "What are you trying to say?"

He pressed a kiss to Sebastian's palm. "That I'm sorry. That I've been an ass. That I've been running scared. That I want you."

Grant pressed Sebastian against the wall, the hard, magnificent length of him grinding against Sebastian's cock. "I want us."

What Sebastian wouldn't have given to have heard Grant say those words before. But as much as Sebastian believed that Grant meant what he said, Sebastian couldn't see where, fundamentally, anything had changed.

A quick nip to Sebastian's bottom lip brought him out of his head. "But I didn't *know* know, not for sure, not until tonight while I sat at home, unable to sleep, or exercise you out of my mind—"

"Now I'm a poltergeist? A demon?"

Grant snatched Sebastian's chin, not hard, but firm, a note of correction in his touch, and kissed him fully and deeply, all dark emotion and light touch. "If only it were that simple."

Sebastian chuckled. Grant didn't.

"What do you want from me?"

"Time. Another chance. Not that I deserve it. But I want that messy, confusing family—you, me, Nana, Tavi—"

Grant broke off, apprehension in his eyes and sweat beading on his upper lip.

Sebastian rested his forehead on Grant's shoulder, drained. Grant's arms came around his head, holding on tight. The pulse at the base of Grant's neck thumping, thumping.

"Say something." Grant's vulnerability became entrenched, deep down in Sebastian's soul, in a place Sebastian had considered unreachable. "*Anything.*"

Sebastian wanted everything Grant offered, but at the same time, Sebastian knew he couldn't dare allow himself to hope because his conditions for their relationship moving forward seemed untenable.

Reaching up, Sebastian took Grant by the wrists and stepped out of his embrace. A muscle popped at the corner of Grant's jaw, and fear—or was that panic?—flared in Grant's eyes.

"I can't take this *I'm in, I'm out* dynamic. It fucks with my head. I can't concentrate at work. Niko's on my ass like a teenager first discovering he's a top, and I can't..."

Sebastian broke off to gather his thoughts and find the unambiguous words he needed to make himself perfectly clear. He held Grant's brittle gaze. "I can't take the back and forth. Either jump off the cliff and let me catch you or turn around and don't..."

Sebastian swallowed the rest of the words that were too large and cutting to speak comfortably. But he *had* to get them out. "... and don't come back."

He leaned against the wall needing the extra support because his lungs forgot how to expand and what little oxygen that remained couldn't locate his brain.

Grant's smile came slow and so devastatingly bright, Sebastian's heart had to put on shades.

"As soon as I sign those bank papers on Friday and Nana's house is secure, I'm out. For good. Out of the closet. Out of porn. And Niko and Black stallion will be a tiny blip in my rearview. I don't care who knows I love you. I'll shout it from the fucking rooftops, take-out billboards, hire one of those stupid planes to fly a rainbow banner all over the goddamn valley if I have to. Name it. I'll do it."

Friday morning. A little more than a day to wait to have the man Sebastian wanted?

Don't forget, Charles promised you the moon and left you with nothing but a fistful of stardust and broken dreams.

But Grant wasn't Charles.

Did Sebastian dare?

"You really love me?" God, Sebastian hated the uncertainty in his voice. Hated that he needed to hear those words again.

"I do."

Maybe it wasn't Grant that had to leap and let Sebastian catch him. Maybe Sebastian had to take the fall.

Sebastian took Grant's hand and started backing towards the bedroom. "Prove it."

———

GRANT ALLOWED SEBASTIAN TO STEER HIM INTO THE BEDROOM. HE knew he was walking. He could see his legs moving, his bare feet hitting the floor, but he felt like he floated. The words Sebastian said to him rattled around in his head, looking for a place to land.

Prove it.

Grant would gladly do just that if he could ever get Sebastian's too small shirt off his back. The fabric clung tight. Grant suspected Sebastian would either have to cut or chew it off of him.

After being apart for the past few weeks, Grant didn't have the patience for a slow tease. As soon as they entered the room, Grant's hands found Sebastian's hips, guiding him backward until his calves hit the bed.

They both took hold of Grant's shirt and ripped it off over his head, chucking their sweatpants in quick order. He was pleased to find Sebastian hard and leaking precum.

Reaching down, Grant took that cock in his hand, liking the way Sebastian's head fell back, the muttered curse dropping from his lips sounding more like a prayer.

He gave Sebastian a shove, knocking him on his ass on the edge of the bed. Sebastian's mattress was extra thick, making it the perfect height to take him right there.

Sebastian must have had the same thought because he said, "Don't move," and leaned over and grabbed a condom and lube from the bedside table.

Wasting no time, Sebastian ripped the wrapper with his teeth and covered Grant's cock, giving him a few hard, fast strokes. "I want you in me."

"What? No foreplay?" Grant teased, though it had been all he could do to wait that long to be inside the man he loved.

Phew. The man he loved. Heady words that made his heart sing and his head light.

Don't fuck it up.

Not the sex part. The relationship part. Emotionally, Grant stood on the edge of the abyss, staring down at all the ragged, jagged places he could fall and get demolished.

But no risk, no reward.

And with the reward as enticing and exhilarating as having Sebastian in his life, how could he not jump?

"You still with me?" Sebastian laid his hands on Grant's hips.

"I am."

Sebastian grinned up at him, the light from his bedside lamp skipping across his features and playing up the mischief in his gaze as he reached for the lube and slicked up Grant's dick.

"What are you thinking about?" Grant asked.

"You really want to know?" The shy, unapologetic smile made Grant think of all sorts of delicious things, all with Sebastian at the center.

With a palm in the middle of Sebastian's chest, Grant laid him back and followed Sebastian down, his cock grazing against Sebastian's taint and slicking up his hole. Grant squirted more lube on his fingers and reached between them, making sure Sebastian was good and ready.

Grant flicked his tongue across one of Sebastian's flat nipples and watched it pucker and peak. "You gonna tell me? Or do I have to torture you in the best, worst possible way?"

Sebastian's eyes flashed, and Grant clocked that thought for future mining. Looked like Sebastian might have an interesting kinky side.

But Sebastian started talking before Grant had a chance to explore that option.

"I was thinking about your shoot with Kattan in the morning."

That was not where Grant thought Sebastian would go with that. Then again, Sebastian had been the one jacking himself off to his and Kattan's first scene. Intrigued, Grant stood and traced his open palm down Sebastian's belly, wanting to see the heat and desire in Sebastian's eyes as the man he loved unspooled his fantasy.

"I'm thinking about how I'm going to watch you fuck him, but this time I'm going to know what it feels like to have you in me. I won't have to imagine it."

"It doesn't bother you to see me with him? Especially now

that we're together?" Grant picked that moment to press into Sebastian's hole, loving the way it stole Sebastian's breath and forced a groan up the back of his throat.

Sebastian blew out a breath as he bared down on Grant's cock, taking him deeper. The grip Sebastian's ass had on Grant had Sebastian's eyes fluttering closed.

"Fuck, no."

Grant chuckled, watching as Sebastian reached down and started jacking himself. What a stunning, seductive, erotic sight having Sebastian on his back, with Grant between his legs, balls deep in the tightest, finest ass...

He didn't want to be anywhere else.

"Besides," Sebastian said between half pants and enraptured moans, "while he'll have your body, I've got a piece of you he'll never have. Your heart. How can I be jealous of that?"

On an inward stroke, Grant fell forward, catching himself on his forearms on either side of Sebastian's head, Sebastian's hard-on jabbing him in the stomach.

"I don't deserve you."

"No," Sebastian said. All hint of humor fled. "That's where you're wrong. You deserve this. And we deserve each other. No reason why we aren't allowed to be happy, too."

Grant kissed him then, turning it deep and tender at the same time. No matter what Sebastian said, Grant found it hard to believe he deserved such a sweet, caring, brilliant man. But he'd take him.

He pulled out slowly and drove back in, Sebastian gripping his hips as the cry of pleasure rang through the room. He would never tire of hearing Sebastian call out.

How did he ever get this lucky?

"I love you," Grant said again, the words thick with emotion.

Sebastian's eyes had rolled into the back of his head. He

opened them and focused on Grant. A smile, one-sided and with a faint curve of his lips. "I could get used to hearing that."

It wasn't a profession of love, but Grant would take whatever Sebastian would give him. Sebastian wrapped his arms around Grant's neck and pulled him in tight to his chest, Sebastian's breath warm in his ear when he said, "Now shut up and make me come."

And as much as Grant didn't want the night to end, Friday couldn't get there fast enough.

16

—————

"All good?" Sebastian asked.

Grant wanted to laugh. Stupid question, but he didn't hold it against Sebastian.

It was midafternoon on Thursday at Black Stallion, and he and Kattan were in the middle of their shoot that should have been over an hour ago if Grant could have stayed hard for more than twenty seconds at a time. How Niko hadn't completely lost it on him, Grant didn't know, especially with what he'd agreed to pay Grant for those scenes.

Kattan walked into the Ready room, buck-ass naked and looking like a God, all muscled and olive-skinned. The epitome of tall, dark, and handsome. But to Grant's dick, it meant absolutely nothing.

Traitor.

"Mind if I have a few words?" Kattan asked Sebastian more than Grant.

Sebastian stepped back, but his hesitation in leaving felt protective, if not a little misplaced. It wasn't like Kattan was going to hurt him, but Sebastian still didn't move.

"It's okay. I'll catch up with you after."

"Yeah, sure."

Sebastian left, but not before giving Kattan a look that said, *Don't fuck this up.*

Kattan slowly closed the door before turning around and facing Grant.

"So, you and Sebastian?"

"Are friends."

Kattan nodded. Whether he believed Grant or not was questionable. Not that Grant cared at this point. If he could get his dick to work and get through this scene, get paid, and make it to the appointment with the bank in the morning, then the whole world could know how he felt about Sebastian.

"It's okay, man. Don't sweat your disappeared dick. Everyone can have an off day."

Grant's laugh spilled out without a lick of humor. "More like off *month*." And in a moment of openness he wouldn't usually have with a guy he barely knew, Grant added, "I don't know what the hell is wrong with me."

Kattan glanced at the closed door and back at Grant as if he knew what—or rather *who*—the problem was, but he wasn't going to be the one to say it.

"I've got something that might help." Kattan dug around in the backpack he'd laid in the corner earlier that morning and came up with an amber bottle.

He rattled the pills and handed them over to Grant. There was no label indicating what the pills were. Grant drank alcohol, but he didn't do drugs, not even recreationally. He eyed Kattan with suspicion. "What are they?"

"Not sure they have a proper name. I get them overseas from a guy."

That didn't make Grant feel any better. "And what are they supposed to do?"

"Make your dick hard as steel. Trust me. Works every time. And the orgasms... holy fuck. Outta this world."

Kattan hadn't had any issues staying hard for any of the scenes he'd shot with Grant. Even now, he remained half erect. At one point, that sight would have been enough to keep Grant hard for as long as necessary, but Grant had come to reluctantly admit that it wasn't *any* dick that he wanted, it was *Sebastian's* dick, as well as the man attached to it.

Grant chuckled. "You think you can take me like that?"

"I can take whatever you can give me." It came out as both a promise and a challenge.

The two Viagra Grant had taken earlier hadn't done a damn thing, so what did he have to lose? Grant popped the top and shook out a couple of pills into his hand.

"A guy your size," Kattan said, "better make it three."

Grant took another, threw them to the back of his throat, and swallowed them dry. "How long do I have to wait?"

"They're pretty fast-acting. Ten, fifteen minutes, tops."

Grant bumped his chin. "Thanks."

"Yeah." Kattan reached for the door handle. "I'll see you out there."

One thing about Kattan, he hadn't lied. Grant had waited the fifteen minutes before pulling up the pictures on his phone that Sebastian had sent him—dick pics and still shots from some of the video feeds of them jacking off earlier on those nights when they couldn't be together but didn't want to be apart.

Between the new drugs, the photos, his imagination, and his right hand, Grant walked out of the Ready room and back on set, fully prepared to kick ass, or fuck ass, as the case were.

His heart rate had kicked up a notch, maybe two, but with the pills, he figured that was expected.

———

SEBASTIAN WATCHED FROM THE SIDELINES. THERE WASN'T MUCH else for him to do during the filming. Most of his job happened behind the scenes. He should probably get back to his office and get some more prep work done for the upcoming Bahamas shoot.

Some of the talent still hadn't sent him their passport details, and despite what he'd told Niko the other day, he wanted to double-check with the caterers that the dietary restrictions he'd sent them had been taken into consideration.

But if Niko thought that Sebastian would be anywhere else besides right there, watching Grant plow Kattan, he didn't know him as well as he should have.

Cat came around the corner to watch as well, one of the perks of the job Sebastian supposed if you were into that sort of thing, which Cat definitely was.

She found him and stepped over, nudging him with her shoulder. "Grant seems to have found his groove."

No lie. It took everything Sebastian had not to reach down and adjust himself in front of her. But considering she'd been the one to find him with his dick in his cum-covered hand the one time he'd let himself indulge, it shouldn't have bothered him.

"He has."

And by the grunts and groans coming from Kattan, and the way his eyes rolled back as Grant pounded into him, Kattan was enjoying the 'groove.'

With Grant behind him, Kattan reached between his legs and started jacking himself, close to the edge. And the way Grant gripped Kattan's hips, the skin blanching beneath Grant's tight hold and the erratic, almost frantic, rhythm Grant had settled into, he would only be a few strokes behind Kattan.

"Fuck, yeah," Kattan bit out, using the hold he had on the

edge of the desk to push back against Grant, taking him deeper still.

With a guttural grunt, Kattan spilled into his hand, the cum shooting out from between his fingers.

Fuck, that's hot.

That Grant and Kattan were such sought-after performers wouldn't come as a surprise to anyone who saw them in action.

The exquisite strain on Grant's face made Sebastian wish he'd been the man to put it there. That was where his jealously began and ended.

But you will have all the time in the world to please him after tomorrow.

And have Grant all to himself.

Though Sebastian wouldn't be opposed if they invited a few special guests to their bed for a three-way now and then. He'd have to talk to Grant about that. Make sure they were on the same page.

And if Grant wasn't?

If he wasn't, Sebastian could live with that. What he couldn't live without was Grant.

"You seem happy."

Cat's observation pulled Sebastian out of the moment, and he took his focus off Grant long enough to give her the side-eye.

He hadn't confirmed what Cat had suspected, but she still knew. Considering Grant planned on coming out in less than twenty-four hours, Sebastian didn't see the point in denying anything. He didn't have to be worried about Cat telling anyone. Her lips were sealed tighter than a CIA operative on a world-saving mission.

"I am. We—"

Cat's eyes went wide, and the horror on her face made his heart skitter to a stop. At Niko's shout, his heart kicked back in.

He turned to find Grant on the ground, seizing. Vin dropped his camera. Niko and Rose ran onto the set.

"Call 911," Kattan hollered out as he kneeled beside Grant.

Sebastian pulled his phone out of his pocket, but his fingers fumbled with the keypad. Cat yanked out her phone and punched in the emergency number.

As he ran for Grant, he heard her say, "This is Black Stallion Studios. One of our guys is having a seizure."

Vin had pulled the furniture back to make room and to keep Grant from hurting himself. Sebastian shoved his way past Rose and dropped to his knees at Grant's side.

Cat must have asked a question because Niko said, "Yes, he's breathing."

Sebastian's heart stumbled. He hadn't even known that Grant not breathing had been a possibility.

Grant writhed on the ground, fully in the seizure's iron fist, his lips pulled back in a frightening grimace, his muscles tight, his eyes rolled and locked into the back of his head.

OhGod, ohGod, ohGod.

"Why's he doing this?" Sebastian asked, not that he'd expected an answer. None of them were likely to know anything more than he did. As far as he knew, Grant didn't have epilepsy, but short of STI screening results, it wasn't like they'd divulged their medical history while they'd been fucking.

Kattan stood back, giving room to the rest of them. Sebastian's gaze cast around, looking for answers he didn't expect to find, then Kattan's eyes locked on his.

Sebastian's stomach free fell twenty floors and hit bottom with a shock that shook him to his marrow. "What?"

Kattan broke eye contact, and Sebastian jumped up. If Kattan had had clothes on, he would have taken him by the collar and shook the answers out of him.

One of Kattan's muscled shoulders went up and down, a half

shrug that somehow came across as apologetic. "I gave him something to help him out."

"What was it?" Now Kattan had Niko's attention as well. Grant was still seizing, but it didn't seem as violent or strong.

Please, God, let him be okay.

"A supplement I got the last time I was in Doha. Just a little something to help with his boner. It's supposed to be all-natural. I figured it couldn't hurt, right?"

Fuck.

"Arsenic is natural, tetrodotoxin is natural—"

"Tetro what?"

"Tetrodotoxin. From the pufferfish?" *Shut the fuck up, Sebastian, that's not what's important.* "Just because something is natural doesn't mean it can't hurt you."

Vin stood and stepped between Sebastian and Kattan. Kattan wiped the spittle off his face from Sebastian's rant. "Hold up, dude. Nobody tried to hurt him. Yeah?"

Vin had to take Sebastian's head in his hands and focus his gaze on him before Sebastian would take his eyes off Kattan. He knew Kattan hadn't tried to hurt Grant, and he knew it had been Grant's decision to take whatever the fuck he took. Kattan had been only trying to help.

"What else is Grant taking?" Vin asked, now that he had Sebastian's attention. In the distance, Sebastian heard the sirens. It wouldn't be long until the paramedics arrived.

"How should I know?"

Vin lifted a brow at the unveiled hostility. "I'm not the enemy here."

Sebastian's gaze flicked to Kattan.

"Neither is he," Vin was quick to add. "Get Grant's bag. Go through his things. See if you can find what else he's taking, if anything, so we can let the paramedics and doctors know."

Sebastian didn't want to leave Grant, even for the few

minutes it would take for him to search through Grant's things, but Vin put pressure in the middle of his chest, pushing him toward the back hallway. "Go. We've got him."

Grant still hadn't regained consciousness, and Sebastian knew he could do more good getting the information they needed than kneeling there holding Grant's hand the way he wanted to.

By the time he got back from searching Grant's bag, he had to run to the studio's back door where the paramedics were loading Grant into the ambulance, the straps tight around his body to keep him from falling off the gurney if he started seizing again.

They locked the gurney's wheels down in the ambulance, and Sebastian started climbing into the back. The paramedic put his hand on Sebastian's shoulder. "Can't let you—"

"He's seizing again," the other paramedic said the same way you might order your morning coffee.

"We gotta go. You find anything?"

Sebastian held up a bottle. "Viagra. That's it."

"How many did he take?"

"No clue."

The paramedic's lips went flat, and if he hadn't been a professional, his eyes might have rolled. "Meet us at Pacifica Hospital."

"John," the paramedic in the ambulance said to his partner, this time, the tension in his voice clear. "We gotta go, man."

Sebastian hopped down. John slammed the back doors, and the ambulance took off, lights flashing and sirens blaring.

Sebastian sprinted for his car.

He couldn't lose Grant. Not this way.

———

Sebastian drove to the hospital in a near panic, running lights, taking corners too fast, and using his horn liberally. He lost count of how many times he'd been flipped off.

He pulled into the drive-through of the emergency room. When the security guard saw Sebastian hadn't brought in a patient, the man told him to go park.

Parking was tight and spaces non-existent. Just when Sebastian had decided to abandon his car and let it be towed or stolen if that were his only options, a car's reverse lights came on, and Sebastian whipped into the empty space and bolted for the emergency-room doors.

A woman stood in line ahead of him at the nurses' station, a toddler in her arms with tears streaming down, his little face all red, his nose bloody, and his cheek scraped up.

Sebastian had the decency and self-control to not shove the poor woman aside and get the answers he needed. When the woman took the clipboard with the admittance forms and walked away, Sebastian bellied up to the counter.

"The ambulance just brought a man in. Grant. Grant Hardy. Where is he? I need to see him."

The woman clicked through multiple screens.

"Is he here? Is he okay? Is he alive?"

All they needed to do was tell him something, anything.

"He's here," the woman confirmed.

"Can I see him?"

"Who are you?"

Fuck. "Look, if I could see him. It doesn't have to be for long, just so I can see for myself that he's okay, that—"

"Are you related?"

Fuckity fuck fuck.

He guessed it didn't matter that he outed Grant to the nurse. It wasn't like she knew him or cared. Sebastian swallowed hard, the truth at the tip of his tongue. "I'm his boyfriend."

He took a step back, and a strong hand caught his bicep as he bumped into another person. Sebastian glanced up at the man beside him. *Niko.*

"What the fuck, Bass?"

What the fuck, Bass?

Sebastian didn't have time to contemplate Niko's question, though the twist in the pit of his stomach told him Niko's reaction wasn't good.

"I can't let you back there," the nurse said.

"But—" How could he get it across to her that Grant would want him there? That they were together? Sebastian gripped the edge of the counter, his knuckles going white as the frustration and the anger and the worry boiled inside. His face went hot with everything he held back. "Look, lady—"

The nurse's eyes shot toward the security guard standing just inside the door. The man straightened and started their way. Niko turned Sebastian toward the waiting room chairs and said, "We'll wait over there."

Sebastian shook Niko off, but Niko got in his face. "Sit your ass down. You won't do Grant any good if you're cooling your jets in jail."

Sebastian allowed Niko to guide him to a blue vinyl chair. It had a tear in the seat, but he didn't much care. Sebastian's fingers fisted in his hair, his head held in his hands. He vaguely became aware of Niko taking the seat beside him.

"You know of any family we can call?"

"He has a grandmother. And an almost foster kid."

When Niko just raised a brow, Sebastian said, "It's in his records back at the office."

Yeah, Niko didn't believe him for one second. "Hand me your phone."

Sebastian handed it over, his brain in a fog. Why hadn't

someone come out to talk to them? Was Grant dead? Was that it? *Fuckfuckfuck.*

"Your passcode?"

He stared at Niko like he'd spoken a foreign language. "What?"

"Passcode?"

"Uh..."

Niko started typing anyway. After a couple of tries, he must have got in because he said, "1234 is *not* a secure password."

The look he shot Niko made his uncle say, "Yeah, I know. Now's not the time."

He thumbed over to Sebastian's contacts. "Who do I call?"

"Nana B."

Niko pressed 'call,' but Sebastian couldn't follow the conversation. All he could think about was Grant.

And the words he'd blurted out to the nurse: *He's my boyfriend.*

Maybe Niko hadn't heard. There had been a lot going on, the baby had been crying, and the hubbub of voices in the near-capacity waiting room could have covered up what he'd said.

Yeah, right. That's why Niko had said, 'What the fuck, Bass?' You can't lie to yourself. He heard. And don't think he won't bring it up again.

Niko dropped the phone in Sebastian's lap. "She's on the way. Fifteen, twenty minutes. I'm going to grab a cup of coffee. You want anything?"

Sebastian shook his head. No way he'd be able to get anything past the stricture in his throat. And even if he'd managed to get anything down, the way his stomach pitched and lurched and heaved, the coffee wouldn't stay put more than a second or two.

He didn't know how long he sat there with his heart in his throat and his head in his hands before Niko sat back down and laid a hand across his back and squeezed his shoulder. "So... You and Hardy, huh?"

A thread of aggravation ran through the words, but Sebastian also picked up on the compassion as well.

"He was going to tell you." There was no point in denying it now, so Sebastian didn't.

"Tomorrow... after he got paid for the shoot." Niko didn't own a successful porn studio because he was slow on the uptake.

The truth came tumbling out. Sebastian couldn't hold it in any longer. He told Niko about the bank foreclosing on Nana B's house. About Tavi. About the Center. Everything. Including Grant's and his relationship. Not the nitty-gritty details, he hadn't lost complete control of his faculties, but close.

"What are you going to do?" Sebastian feared the answer, though he knew what it would be.

"You know I have to fire him, right? You more than anyone else at Black Stallion knows what's at stake if we don't abide by the rules we set up for the company. There's a reason our viewers pay a premium for our videos. We can't let them down."

The pause weighed heavy on Sebastian, more was coming, and his nerves fired and pinged, waiting for what Niko would say next. "I should fire you, too. If you weren't my brother's kid—"

Sebastian chuckled—a hollow, caustic sound that ripped through his vocal cords, cutting off whatever else Niko had been prepared to say. A few people in the waiting room glanced their way. The toddler even quieted his crying for a brief, relieving moment before it began wailing again. *Mother of God, would someone see to that kid?*

"Do what you've got to do. I don't care anymore."

Sebastian was officially out of fucks to give. Niko and Black Stallion could kiss his hairy, Greek, gay ass for all he cared. He'd like to see how the Bahama shoot went without him there to run roughshod over the whole event. Without him there to manage the talent, the production schedule, the host resort, and countless other things that always popped up threatening to derail a shoot. If Niko got one scene shot, he'd be lucky.

The front doors slid open, and Nana B came scooting in. Sebastian met her in the middle of the waiting room and wrapped her in a hug.

"How is he?" Her voice didn't waver, but her puffy eyes and red nose gave her away.

"They won't tell us anything."

She grabbed his hand and towed him up to the nurse's station. "I'm Betty Hardy. You have my grandson."

The nurse glanced up at her. "I'll let the doctor know you're here. If you'll have a seat, they'll get to you as soon as they can."

"Can you at least tell me if he's alive?"

The nurse's face softened. "I don't have that information." Someone hobbled in through the emergency room doors, his hand on his side and blood dripping through his fingers. The nurse called for an orderly and a wheelchair before turning her attention back to them. "Please, have a seat."

17

———

THE NUMBER OF PEOPLE IN THE WAITING ROOM WANED, AND AS Kattan, Vin, Rose, and Cat arrived, they commandeered a corner of the waiting room to have all to themselves.

"Is Tavi coming?" Sebastian could send someone to pick him up or—

"He was at Pigments when I got the call. He doesn't know yet."

"I'll call him." Though worried, Sebastian's brain kicked into organization mode. "And Vondra at the Center." She would have been watching the Center for Grant while he'd been gone for the shoot.

He went to get up and make all the arrangements because that was something he could do. Something he was good at. Then Nana put a staying hand on his arm.

"That can wait, dear. First, you need to introduce me to your friends."

They all glanced around at each other, not knowing what to say. How do you tell someone's grandmother that their beloved grandson shoots gay porn? And not only shot gay porn, but he was a sought-after porn star?

You could probably spare her the details.

Even if she was fine with Grant being gay, knowing he was into porn was a higher bar to clear.

Sebastian started with the basics—that Grant was an 'actor' for their studio—and he introduced them all around, being careful not to give anything away. "And this is my uncle, Niko. He owns the studio."

"And what studio is that, dear?" She'd addressed her question to Niko, who'd lost a few shades off his solidly Greek complexion.

"I doubt you would have heard of it."

"Humor an old lady."

Whether she was trying to pass the time as best she could to keep her mind occupied until she learned something about Grant, or if she suspected they weren't being entirely truthful, Sebastian couldn't be sure.

"Black Stallion." Niko didn't equivocate, but he also didn't elaborate. If that was something Grant wanted to tell his grand-mother, he could tell her himself when he could.

If he could.

Stop. It. You can't think like that. You should knock on wood or burn sage or do whatever people do these days to banish dark thoughts. He felt like that was something he should know. He lived in Southern California after all.

Nana's eyebrows went up. "The gay porn studio?"

That got a surprised chuckle out of Cat, and suddenly the makeup artist was paying more attention to the conversation. Sebastian glanced at Niko, who shrugged as if to say, *You confirm it, not me.*

"That's the one," Sebastian admitted, and because he couldn't let it rest, he asked, "did Grant tell you?"

"Lord, no. Bernadette Stevens told me about it." When they

all gave her a *Who the hell is that?* kind of look, she said, "She's Father Stevens' wife at The Church of the Valley."

Great, just what they needed, to be on the radar of a local church activist group. "She saw Grant in a bunch of the videos that she and her husband watch."

Considering the circumstances, Cat's grin probably couldn't get any wider. Vin suppressed a chuckle as well.

Nana glanced up at Niko. "They're a big fan of your work."

"So, have you...?" How do you ask someone if they'd seen their relative in porn?

"Oh, no, dear. I figured if Grant had wanted me to see them, he would have told me about them."

"You're okay with it?" Sebastian couldn't believe she was taking all this so well. Sebastian's mother had an apoplectic fit one awkward Christmas when she'd found out Niko had hired Sebastian at the studio, and Sebastian wasn't even in any scenes. He still couldn't bring up his work without her turning scary shades of red.

"He's an adult. And he's being safe." She glanced at Niko for confirmation. When he nodded, she said, "Why wouldn't I be?"

Sebastian leaned over and wrapped her in a hug. "He's so lucky to have you. Him and Tavi both."

"I'm surprised because I thought Bernadette had said he'd quit."

Sebastian wasn't getting into that. He stood. "I think I'll go make those calls."

"*Bass.*" Nana had never used his nickname before, and with that disapproving tone, it stopped him before he could escape. Then all the pieces must have clicked into place in her mind. Grant telling her he'd get the money to pay off the bank. Him being vague about how he was going to manage that when they both knew he poured almost all of the donations the Center received into running the Center and developing new programs and scholarships and took very little of that to pay his own salary.

"It's for my house, isn't it?"

"Look, Nana..." Sebastian took her hand, her skin had gone cold, and her bony fingers felt frail in his hands.

"This is all my fault," she said. "All mine."

The tears were back as well as the blotchiness to her cheeks. Rose found a box of tissues. Nana plucked one out of the top and blotted her eyes and wiped her nose. "I should have asked more questions. I don't have a problem with him shooting porn if that's what he wants to do for himself, but for him to have to go back after he'd left it behind... For me... And now..." Between the sniffles and the hiccupped breaths, it became harder and harder to understand her. "He's here and... and..."

She buried her face in her hands, and Sebastian pulled her out of the seat and stood with her in his arms. "It's going to be okay. He's strong and healthy, and we're going to make sure he gets well so we can both kill him. Deal?"

Nana laughed through the tears. "I get to go first."

———

A couple of tense hours passed before a nurse called Nana into a consultation room to speak to a doctor, the nurse's demeanor giving abso-fucking-lutely nothing away. Nana squeezed Sebastian's hand and toddled away behind the nurse.

Kattan huddled in one of the chairs, looking positively green with guilt.

"It's not your fault," Sebastian reassured him, even though he wanted to take his anger out on Kattan. A natural reaction, but Grant bore the brunt of that responsibility. He'd known what he'd taken before. Ultimately, Grant had decided to take the pills. If Sebastian wanted to be mad at anybody, he should be mad at Grant.

"You had no way of knowing he'd have a bad reaction to the combination of pills he took, and it's entirely possible that that isn't even the issue."

"His grandmother said he doesn't have epilepsy. It was the pills."

"Probably." Which only made Kattan greener. Sebastian glanced around and found the nearest trash can in case Kattan needed it. "Hopefully we'll have some answers soon."

The double doors Nana had disappeared through swished open and spat her out. She had a tissue in her hand, and she was drying her eyes. Sebastian stood and swayed on his noodle-y legs. Kattan caught him, preventing him from going to his knees.

"How is he?" Sebastian called out from across the room. He couldn't wait for her to get any closer. He found his legs and met her half way, his hands on her shoulders, holding her away from him so he could see her face. Her wrinkles were mottled with red and her eyes were wet with unshed tears. "Nana?"

Vin, Niko, Rose, Cat, and Kattan all gathered around. Niko held his hand out to her and helped her into a chair. "Give her room to breathe, people."

She can breathe after she tells us what's going on, Sebastian wanted to say, but the words never made it past his lips, so at least a tiny portion of his frontal lobe must still be functioning.

Kattan's hands gripped the back of Sebastian's neck, his tension tight and almost tangible. "Well?"

"They moved him up to ICU."

Grant was alive. Anxiety quickly swamped Sebastian's relief. Grant was in ICU. Which meant he was still critical. They didn't send people to ICU for a paper cut.

Because Sebastian couldn't find his voice, Niko asked, "What did the doctor say?"

"He's in a medically induced coma. They couldn't control the seizures, so they put him under until they can get more blood results back and determine if it's a drug reaction, or if there's another cause."

"But they think he's going to be okay?" Vin had Cat tucked under his wing, her voice almost as shaky as Sebastian's. But then again, Grant had always been one of her favorites.

"They don't know for sure, but they are cautiously optimistic."

"Whatever the fuck they mean by that." When Niko cut Vin a look, he said, "What? Doctors need to tell it to people straight, not shroud their meaning and cover their ass."

Niko put a staying hand on Vin's shoulder. The look he shot him said, *That's not helping.*

"Have—" Sebastian's voice squeaked when he spoke, and he had to try again. "Have you seen him?"

Nana dabbed at her eyes again, though her complexion was clearing up. "Just for a few minutes. He looked peaceful."

"Can I see him? Please?" Sebastian didn't care that the words came out sounding like he was begging. He was. He would grovel, get down on his knees and lick the doctor's shoes if he thought it might help.

"I'll see what I can do." Nana eyed him, her rheumy blue eyes still as sharp as her mind. "So... boyfriend, huh?"

Sebastian choked on air. Vin gave him the same *What the fuck?* look Niko had when he'd first heard. Cat smiled, she knew the score, and Rose kissed him on the cheek. "Good for you two."

"Who told you?" His eyes went to Niko, even though Niko hadn't been alone with Nana to tell her the gory details of her grandson's sex life. Niko gave a short shake of his head, indicating she hadn't heard it from him.

"One of the nurses. Can't remember which one. Said you were trying to see him."

"It's new," Sebastian said, not knowing what else to say.

"But you love him." More statement than question. And yeah, he did love Grant, but he'd barely been able to admit that to himself, much less to Grant. He'd be damned if his friends were going to hear it from him before Grant did. "He's very special to me."

Which seemed to be enough for Nana.

Nana stood, and everyone shifted, making way for her to pass. "Let me go talk to the nurse, and I'll see if I can get you in."

———

SEBASTIAN SAT IN THE HOSPITAL ROOM WITH NANA, HIS FINGERS entwined with Grant's, even though Grant was still in an induced coma almost twenty-four hours later.

They were on the tail end of visiting hours and would be kicked out of the room soon. Not that Sebastian was going anywhere. He'd staked his claim in a corner of the ICU waiting room where he stayed between visiting hours while Nana went home to shower and change and check up on Tavi—who hadn't been pleased he'd been kept away from the hospital. But when visiting was so restricted, and with Grant not even being conscious, there hadn't been a point.

Not that Tavi agreed, but he didn't have transportation, so what could he do?

Nana had gone to the bank that morning, keeping Grant's appointment, but essentially letting them know that they weren't going to be able to catch the loan up to date the way they'd hoped they would.

"What are you going to do now?" Sebastian asked.

"Move out." Her eyes remained dry, and her tone matter of

fact. She'd seemed to come to terms with losing her home, though Sebastian was still a little wobbly in the knees about it. "The sooner, the better."

"I thought you'd have a little time before you had to get out."

"I do, but that's in my past. I'm ready to move forward. Truman has agreed to let Tavi stay with him until I can find a job and a more permanent living situation, but until then, Bernadette has a room at the church where I can stay and..."

"Stay with me."

When her brows went up, he added, "I mean at my rental house. I told Grant about it a while ago, but he'd refused to consider it. It's a cozy two-bedroom with an apartment over the garage, not too far from the Center and Pigments. The tenants moved out a month ago. I've kept it off the market, just in case... you know, in case Grant needed it after all."

Nana patted his knee. "That's very kind of you, dear. But I can't afford a place like that on my pension."

"I wouldn't take your money. I couldn't. You don't have to stay there forever if you don't want, though if you do, I'd be fine with that. You need a place to live, and Tavi needs to stay with you and Grant. The kid doesn't need any more instability in his life than he already has."

"I don't think Grant would approve."

Sebastian glanced over at Grant, at the peaceful way his chest rose and fell and the slow, steady beat of the EKG, then glanced back at Nana with a wary, wily grin on his face. "I don't think he's in a position to have a say in the matter. Do you?"

"You're sneaky," Nana said, but that was excitement in her voice, not censure. "What's your plan?"

"We pack you up tonight and move you and Tavi in tomorrow. We'll move you in before the doctors try to wake him up again."

A nurse popped his head in the door. "I'm going to have to ask you to leave."

Sebastian stood and planted a kiss on Grant's forehead, the skin so warm under his lips that it was easy to think Grant would wake up any minute and take him in his arms, but he knew that wasn't going to happen any time soon.

Nana cupped Sebastian's cheek when he turned around and gave it a gentle pat. "You're a good person."

"That remains to be seen. You have to promise not to tell Grant I own the house."

"You can't keep it a secret forever, dear."

"I won't. Not forever. Just until he's stronger and has the energy to kill me once he finds out I went behind his back."

———

GRANT WOKE TO FIND SEBASTIAN AT HIS BEDSIDE. THE BRIGHT lights above his bed forced him to close his eyes again. He tried to raise his arm to shield his eyes, but they weighed a ton, and he couldn't be bothered.

His voice croaked, and Sebastian held a cup with a straw up to his mouth, placing a helping hand behind his back so he could get the cool water down.

"What..." His train of thought derailed and crashed, a tumble of words in his head that had no meaning. He wasn't at home but beyond that...

Sebastian's hold on his hand roused him back into consciousness. "There you are. You going to stay awake for me?"

Had he been asleep? Every muscle in his body ached, his brain throbbed as if it had its own heartbeat, and it felt like he hadn't slept in a month. He opened his eyes again, squinting against the light. He wanted to speak, but moving his tongue to talk required too much effort.

Sebastian came into focus, mostly. The soft beep of a heart monitor gave away Grant's location unless Sebastian was into medical play and a hell of a lot kinkier than Grant had ever thought.

What happened? The last thing he remembered... he remembered... nothing.

The questions formed on his lips, but before he could utter them, Sebastian said, "You had a seizure. A series of them. You're at the hospital. The doctors had to sedate you to keep them from continuing. The best they could tell is you had a bad drug reaction from mixing the Viagra with whatever the hell Kattan gave you. They're still trying to figure it out."

Slowly, it came back to him. The hot studio lights on his bare skin. Kattan's hips in his hands, Sebastian watching in that way he had that said he would never get enough.

"How long?"

"It's Saturday night, you've—"

Saturday? Grant grabbed the bed rail, trying to pull himself up. "Help me."

With a hand on his shoulder, Sebastian pushed him back down to the mattress. "Where the fuck do you think you're going? You're not allowed out of bed until a nurse or doctor okays it."

"Then press the damn call button and get—" Get... get something. Fuck. Had those pills dissolved his gray matter? The thought vanished, but he couldn't shake the feeling that there was somewhere he needed to be. Somewhere important.

"Nana? Tavi?"

"They're fine."

Had Sebastian hesitated before answering, or was that just a cruel trick his muddled mind played on him?

Then his mind started clearing, layer by layer, a dense fog

lifting, burning off as the sun started to shine. "The shoot. Did I finish?"

"Nearly."

Which meant no. Which meant no payment. Which meant...

Grant struggled to sit up again. "The bank. I've got to—"

"The only thing you have to do is lie back down and get your rest. It's Saturday night. Nothing is open. Besides, the bank is sorted."

Why couldn't Sebastian look him in the eye?

"*Sorted*. What does that mean?"

Sebastian offered him more water, but it seemed like a diversion more than anything else. He pushed it away. "*Bass*."

His boyfriend turned a pale shade. Maybe *he* should be the one in the hospital bed. "Nana turned the house over to the bank yesterday."

"*Fuck me*." The hand Grant tried to run down his face ended up smacking him in the forehead, a heavy blob of skin and muscle and bone that he had little control over.

Much like the rest of your life.

"Help me get out of here. I've got to make calls. I have to find a place for them to stay. They can have my place until I can find something better, and—"

"It's handled," Sebastian said before Grant could go completely off the rails. "We moved her and Tavi in today. Everyone pitched in. Pigments closed to help, and Vin and Cat came as well. It was a big job, but with that many people, it went quick."

"You did that?"

Sebastian didn't deny it. "It's going to be okay. It's a setback, not the end of the world."

"Where are they staying?"

"A friend's." Again, that hesitation, or Grant's mind whirring at sub-optimal speed. "It's available for as long as they need it, so all you have to worry about is getting well. Okay?"

Grant's eyes fluttered closed without his permission, the unrelenting exhaustion dragging him under. How could he be so sleepy when he'd slept for almost two days straight?

"Can you still hear me?"

Grant grunted and felt Sebastian's lips on his cheek and the brush of Sebastian's warm breath by his ear. "I lo—"

Whatever Sebastian said next was lost to the drugs and the blackness that rolled in and swamped him.

18

<hr>

"HOW ARE YOU FEELING?"

It was Sunday evening, and Grant had quickly transitioned out of ICU the night before to a regular room, and now he'd be sprung as soon as the hospital completed his discharge paperwork.

"I feel like I ran a marathon I never trained for."

Grant didn't know how else to describe the soreness in his muscles and the concerted effort it took to sit up and not curl up on the hospital bed and sleep for the next week or two.

But with the fundraiser coming up on Saturday, he had too much to do to sleep.

Sebastian eyed him from the chair, his socked feet propped up on the side of the bed. "The doctor said you need to take it easy. That it'll take some time for your body to acclimate to the anti-seizure medication. Until then, you're going to be a little groggy."

"Fucking meds. My head feels like someone filled it with cotton, and all I want to do is sleep. The Center needs me and—"

"The Center is fine. And the doctors said they could start

weaning you off the drugs soon, so it's a temporary thing. Besides, Nana says Tavi is filling in at the Center, and Truman has sent some of his people from Pigments to help out in the evenings. All you have to do is get better and put Vondra on the payroll. She's stepped up and gotten shifts covered at the Center while you've been out."

"If that grant ever comes in, it'll be the first thing I do." Grant motioned to his jeans on the arm of Sebastian's chair. "Toss me those."

He underhanded them to Grant. Sebastian had been quiet all day, which wasn't like him at all. At first, Grant had chalked it up to concern over his hospitalization and being tired himself, but that wasn't it. A couple times, he'd started to say something, then stopped and waved Grant off when he'd asked what was wrong.

Was Sebastian having second thoughts about the boyfriend thing and didn't know how to break it to him?

He slipped into his jeans, zipping and fastening them before reaching for his shirt. "Spill."

Sebastian didn't even pretend not to know what Grant was talking about.

"What is it? You look like you're going to be sick."

Sebastian swallowed hard. "Remember when you said you loved me?"

"Yeess." Grant dragged the word out, not liking how Sebastian started the conversation. It made his chest tight and dread sit like lead in the pit of his stomach.

"Well, after you hear what I have to say, you may want to take it back."

"Unless the next words out of your mouth are that you're a serial killer or like to kick puppies for fun, I don't think whatever it is you have to say is going to change my mind about how I feel about you."

Sebastian winced.

"Okay. The serial killer thing I could maybe live with as long as the puppies are safe."

That got a strangled laugh out of Sebastian like he hoped it would. He took Sebastian's hand and pulled him out of the chair and into his arms. "Tell me."

Sebastian broke away and paced the room, his hands raking through his hair, making it stand up on end. He stopped by the door and turned to face him. "Niko knows."

The agitation and consternation settled onto Sebastian's features. Beneath it lay a touch of panic making him look raw and vulnerable.

"About us, or about me being gay?"

Grant tamped down on his rising panic. His Nana had lost the house. He had no need for Black Stallion anymore. What did it matter that Niko knew the truth now?

But Grant had been in the closet so long that acid poured into his belly to gnaw at that chunk of lead sitting there.

"Both. I'm sorry. I didn't mean to say anything. It's just that when they brought you in and I couldn't get to you, and they asked who I was and I said I was your boyfriend and Niko wasn't there, but then he was and... *fuck*."

Everything spilled out in one long run-on sentence, that, combined with the drugs in Grant's system, made him hard to follow, but he got the gist.

"Bass."

Sebastian clamped his hands behind his neck and met Grant's eyes for the first time since the verbal vomit. "Yeah?"

"Take a breath."

Sebastian closed his eyes and sucked in a lungful of the antiseptic-scented air and blew it out, but he still looked on the verge of a meltdown.

"Come here." Grant held out his arms, and Sebastian stepped into them.

"I'm sorry." The apology came out muffled as Sebastian buried his face in the crook of Grant's neck.

Sebastian held on tight, and his breath caught.

Fuck. "It's okay. You—"

Sebastian pulled back. "No, it's not okay. I—"

Grant took Sebastian's face in his hands and kissed Sebastian to shut him up. When they came up for air, Grant said, "It's over. I'm out. I'm not mad. I'm..."

He didn't know what the hell he was. All those years of being in the closet, of looking over his shoulder, of having to remember who knew and who didn't. All the worry, all the angst, all the paranoia, evaporated. That acid that had spilled into his gut dissolved the lead, and his stomach felt lighter, and the tightness in his chest eased.

"I'm free, Bass. Free to be the man I want to be. Free to love who I want and not fear who knows it."

"You're not mad?"

"No."

Sebastian's head dropped to Grant's shoulder. "Thank fuck. I thought I'd ruined us."

"I'm glad everything is out in the open. We don't have to lie or hide any secrets. We can move forward with a clean slate. And it feels incredible."

"You sure that's not the drugs talking?"

"Positive."

Why wasn't Sebastian smiling? The grin on Grant's face had the muscles in his cheeks starting to cramp. Grant trapped Sebastian's chin between his thumb and forefinger. "Now what?"

"I have a confession." Sebastian glanced away, then took a breath and met Grant's gaze head-on. "I love you."

The tightness in Grant's chest returned for an entirely

different reason. He'd thought Sebastian loved him. You don't camp out at the hospital for days for just anybody, or arrange to move someone's family in a day, or all the other things Sebastian had done for him while the seizure had sidelined him.

But hearing those words... It fucking floored him.

The feeling that that wasn't what Sebastian had been about to say lay buried beneath Grant's elation. He made a mental note to press Sebastian later, but they had all the time in the world for that.

"I love you, too."

Sebastian backed him into the bed, his hands sliding up Grant's chest and locking behind his head as he bit down on Grant's lower lip before swiping the sting away with a flick of his tongue.

Grant fisted his hand in Sebastian's hair, angling his head and taking the kiss deeper. If they hadn't been in the hospital, he'd already have ripped Sebastian's clothes off him.

Despite the drugs running through his system, Grant's cock got heavy and pressed against his zipper. *Thank fuck* the drugs hadn't affected his hard-on, because as soon as he got Sebastian alone, he planned on proving how much Sebastian meant to him.

A knock came on the open door, and where Grant would have pushed Sebastian away three days ago, he simply broke the kiss and tucked Sebastian under his arm and pulled him into his side.

Niko stood in the doorway, pressed and polished as if ready for a fancy night on the town.

"Hot date?" Sebastian ribbed his uncle. "Who's the lucky guy?"

A grunt was all the answer Sebastian got. Niko reached into the breast pocket of his suit coat and pulled out a thick envelope and handed it to Grant. "I wanted to drop this by."

"What's this?" Grant removed his arm from around Sebastian and thumbed through the crisp hundred-dollar bills in the envelope.

"Payment. For the scene."

Grant pushed the money back into Niko's hands. "I'm not taking money for something I didn't finish."

Not to mention the guilt he felt for deceiving a man who'd been nothing but kind to him, almost weighed as heavy on him as the drugs.

He wanted to express that, but he'd have to do it at a time when his brain wasn't so foggy.

Niko held the money out again. "Take it. You're going to need it while you get back on your feet."

"I'm not taking money I didn't earn, and I'm not taking handouts."

Niko's lips turned down at the ends, but he stuffed the envelope back into his pocket. "If you change your mind, you know where to find me."

"Forget it. Bad enough my Nana had to accept charity from her friend. I'll figure my stuff out on my own."

And yeah, he kinda sounded like a dick. He stuck out his hand for Niko to shake and softened his tone. "Thank you, though."

A look passed between Niko and Sebastian, and Sebastian's grip around Grant's waist got tighter. But Grant was too tired, physically, and emotionally, to chase that rabbit down its hole, even though he didn't want to let it pass. He was missing something. He just didn't know what. Fuck, he couldn't wait until the drugs were out of his system. "What?"

Sebastian pressed a kiss to his temple. "Nothing. Right, Niko?"

After a slight hesitation, Niko pasted on a smile and clapped Grant on his upper arm. "Good to see you up and around."

———

THE FILMING SCHEDULE AT BLACK STALLION HAD BEEN LIGHT during the week. With the Bahama shoot coming up, everyone's energy refocused on that, so Sebastian slipped away early to help Grant load his things into the box truck he'd rented for his move to Sebastian's house.

Nana's house.

Fuck. Sebastian really needed to tell Grant that he owned the house before Grant heard it from someone else. Too many people knew the truth for it to stay a secret for long.

And it wasn't like he didn't want to Grant to know. It was that things were all kinds of crazy with Grant only a few days out of the hospital, and with his upcoming move, and the carnival and masquerade in two days, he'd put off telling him.

Sunday. He'd tell Grant first thing Sunday and deal with the fallout then.

He glanced at the take-out he'd picked up along the way, his appetite suddenly gone. Grant was going to kill him when he found out Sebastian had gone behind his back.

Epically bad decision.

But what was he supposed to do? Let Tavi go home with Truman and Nana go live in a room at the church? Fuck that. No way would he allow them to be split up when it was within his power to help them.

He parked beside the box truck, it's ramp down and angled toward the stairs to Grant's apartment. With the food in one hand and his change of clothes in the other, he took the steps two at a time. It had only been twenty-four hours since he'd last seen Grant, but it felt like weeks.

Despite the heat, Grant's door stood wide open, and Sebastian stopped at the threshold. Packed boxes were stacked in the dining area and den, the apartment already had that 'gone' feeling.

He stepped inside and closed the door. Grant didn't even look up from where he sat on the couch, staring at the envelope in his hand.

"What's that?" Sebastian gestured to the envelope and set his gym bag on the floor and the food on the coffee table.

"It's from the Forsythe Foundation."

"About the grant you applied for?"

Grant nodded.

"Well? What did they say?"

"I don't know. I haven't opened it."

Sebastian sat down beside him. "Why the fuck not?"

"I'm afraid of what it's going to say." Grant scrubbed a hand across his stubbled jaw. Sebastian wanted nothing more than to feel the stubble on his skin, to let it raise goosebumps on his flesh in anticipation, but he tamped down the urge to take Grant to his bedroom and instead took the envelope from his hand.

"Want me to open it?"

Grant planted his elbows on his knees and covered his face with his hands, his voice coming out muffled when he said, "Go for it."

Sebastian ripped through the flap. Grant's hand went to Sebastian's thigh, his grip tight as Sebastian pulled the single sheet of paper out and unfolded it. He linked his fingers with Grant's and read: "Mister Hardy, we are pleased to—"

Grant whooped and jumped to his feet, grabbing the paper from Sebastian's hand. Sebastian stood and read the rest of it over Grant's shoulder.

"You did it," Sebastian said.

"I can't fucking believe it. Do you realize what this money will do for the Center? More scholarships, more services. I can hire Vondra or someone else to help staff and—"

"And you don't have to move out of your apartment, now that you can pay yourself a salary."

"No. I still want to move. I need to be there for Tavi. Leaving him with my Nana had always been a temporary fix. Besides, the home inspection is next week for my foster parent application and what money I save on my apartment, is that much less I need to live on so I can put more money into the Center and—"

Sebastian pulled him in for a kiss. "I'm so happy for you. You deserve this."

"No, but the kids do." Grant didn't let Sebastian go. Instead, he pulled him tighter against him. "Though I'm going to miss having a place where we have some privacy."

"With Nana taking the apartment above the garage, and Tavi's room at the opposite end of the house from the master, I think we'll have enough privacy... if you can tone it down a notch or two."

Grant leaned in, his shirt damp with sweat from loading some of the boxes already, but that only made Sebastian remember the times they'd been sweaty together, and he cast a glance at the bedroom to see if the bed was still intact.

Grant whispered in Sebastian's ear, "I thought you liked me loud."

"I do." Sebastian took Grant by the hips and walked him back into the bedroom. "Fuck privacy. We can get Tavi a set of noise-canceling headphones if he doesn't want to hear you yell out when I'm fucking you."

Grant's gaze went dark, and his smile went wicked. "I like the way you think."

Then Grant switched their positions, and he pushed Sebastian toward the bed. "Except this time, you're the one who's going to be calling out."

———

They laid on top of the bed, the sheet tangled around their legs as their sweat dried, and their bodies cooled. Despite Sebastian's suggestion of the headphones for Tavi, it wouldn't quite be the same once he moved. Grant ditched the condom and rolled onto his side, itching to run a finger through the cum pooled on Sebastian's belly.

Grant flicked his tongue over Sebastian's exposed nipple, and Sebastian's hand went to the back of Grant's head and held him there. "Fuck. I love it when you do that. Give me ten or fifteen minutes, and I'll be good to go again."

"We don't have fifteen minutes. Not if we want to get my stuff over to the house and the truck back to the rental place before they close tonight."

"Shit. Forgot about that."

"But maybe we could leave the mattress one more night."

Sebastian pulled Grant in and kissed him long and deep. "That's the best idea I've heard all week. Except how will you get the bed to the house?"

"Truman's got a truck. I'm sure he'd let me borrow it. That way you can meet me here tomorrow night, and we can have tonight and tomorrow night for just you and me."

Sebastian kissed him again. A flicker of unease in Sebastian's eyes came and went. Grant would have asked him about it, but he didn't want to spoil the moment.

"We won't get any sleep."

"Sleep's overrated."

Grant sat up and tossed Sebastian a cum-rag off his bedside table. "Come on, let's shower and get going. The sooner we get things moved, the sooner I can get you back in my bed."

They showered, and Sebastian pulled on the spare clothes he'd brought with him. They ate the food Sebastian had brought, though it had long gone cold.

They packed up the remaining boxes, the couch and coffee

table, and the rest of the furniture sans bed, and were on the road to Grant's temporary home in under two hours.

The drive took less than fifteen minutes, and Grant backed the box truck into the driveway of the fifties-era home. The quiet, tree-lined street was just the kind of neighborhood that Tavi would have complained about a month ago. But the kid came out of the house with a smile on his face, and Grant knew without a doubt he was doing the right thing.

"Damn," Sebastian said as he patted down the pockets of his shorts, "I must have left my phone back at your apartment."

"We can pick it up when we go drop off the truck. We have to stop by the apartment to get my car anyway. Or we can go back now if—"

"No. It's fine."

In the side mirror, Grant watched as Remy came out of the house, taking Tavi's hand when he thought no one was watching.

He turned to Sebastian. "Tavi and Remy? They a thing?"

"I think? Though he hasn't said as much."

"I wondered." Grant scrubbed a hand over his face but couldn't keep the grin off of it. "Somehow, when I pictured being a father, I figured I'd have more time to come to terms with my kid dating."

"This mean you're gonna be standing at the front door with a shotgun, asking Remy what his intentions are?"

Grant chuckled. "I think with these two, we're past that stage."

They popped their door latches and climbed out as a Jaguar F-Type pulled into the driveway. Niko climbed out, two Tupperware containers in his hands.

Sebastian stepped beside Grant, linking their fingers. Grant glanced down at their joined hands, loving how they fit together and how he didn't give a damn who saw.

Niko came around the hood of his car and handed the containers to Sebastian. "Had dinner at your mom and dad's. It's your favorite. She made me promise to bring it to you. I figured it would be just as easy to drop it by here on the way home as take it by your place."

Sebastian opened a corner and sniffed.

The savory scent of Mousaska made Grant's stomach growl. "There better be enough for all of us, or we're going to have to fight over it."

Sebastian didn't smile. He looked pained.

Grant squeezed his shoulder. "Bass, you okay?"

The smile Sebastian offered up didn't reach his eyes, hell, it barely moved his lips. "Sure, why wouldn't I be?"

Which didn't answer the question. Niko backed away, hitching his thumb over his shoulder at the passenger in the car. "I need to be going."

The two exchanged a look that Grant couldn't quite read, but something was off. Then he remembered the other silent exchange between Niko and Sebastian back at the hospital. No, he wasn't imagining things.

It didn't hit him until Niko had his door open what had been bothering him. "Hey, Niko."

Niko stopped, one leg in the car. "Yeah?"

"How did you know where to bring the food?"

Niko's eyes shot to Sebastian's, his smile weak. "Sebastian texted the directions to me."

Niko started getting into the car.

"When?"

"I don't know. Ten or fifteen minutes ago. His parents don't live far."

An audible breath whooshed out of Sebastian, and Grant glanced over. In the background, he heard Niko's door close, and

Grant became vaguely aware that Niko backed up and drove away.

He turned to Sebastian. "You don't have your phone."

"No."

"Niko didn't text you, did he?"

Sebastian's eyes closed, and he pinched the bridge of his nose. Tavi and Remy came out from behind the truck, and Tavi said, "You want us to start unloading?"

Grant took the containers from Sebastian and handed them to the boys. "Why don't you two go in and eat. We'll be along in a minute."

"Sweet," Remy said. "I'm fucking starving."

Grant refocused on Sebastian, not even caring about the language. In fact, he had some language of his own for Sebastian.

He waited with his hands on his hips until the front door closed. "What the fuck, Bass? You want to tell me how your uncle just happened to know where we moved to?"

"I can explain."

Grant crossed his arms over his chest. "This should be good."

"I was going to tell you—" Sebastian glanced up at him. "Would you stop looking at me like I pluck the wings off butterflies for fun?"

It felt more like Sebastian had sucker-punched him because Grant couldn't breathe without knowing what Sebastian was going to tell him next.

"Fine," Sebastian said when Grant didn't say anything. He couldn't. Not when his lungs lay paralyzed in his chest, and his heart felt like it had Sebastian's size nine boot print on it. "This is my place."

"You're the *fucking friend*." He should have known everything had fallen into place too easily.

"Yeah."

"You lied."

Sebastian's chin went up. "By omission, maybe."

"Fat fucking difference." Grant laughed, a high-pitched irreverent sound. He couldn't believe it. "You went behind my back, knowing, *knowing*, how I felt about this?"

"It seemed like a good idea at the time."

"And now what? I'm the only one who didn't know? Is that it?"

"Tavi doesn't know."

"You played me for a fool."

Sebastian reached out and took his hand, but Grant snatched it back. He didn't want to be coddled or cajoled. "Don't touch me."

Sebastian held his hands up. "Listen. I was going to tell you, but things were going so well. I didn't want to spoil things, and I didn't think it was a good time."

Grant paced the length of the truck and back again, not believing his ears. "Any time before I moved in would have been a good time."

"Babe." Sebastian reached out again. Grant caught Sebastian's hands, wanting to push him away, but couldn't.

Why the fuck did Sebastian have to lie?

"*Babe*." Sebastian's word came out more like a plea. "Let's talk this out. All we need—"

"I love you, Bass, but I *need* you to not be here right now."

Sebastian's hands dropped to his sides. "Let me get this straight. You're kicking me out of my own house?"

"Looks that way."

19

Grant arrived early at the Center Saturday morning. He hadn't slept the night before—the new house too quiet, the lack of noise unsettling. He'd spent most of the night searching online for a new place they could afford to rent, but he hadn't had any luck.

The carnival was set to start around noon, and the masquerade set for later that evening.

A lot of last-minute details he needed to see to and—

Bullshit. Don't lie to yourself. You're not losing sleep over the fundraiser. You're losing sleep over Sebastian. You. Love. Him.

Yeah. But that didn't make Sebastian going behind his back right.

Tavi wandered in and plopped into the chair across from Grant's desk. He hadn't seen that dark, brooding expression on Tavi's face since Connor Brewer had first brought him to Grant's door.

Grant pushed away his keyboard. It wasn't like he'd been getting any real work done. "What?"

"Anybody tell you you're acting like a bag of dicks?"

Any other time, Grant might have thrown his head back and

laughed, but nothing in his life seemed very funny at the moment. He crossed his arms and leaned back in his chair. "A bag of dicks?"

Tavi held his arms out wide, indicating size. "Big fucking bag." The language returned with the scowl. "You need to apologize to Sebastian. If you do it real sweet like, maybe he'll take you back."

"It's none of your business, kid."

"When you're shitty to my friends, I'm not standing by and not calling you out on it."

"You've got the wrong man. He's the one who fucked up."

"*Right.*" If Tavi could bottle up that sarcasm and sell just a fraction of it, he'd knock some of the contenders off the Forbes' richest list. "You know, everyone needs help sometimes."

"You don't think I know that?"

Tavi leaned forward, that edgy street vibe licking the surface. Grant had to give the kid points for holding his ground and saying his piece even if Grant didn't agree.

"You don't act like it. You don't see us kids fighting the help, do you? Do you think I don't know that Truman doesn't need an apprentice? That he's just trying to help me out?"

"Look, Tavi—"

"I'm not done. I'm not fighting the help because it's an opportunity I can't pass up. I'm not asking why. I'm taking it and running with it."

"That's different."

"Not so much. The Center, it's all about doing for others. Why won't you let others do for you? Why are you the exception?"

Grant steepled his fingers and rested his chin on his thumbs. He couldn't be prouder of the kid if he were his own.

Clearing his throat, Grant said, "Maybe you have a point."

Tavi relaxed back into the chair. "Damn right, I do."

Grant cocked his head as if he heard something. "Is that Vondra calling you?"

"She won't be here for another hour, but I get it. You want me to scram."

Though Grant hated to admit it, he said, "There's this kid I know—one that's too damn smart for his skinny britches—but he gave me a few things to think about."

The street kid façade faded away, and Tavi's shy smile flicked across his face. He hopped out of the chair and made it to the door before hitching his fingers around the door jamb and spinning back around.

"And for the record, you coulda told me about you two. I can keep a secret."

"You mad?"

"No. I kinda feel sorry for you. A shitty day on the streets was a helluva lot better than my best day in the closet."

"Yeah, well, I'm starting to figure that out." Grant turned back to his computer. "Now, go on and let me get some work done."

Tavi left, and Grant shook his head. *Schooled by a fifteen-year-old.*

Grant didn't even have a chance to open his document with all the checklists for the day when his phone buzzed.

Niko.

He almost sent the call to voicemail, but he owed Niko too much, an apology being the least of it, so he pressed the green icon and answered.

"What's up, Niko?"

"We need to talk."

On some level, Grant had expected this reckoning. He just hadn't expected it so soon. And today of all days. "Can it wait un—"

"No. I'll see you in thirty."

Niko hung up before Grant could answer, feeling like he'd been summoned by the king. Even if it was only by the king of gay porn.

He glanced at his watch. That early on a Saturday, he could probably make it across the valley in the thirty minutes if he left right away.

Pocketing his phone, he grabbed his keys and found Tavi sorting the masks for the masquerade by dominant color and putting them in boxes to hand out.

"I've got to run across the valley. You going to be okay here by yourself until Vondra gets here?"

"Yeah, I'll try not to burn the place down," Tavi said.

"Cute."

"You going to Black Stallion?"

"Yeah."

"I wanna go."

Grant laughed at that and started backing out of the art room. "Not on your life."

"You going to talk to Sebastian?"

Whatever Grant planned to do, he had no intention of discussing it with Tavi. "Don't know yet."

Karma was a bitch.

Grant knew this because on the one day he needed time to gather his thoughts before he spoke with Niko, and especially Sebastian, the traffic across the valley proved almost non-existent, and he found himself in front of the studios with ten minutes to spare.

He would have sat in the car and waited out those ten minutes, but he figured if he didn't know what he was going to say now, another ten minutes wouldn't make any difference.

Vin's car sat in the parking lot, but Sebastian's was absent, though it wasn't unusual for Sebastian to park his car in Niko's garage.

Grant rubbed his hands together, but it did nothing to bring back the circulation in them. If he hadn't been able to feel the thud of his heart against his chest, he would have thought it had stopped.

Even before his first shoot he hadn't been this nervous.

But this meeting should close the book on Black Stallion for once and for all, and if he could get out of there without seeing Sebastian, well, maybe that was for the best.

For now.

He just needed to get through the next sixteen or so hours. Then he could focus on making it up to Sebastian for being a gigantic bag of dicks, according to Tavi, who'd put it so eloquently.

That early, he had to be buzzed into the office wing. The hall lights were dim, and the offices quiet, though light spilled from Niko's open office door.

He had to bypass Sebastian's office to get to Niko's. He tried the handle along the way. Locked.

What the hell would you have done if it wasn't?

No clue.

Stopping outside Niko's door, Grant drew in a deep breath and blew it out before rapping on the jamb.

"Come in." Niko glanced up from the file full of headshots he'd been going through.

Grant stepped over to the desk and reached his hand across. Niko shook it.

Great, now Grant's palms had gone sweaty.

He took a seat and cleared his throat, the high-end leather chair smelled like Sebastian's couch, and his jeans got tight in the crotch.

Now *you get hard.*

Where the hell was that when you needed it?

"Thanks for coming. I know it was short notice and—"

"Can I say something before we get started?" Grant wanted to get a few things off his chest before Niko blasted him.

Niko sat back, gesturing for him to continue.

"First, I owe you an apology. You and Black Stallion have been nothing but good to me, and you didn't deserve the deceit."

"No, we didn't." Niko's voice remained even, but that hit harder than if he'd yelled and screamed and thrown his coffee cup across the room.

Grant tried to swallow, but his spit had dried up, and he wouldn't have been surprised to find desert sand between his molars. "About the other... the hospital bill..."

Why don't you let others do for you?

Tavi's words looped around in his mind. They had played on repeat the entire drive over, and it was a valid question Grant couldn't quite find the answer for.

But finding out Niko had covered his hospital bill was a whole other level of charity he had difficulty reconciling in his mind. Niko owed him nothing. Yet, he'd paid.

"You didn't have to pay my bill."

"You've made good money for the studio, and while I don't condone the lying, you're still a part of the Black Stallion family. We take care of our own."

"I appreciate that. And I'll pay you back. Monthly install-ments if that's okay. It'll take—"

"*Grant.*" Grant recognized that face, it was the one Niko usually had when Sebastian had exasperated him, and Niko was doing everything in his power to keep it together. "Keep your money. You more than earned it."

"Yes, sir." Grant had never called Niko 'sir' before, but some-how, it seemed appropriate. "Thank you."

The silence stretched out, and Grant shifted in his seat, catching himself before glancing at his watch. "Was there a reason why you called me here?"

"Yeah." Niko pressed the intercom button on his desktop phone. "Bass. My office. *Now*."

20

Sebastian leaned his palms flat on the table at the back of the studio, screwing on his most desperate, *If you do this for me, I'll owe you forever* faces.

"Please, Vin, I'm begging you."

"Absolutely not."

"Just this once."

Vin glanced up from the array of video cameras he had laid out across the table, a lint-free cloth in his hand as he cleaned the cameras' lenses.

"Exactly how many live bachelor auctions are you planning on having?" Then he held up his hands before Sebastian could answer. "Don't answer that. It doesn't matter how many times you ask me to auction myself off like cattle. I'm not doing it."

"Not like cattle. Like a hot, young, gay man who anyone would be lucky to bid on."

Despite his vehement denials, Vin's reluctant eye roll said he was reconsidering. Sebastian could tell. At least that's what he told himself. Grant's fundraiser would be a success if it killed him.

Sebastian switched tack. "What are you afraid of?"

He didn't expect an answer. It was more of a jab than anything and a little more mature than flat out calling Vin a chicken. Then Vin's shoulders fell, and he leaned in and said, "Who the fuck is going to bid on me? I'm a nobody. You've got actors, models, athletes... This fiasco will be like middle school all over again, waiting to be picked last for the team in PE. Except for dodgeball. I kicked ass at dodgeball." Vin waved his hand dismissively. "Anyway, I don't want to be the only one no one bids on."

Wow. Vin seriously had no idea how fucking sexy he was. It didn't matter that no one knew who he was, he'd get top bids, Sebastian had no doubt.

"What if I promise to bid on you if no one else does?"

Vin scoffed. "I don't want a pity bid any more than I want a pity fuck."

"Trust me, Vin. Anybody who fucks you, it isn't out of pity." Sebastian caught Vin's chin and lifted it toward the light inspecting him closely. "Add a little guy-liner and wear something that shows off your tattoos, and you'll bring top dollar. Promise."

Vin had stopped saying no. Maybe all he needed was one last push. "Please? It's for the most amazing kids."

"*Fuck.* You had to bring the kids into it, didn't you? Low blow, man."

Sebastian wanted to jump across the table and wrap Vin in a bear hug, but he'd probably end up on the ground with Vin sitting on his chest and his arms pinned to the ground. You can take the kid off the streets, but you can't take the street kid out of the man.

Vin pointed a dust cloth covered finger at him. "I'm not fucking anybody. No matter how much they pay."

"I'm not a pimp."

"That remains to be seen."

The speaker overhead pinged, and Sebastian's good mood vanished knowing the next thing he heard would be Niko's voice. If that man wasn't his uncle...

"Bass. My office. *Now.*"

Vin cut Sebastian a look. "What the fuck did you do now?"

"No idea." Sebastian clapped Vin on the shoulder. "Thanks, man, I'll text you the deets. I owe you one."

"A big fat one."

On the way to Niko's office, Sebastian didn't worry about what he'd owe Vin. Knowing him, Vin would hoard that favor and spring it on him at a much later date when something vitally important was on the line.

Instead, his mind drifted to the best way to avoid Grant at the fundraiser they were putting on together. If he were lucky, there'd be many more little disasters that popped up, like this last-minute cancellation in the bachelor auction, and he'd have a valid reason to avoid Grant.

Yeah, but you don't want to avoid him.

As if to prove that, his hand drifted to his phone in the front pocket of his pants, and he checked his messages for a text from Grant that he knew wasn't coming any time soon.

Or at all.

No, he didn't believe that.

Grant's parting words replayed in his head on that never-ending loop. *"I love you, Bass, but I need you to not be here right now."*

Which meant there would be a time when he did want him to be there. Right? *Right?*

Grant would be in touch, Sebastian had to believe that and cling to it as his heart lay flaccid in his chest, forgetting how to beat. He just had to give Grant some time to cool off.

No amount of apologizing or groveling or begging for forgiveness would help if Grant weren't ready to hear it.

Sebastian stepped through Niko's open office door, his eyes still on his phone, on the message that wouldn't come.

A sharp intake of breath had Sebastian glancing up. *Grant.* "What are you doing here?"

Sebastian couldn't help that the words came out sounding like an accusation. By the confused expression on Grant's face, he'd had nothing to do with why Niko had called Sebastian to his office.

Which hurt way more than Sebastian wanted to admit.

He shoved his phone deep into his pocket and wiped the *what the fuck?* look off his face and attempted to replace it with a neutral one as he turned his attention to Niko. "You wanted to see me?"

Niko planted his palms on his desk and stood. "Yeah." He waggled a finger between Sebastian and Grant. "I don't know what's going on between you two, but you need to work it the fuck out."

"Excuse me?" Grant said when it looked like he wanted to use more choice words. Frankly, Sebastian didn't know what held him back.

"I don't know what you're talking about." Which wasn't the truth, but Sebastian didn't see where his and Grant's issues were any of Niko's business.

Niko came around his desk and sat on the front edge, his arms and ankles crossed. "I've had enough of you moping around." Niko's pointed look leveled on Sebastian. Then his gaze swept over Grant as well.

Moping? "It hasn't even been two days."

"Which is two days too long. You're distracted, ill-tempered, and generally a pain in the ass to be around. So, whatever this is, it ends here and now."

"What are you going to do?" Grant asked. "Lock us in a room until someone comes out the victor?"

Niko reached into his pocket and pulled out his office keys. "Exactly. Now you two kids kiss and make up, or whatever you need to do to make things right. I don't care what it is as long as Sebastian leaves this room with a smile on his face."

Grant folded his arms across his chest. Sebastian held little hope that he'd be leaving the office grinning any time soon.

But Grant didn't move to stop Niko, so maybe he had something to say, or at least he'd be willing to hear Sebastian out. The more Sebastian thought about it, the more he liked the idea. At least this way, Grant couldn't leave without hearing what he had to say.

Grant stood. "I've got the fundraiser tonight. I don't have time for this."

"Then I suggest you two make up fast." Niko strode to his door and turned, the knob in his hand. "No make-up sex on the desk."

Niko left, then popped the door back open and stuck his head in. "The horizontal filing cabinet and couch are fair game."

———

THE DOOR CLOSED, AND THE KEY TURNED IN THE LOCK.

"I can't believe he locked us in."

Sebastian knew about the spare key in the back of the top desk drawer, but he wasn't going to tell Grant that.

Grant stepped over to the horizontal filing cabinet beneath the window and checked it for sturdiness before turning back around. "I think it can hold you," he deadpanned. "Looks like Niko has it bolted to the wall."

The first semblance of a smile all morning ghosted across Sebastian's face. How pissed could Grant still be if he still wanted to fuck him? "Is that right?"

Grant leaned back against it, looking Sebastian up and

down, a lick of that heat Sebastian loved seeing there lurking beneath the hurt. "The height's not bad either."

"Do I just drop trou now, or do you want to finish our fight first?"

"Fuck, Bass. I don't want to fight with you."

Sebastian was almost afraid to ask. "What do you want to do?"

"I want to apologize."

Wait. "What?" That one word came out on a rush of air. Sebastian couldn't be sure he heard Grant right, but he must have because the blood whirred past Sebastian's ears as his heart decided it might have reason to beat again.

Grant held out a hand. "Come here."

Sebastian didn't remember making the conscious decision to go to him, but he found himself between the V of Grant's legs, nonetheless. "I'm so fucking sorry, Grant, I—"

Grant placed a finger against Sebastian's lips. Sebastian flicked his tongue out and licked the tip of the finger pad. Grant's pupils dilated, and his nostrils flared. "No fair."

"If I want to win you back, it's no holds barred."

Grant's eyes drifted closed, and when he opened them, the intensity nearly stopped Sebastian's heart. Sebastian really needed to see a cardiologist. Maybe something was wrong with him.

Grant cupped the back of Sebastian's neck and rested his forehead against his. "You don't have to win me back, Bass. I never went anywhere. I just needed some time to figure my shit out."

Sebastian broke the hold, not because he didn't welcome Grant's touch, but because he wanted to see Grant's face when he answered Sebastian's question. "And did you? Figure your shit out?"

"I think so. You see there's this kid—"

Sebastian couldn't help the surprised—and relieved—laugh that escaped him. He knew there was a reason he loved Tavi. "A *kid*, huh?"

"A disgustingly wise kid. One who isn't afraid to call me out on my bullshit and show me where I'm wrong."

"And where were you wrong?"

Grant tucked a finger in Sebastian's waistband and tugged him closer. Close enough to feel the heat radiating from Grant's body and smell the fresh soap on his skin.

"While going behind my back was a shitty thing to do, it came from a good place. I'm used to being the one taking care of myself and my grandmother. Ever since my dad kicked me out, it has been the two of us against the world for so long that I forgot that the world wasn't the enemy... that *you're* not the enemy. And that there's nothing wrong with accepting help when you need it."

"That's all I wanted to do. I could have found a better way to do that, though."

"I know. But the house is perfect. Nana has her own space, but she's close enough to easily stay involved in Tavi's life. Which is a great gift to both of them. So, I'm sorry for being an ass, and thank you for having my family's back."

Sebastian's heart beat so hard and so fast, it was a testament to his strong bones that his sternum didn't crack under the constant battering. The smile made his cheeks hurt, but he didn't care if he grinned like a fool. "You're welcome."

Grant straightened and reversed their positions, his fingers going to the buckle of Sebastian's pants and tugging the end free. Leaning in, he covered Sebastian's mouth with his, the tender brush of lips, and the soft stroke of his tongue made the back of Sebastian's eyes sting.

Grant broke the kiss and peppered Sebastian's jaw with

tantalizing nips and open-mouth kisses that made Sebastian's head light and his dick hard.

Grant didn't stop there. He unfastened Sebastian's pants and slipped them over his hips, letting them drop to the floor around his ankles.

Aw fuck. Sebastian was nearly certain Niko had been kidding about having sex in his office, but—

Grant dropped to his knees and nibbled the slash of bare skin over Sebastian's exposed hip as he pulled down one corner of Sebastian's briefs with his index finger. Sebastian's hands went to Grant's hair.

"What are you doing?" Sebastian hardly recognized the smokiness in his voice.

Grant glanced up at Sebastian with unabashed mischief in his eyes and pulled Sebastian's briefs down to mid-thigh, freeing his cock. Precum already leaked from his slit.

A sinful smile played at the corner of Grant's lips as he took Sebastian in his hand. "I figure the best way to ask your forgiveness is on my knees."

In the crowded ballroom, people dressed in their finest evening wear laughed and joked and ate and opened their wallets for a good cause.

Grant stood at the back of the venue, the blue sequined mask Tavi made covering his eyes. He wrapped his arm around Sebastian's neck and tugged him against him, plopping a fat, wet kiss on Sebastian's temple with a loud smack, his heart beating right and true with Sebastian at his side.

Sebastian chuckled. "What was that for?"

He gazed out over the hundred-plus dinner crowd who

somehow Sebastian had convinced to part with two-hundred dollars per plate for their meal.

Before bringing Sebastian on board for the fundraiser, Grant had pictured ten-dollar donations for a plate of barbecue. "You're unbelievable."

"Please tell me that's a good thing." Though by Grant's smile, Sebastian already knew the answer.

"Between the money coming in from the dinner and the silent and live auctions, I can't wait to start implementing new programs for the kids. Just imagine the kind of money we could raise if the Center had a guy like you on staff full time."

"Is that a job offer?"

Grant heard the joke in Sebastian's tone, but beneath it was a hint of seriousness. He turned to Sebastian. "You would want to work for the Center full time? What about Niko? He'd—"

"He'd have to learn to live without me. Maybe that's not such a bad thing."

"The grant money allows for salaries, but I couldn't pay much, nothing near what Niko can pay you."

"I don't care about the money. I care about these kids, and this crazy compulsion of yours to make their lives better."

Grant took half a step back so he could get a good look at him. "Wait, you're serious."

"I am. Unless..." Sebastian shrugged. "You don't want me. I've been known to drive you crazy."

Grant leaned in and whispered in his ear, "And bring me to my knees."

The flush ran up Sebastian's face and disappeared beneath the mask. "Have I told you how much I love the way you apologize?"

Grant felt the heat in his cheeks and the heaviness in his cock at the reminder he'd had Sebastian's dick in his mouth back in Niko's office earlier that morning. As much as Grant enjoyed the evening, he couldn't wait to get Sebastian home and in his bed.

Where he belonged.

With a hand on Sebastian's waist, he pulled him in closer, his hard-on brushing against Sebastian's hip. "Come home with me."

"Tonight?" Sebastian's matching blue mask rose with his eyebrows.

No. What Grant wanted to build with this incredible, caring, compassionate man went way beyond a fast fuck and Sebastian crawling out of Grant's bed in the morning and going back to his place. What he wanted from this man was forever.

"Every night."

Even with the mask, Grant caught the flash of moisture in Sebastian's eyes. Then they narrowed. "What are you saying?"

The trepidation in Sebastian's words cut, and Grant's breath hitched knowing it was his fault for putting that doubt there.

"I love you, Bass. I want you in my bed, my house, my life. You're wrapped so completely around my heart it doesn't know how to beat without you there. So yeah, I want you for tonight, and I want you for always. What do you say?"

Sebastian pulled up his mask and Grant's as well, placing a kiss on his lips so sweet and tender and true that Grant knew the answer before it spilled from his mouth. "Yes."

———

A HAND CAME DOWN ON SEBASTIAN'S SHOULDER, AND HE KNEW from the grip that it belonged to Niko.

Sebastian stepped away from Grant, not wanting the world to intrude on their bubble, but they had a bunch of people that needed their attention. The carnival had gone off without a hitch thanks to some great organization by Nana with help from

Tavi, who'd taken that part of the fundraiser over while Sebastian had stayed at the hospital with Grant.

Niko bumped his chin toward the stage. "They're calling for you, Grant. It's time to start the live auction."

Most everyone had finished their dinner. Vondra stood on stage in an emerald evening gown that made her look more like a movie star than the actual movie stars in attendance.

Many of the guests had turned their way, waiting for Grant to take the stage.

Grant caught Sebastian's hand and kissed his cheek. There were some claps and wolf-whistles, and the heat rolled up the back of Sebastian's neck.

Grant had barely stepped out of the closet, but clearly, he had no intention of returning.

Grant jogged down the center aisle between the tables and took the stairs up to the stage two at a time, taking the microphone from Vondra and sucking in a deep breath before addressing the crowd.

"You two get everything sorted?" Niko asked.

"We did. Thanks for that."

Niko clapped him on the back. "Glad I could help."

Sebastian didn't see where Niko ran off to since he turned his focus to the stage. To Grant.

Grant adjusted the microphone and removed his mask, wiping his hands on the legs of his rented tux. "Hello, everyone."

Grant had to clear his throat, the nerves, and tension making his voice tight. "Thanks so much for being here tonight and supporting The Cory Center." Grant's eyes drifted across the tables, over all the guests.

"The work we do at the Center is vital to our marginalized LGBTQ kids. Your love and support are invaluable, and on behalf of myself and the kids, I want to thank you from the bottom of my heart."

Under the stage lights, Grant blushed at the claps and cheers. For a guy who'd comfortably worked naked under the lights at Black Stallion, Sebastian found Grant's stage fright adorable.

Then Grant's gaze landed on Sebastian, and everyone's attention turned to him where he'd been minding his own business at the back of the room.

"Most importantly, I want to thank my boyfriend, Sebastian Stavros, for putting together such an amazing event. I love you, Bass. I couldn't have done it without you."

Sebastian's chest tightened, and the backs of his eyes stung as everyone clapped. The masquerade had been a marvelous idea since the mask hid the tears that threatened to fall.

"And now, for the event you have all been waiting for." Grant turned to the edge of the stage. "Please give a round of applause for our auctioneer, Vondra Mumbee."

Vondra came back on stage to a hearty round of applause from a bunch of people whose purse strings had been strategically loosened by the liberal flow of alcohol at the open bar generously funded by Niko.

Even without the auction, Sebastian would call the fundraiser a success. Whatever money they took in from this point on was pure gravy.

Sebastian leaned against the back wall watching Vondra charm the crowd as she announced the first person up for auction that evening, the first baseman for the Grizzlies Double-A affiliate team.

A hand came around Sebastian's waist, and Grant leaned in, his lips by Sebastian's ear when he said, "Can I take you home and have my way with you yet?"

And fuck if that didn't have the semi Sebastian had been sporting since that morning spring to attention. He needed to adjust himself, luckily the crowd's attention was focused on the stage and on a tall, fit athlete decked out in his finest. Any other time the man might have turned Sebastian's head, but Grant was the only man Sebastian wanted now.

"If we could get out of here without anyone noticing, I'd take you up on that. We've only got about another hour or so, and then—"

"And then I'm bending you over the back of my couch and—"

Sebastian turned in the curve of Grant's arm, the smile tugging on his lips. "I'm sure Tavi or Nana would love to see that."

Grant's eyes closed on a string of muttered curses. "I forgot I don't have my own place anymore."

"We could take advantage of the double shower in the master."

The grin that overtook Grant's face couldn't get any bigger. He planted a quick kiss on Sebastian's lips. "Your brilliance is one of the many things I love about you."

Love.

Never in a million years had Sebastian ever suspected those words would tumble from Grant's lips and be aimed at him.

They watched the auction from their vantage point at the back of the room. The grip of Grant's hand at Sebastian's hip growing tighter as the bid on the second to the last person, the most fabulous and flamboyant drag queen that side of Los Angeles, climbed higher and higher. She pranced around on stage in a form-fitting sequined red sheath dress and sky-high Louboutins, shaking it for the crowd and hamming it up.

When bidding slowed, Vondra called once, twice. Vondra slapped down the gavel. "Sold to bidder number forty-five for six thousand, four hundred dollars."

"Holy shit." Grant huffed out an incredulous chuckle. "The

only thing I find more attractive than your heart and your ass is your genius."

Grant eased Sebastian back against him, Grant's erection rubbing against Sebastian's very lucky ass cheek. "There's only one more person. No one will notice if—"

"Vin's next. I promised I'd bid if no one else did."

21

NIKO CAME OUT OF THE MEN'S ROOM TO THE SOUND OF WOLF-whistles. How Sebastian had managed to pull together such an engaged auction crowd in such a short period of time, he'd never know.

He stepped into the backstage hallway and leaned against the wall, having a direct line of sight down the stage to the crowd beyond.

His smartwatch buzzed, and he glanced down at the incoming text from a nearly anonymous one-night stand who wanted to extend it to two nights, if the *Sup?* meant anything.

They'd both had a good time, but there had been little connection besides the physical.

Maybe if you tried dating someone who wasn't twenty years your junior, you'd find something to talk about besides anime and Pokémon Go.

It hadn't been that bad.

But nearly.

Apparently, Niko had a type, so sue him.

But contrary to popular belief, he needed more from a man than a hard dick and a tight ass.

He let the text go unanswered as the man at the center of the stage caught his eye. Niko didn't know if it was the fit of the tuxedo slacks, the way the tattoos peeked out from beneath the white sleeves rolled three-quarters of the way up the man's forearms, the messy-gelled hair, or the quiet confidence in the man's walk that caught his attention the most.

Or that fine ass.

Tight and high and round...

Who the hell was this guy?

The stirring beneath Niko's pant front made him glad the hall was clear of other people.

Reaching down, he adjusted himself, all the while imagining what it would feel like to have his cock lined up in the crack of the finest ass he'd seen in a very long time.

But imagining was all he was going to do. He made a vow to himself then and there to make an effort to date men closer to his age. Southern California had no shortage of handsome gay men that fit that profile. He just had to find one he clicked with.

In the meantime, while the bidding quickly grew from a few hundred dollars to over four grand, Niko would allow himself to fantasize.

Vondra worked the crowd, the bidding becoming fierce between an older woman who had to be in her sixties and... Niko shifted and brought the other bidder into view.

Pierce Hatchett.

Of PornU Studios.

Niko recognized him even behind the mask.

Hatchett was the kind of studio owner who gave porn studios a bad name.

Cut corners.

Shoddy camera work.

Low pay.

Exploitative contracts.

Questionable health screening enforcement, putting his talent at risk.

Niko couldn't figure out why Hatchett would be so dead set on winning the bid.

Intrigued, Niko made his way down the hall and into the ballroom. At the back of the room, Grant stood behind Sebastian with his arm hooked around Sebastian's shoulder as he whispered something in Sebastian's ear that made his nephew smile.

As much as Niko hated losing Grant as part of his stable of performers, seeing his nephew happy almost made up for it.

"Five thousand dollars." Hatchett hollered out, one of those smug, supercilious smirks on his face that Niko wouldn't mind wiping off with his fist.

Frankly, it surprised Niko someone hadn't beat him to it.

"Do I hear a fifty-five hundred? Fifty-five?" Vondra called out from the stage.

Niko shifted his attention from Vondra to the man in such high demand he had a tightwad like Hatchett opening his wallet.

Vin.

Fuck.

Niko sucked in a breath and swallowed a string of curses. As much as he tried to bank it, that semi he hid behind his clasped hands only got worse. It was all kinds of wrong.

Vin was off-limits.

"You okay, sir?" A waiter with a tray of full champagne flutes stopped next to him.

"I'm good." Niko took one of the proffered glasses and slammed it back, the bubbles working up the back of his throat and tickling his sinuses.

As he watched, the bidding increased but slowed as the price eased closer to seven grand, the excitement in the room palpable. As good as this was for the Center, it was a bad deal for Vin if Hatchett won.

And a bad deal for Black Stallion.

Niko had warned Hatchett off Vin numerous times. He couldn't allow Hatchett to poach his best cameraman.

Niko was the one who'd plucked Vin off the streets as a damaged teen. The one who'd put in the time, the effort, the emotional support to get him back on his feet again.

Hatchett couldn't have him.

Vin was Niko's.

Yours? Do you hear yourself?

Not *his*. The studio's.

"It's to you, number five. Seventy-two hundred. Going once..."

Niko watched as Hatchett straightened. Over seven grand was a lot to pay to have Vin to himself. As determined as Hatchett must be, even that number gave the man pause. But as closely as Niko eyed Hatchett, he saw Hatchett's shoulders go back a fraction, and his expression shift, the determination settling into his features.

When Hatchett opened his mouth, Niko pulled off his mask and called out above the buzz in the room. "Ten thousand."

Vin did a double-take.

The room went so quiet. Niko swore he could hear the squeeze of his adrenal glands as they pushed adrenaline into his system.

This was nuts.

Fucking crazy.

But Hatchett wasn't going to win this. Hatchett's pockets were deep, but not as deep as Niko's. Not by a long shot.

Hatchett stuffed his hands into his pockets and rocked back on his heels as he regarded Niko over the heads of the men and women seated at the tables.

"I need your number, sir, " the auctioneer said.

He hadn't registered for the auction. He'd had no intention of participating. Pushing off the wall, Niko walked farther into the room. "Sebastian will vouch for me."

He glanced back at his nephew, who looked like he was fighting a grin, and not too successfully at that.

"It's okay, Vondra," Sebastian said.

Though immature, the *fuck you* grin Niko shot Hatchett deeply satisfied him. Being related to the event organizer had its privileges.

"Ten thousand going once. Going twice." Vondra glanced between Hatchett and the older woman, both of them shaking their heads, indicating they were out of the bidding. She landed her gavel. "Sold for ten grand. That concludes our auction. If the winners will settle up at the table at the back, you can meet up with your date at the back of the room afterward."

Whatever else the woman had to say was lost on Niko as Vin disappeared backstage with an expression Niko couldn't read, even after knowing him for years.

At the back table, Niko parted with his credit card and settled up. Grant and Sebastian came over and shook his hand, but he had more important business to attend to.

The crowd thinned as the event-goers picked up their silent auction items and headed home.

Niko waited at the back of the room for Vin.

And waited.

And waited.

Until only a few stragglers and catering staff remained in the ballroom. The staff going from table to table, gathering up dirty dishes and soiled linens.

Another text came through on Niko's smartwatch. His one-night stand. Niko pulled out his phone, and with a short, curt text made it clear he wasn't interested in another hookup.

"Hot date?"

Niko glanced up from his phone and slid it into his pocket. Vin had changed into a pair of soft denim jeans that hugged his hips and thighs... and his package.

Niko dragged his eyes upward, to the tight T-shirt that spanned Vin's chest and banded his muscled biceps. Vin's gelled hair looked like he'd spent the last twenty minutes running his hands through it, and his face looked like he hadn't smiled in years.

"What's wrong?" Niko asked.

"What the hell was that all about?"

Niko didn't play dumb. "I didn't want Hatchett getting his claws on you. He's never made it a secret that he'd steal you away from Black Stallion if given the opportunity."

Somehow, Vin looked more disappointed than pleased.

"What? You wanted to go to dinner with him?"

"I'd rather lick the grime off the toilets seats at Grand Central Station than go out to dinner with Hatchett, but my phone number is no state secret. It's not like he can't contact me any time he wants."

Niko didn't say anything to that. His attention diverted to Vin's eyes and the dark guy-liner, making him look even more like the mid-twenties man that he was.

Yet another reminder that Vin was strictly off-limits.

But yeah, tell that to Niko's dick. The dick that refused to take orders from the rest of him.

"So why did you outbid him by almost three grand? Did you do it to prove a point?"

"And what point would that be?"

Vin's annoyance showed through with the tense shrug of one shoulder. "You tell me, *Mr. Stavros.*"

Mr. Stavros.

Vin hadn't called him that since the first couple weeks after

Niko had pulled him off the streets. And why the hell did hearing the defiance—because that tone certainly hadn't been deferential—make Niko want to do all sorts of naughty things to him?

Niko's gaze darted from Vin's eyes to his lips and back again before Vin had the chance to notice.

"Look," Vin said. "This was just a charity thing. I get it. You don't have to worry about me thinking it's anything other than what it was—a chance for you to flex your wallet, show Hatchett up, and do some good for the Center."

Vin was partially right. Niko would have drained his bank account if it meant Hatchett didn't win. But that was only a part of it and the kids, well... he was glad they'd benefit, but that wasn't why he'd forked over that kind of money.

"What are you trying to say?"

Vin met Niko's eyes, and it was all Niko could do to maintain eye contact and not let his gaze wander back to those lips.

"I'm saying you don't have to go out on a date with me. Bass talked me into doing this anyway."

Niko didn't know what came over him, the devil on his shoulder or the devil in his pants, but one of them over-rode his better judgment.

Vin was forbidden.

Niko shouldn't.

Couldn't.

Wouldn't.

But then he leaned in and whispered in Vin's ear. "Oh, no. You've got me all wrong. I want that date. Friday. Seven o'clock."

Then he stood straight and clapped Vin on the shoulder. "Pick me up at my place."

Niko walked away, knowing he'd either made the best or the worst decision of his life.

A LETTER TO MY READERS

Dear Reader,

Black Stallion Studios is at the height of production, and taking their talent and their cameras on the road... But not before Vin finally gets his date with Niko. Will it be everything he's wanted, or will it be the disaster he feared?

Niko took Vin in when Vin's family kicked him out.

He gave an aimless street kid direction, a career, a life.

But Vin Andino is now a grown man, and he wants more. What he wants is Niko.

Black Stallion Studios' owner Niko Stavros has a thing for younger men, but with wealth and power comes responsibility, and there are rules even he won't break:

1.No f*cking the employees.

2.No f*cking Vin—That would be wrong... Right?

After a bachelor auction, Niko sees Vin in a new light, and while the whole studio crew is out of the country on location, Niko tiptoes up to the forbidden line.

But Vin has a secret, and his past threatens to blow up his life, and Niko's.

Can love bring them together and allow them to let go of the past?

Or will the revelation tear them apart?

Best Boy is a sexy read with all the feels. Get you copy here: https://books2read.com/BestBoy

Romantic Suspense

Lazy S Ranch Series
Cowgirl, Unexpectedly (Book 1)
Must Love Horses (Book 2)
Hot on the Trail (Book 3)
Cowboy, Undercover (Book 4)
Cowboy, Unbridled (Book 5)
Cowgirl, Unbroken (Book 6 Coming soon!)

Wright's Island Series
Don't Look Back (Book 1)
In Her Defense (Book 2)

Steele-Wolfe Securities
Wyoming Confidential (Book 1 Coming soon)

Contemporary Romance

Rockin' Rodeo Series
Luck of the Draw (Book 1)
Photo Chute (Book 2)
Reined In (Book 3)
Rockin' Rodeo Series Collection (Books 1-3)

MM Romance

<u>*Black Stallion Studios Series*</u>
One Shot (Book 1)
Key Grip (Book 2)
Best Boy (Book 3)

ABOUT THE AUTHOR

Vicki Tharp makes her home on small acreage in south Texas with her husband and an embarrassing number of pets. When she isn't writing, you can usually find her on the back of her horse—avoiding anything that remotely resembles housework —smelling like fly spray and horse sweat.

Join my newsletter at: http://eepurl.com/croJgz
Join my street team and receive free Advance Reader Copies of my upcoming books at: http://eepurl.com/cWhXbD
You can find my website at: www.VickiTharp.com
I love to hear from readers. You can email me at vwtharp@VickiTharp.com

Or you can stalk me at:

facebook.com/VickiTharpAuthor

instagram.com/author_Vicki_Tharp

bookbub.com/authors/vicki-tharp

amazon.com/author/vicki_tharp

twitter.com/vwtharp